THE THIRTEENTH FAE

OTHER BOOKS BY ANNA DURAND

THE THIRTEENTH FAE

Undercover Elementals, Book Six

ANNA DURAND

JACOBSVILLE BOOKS · MARIETTA, OHIO

THE THIRTEENTH FAE

ISBN: 979-8-9852412-0-4 (paperback)
ISBN: 979-8-9852412-1-1 (ebook)
ISBN: 979-8-9852412-2-8 (audiobook)

Manufactured in the United States.

Jacobsville Books
www.JacobsvilleBooks.com

Publisher's Cataloging-in-Publication Data
provided by Five Rainbows Cataloging Services

Names: Durand, Anna.
Title: The thirteenth fae / Anna Durand.
Description: Marietta, OH : Jacobsville Books, 2022. | Series: Undercover elementals, bk. 6.
Identifiers: ISBN 979-8-9852412-0-4 (paperback) | ISBN: 979-8-9852412-1-1 (ebook) | ISBN 979-8-9852412-2-8 (audiobook)
Subjects: LCSH: Fairies--Fiction. | Magic--Fiction. | Curses--Fiction. | Romance fiction. | BISAC: FICTION / Romance / Paranormal / General. | FICTION / Romance / Fantasy. | FICTION / Romance / Suspense. | GSAFD: Love stories. | Occult fiction. | Fantasy fiction. | Suspense fiction.
Classification: LCC PS3604.U724 T55 2022 (print) | LCC PS3604.U724 (ebook) | DDC 813/.6--dc23.

Chapter One

Tris

"I NEED A STONE THAT WILL CHASE AWAY AN OBSESSED SUCCUBUS," I TELL my friend Lindsey. "Don't you have something like that? I mean, you've got bins full of junk that came out of the ground. Maybe granite would do the trick? Don't laugh at me. This is not funny. I'm being stalked by a genuine sex addict who wants me so bad that I don't know what she might do next."

Lindsey laughs.

"Hey, I told you not to do that."

She clamps her lips between her teeth until the quivering of her contained laughter stops. "I'm sorry, Tris. You seem genuinely upset about this, but I kind of doubt a succubus is stalking you. Those ladies have no trouble finding bedmates."

"Max is an incubus, but he nearly starved himself into oblivion. Couldn't 'get a leg over' with anyone." I still think that British term is dumb, especially since Max has never been to England. The Unseen made him British. Go figure. It changed my accent too, but I haven't starved myself because of that. "Someone has been following me. I can feel it. Must be that crazy salamander chick."

Lindsey's expression turns contemplative. "You know, I never thought about it until just now, but I guess a succubus and an incubus would both be salamanders. Wonder if the girls turn into cute little red lizards or if they have a different color."

I roll my eyes and groan. "Lindsey, I need help. I'm seriously having a problem."

"Let's ask Nevan."

"No, Lindsey—"

She twists her head around to shout, "Nevan! Get your butt out here!"

We're standing inside the rock shop that Lindsey and Nevan own, and the corrugated metal building has no insulation of any kind as far as I know. That means it echoes when she hollers at her husband. It makes my ears hurt. Do all mothers develop the ability to yell for their husbands that way? I don't think I'll ever understand humans. Nevan used to be the king of the sylphs, but he gave it up to become a mortal and marry Lindsey. That means he's not exactly normal.

Yeah, he's a freak with an Irish accent.

Nevan emerges from the back room, halting just behind the sales counter beside his wife. And he has their kid, Liam, hugged to his side. "What is it, darlin'?"

"Tris thinks he's being stalked by a succubus who can't get enough of him."

Nevan stares at me for a few seconds. Then he busts out laughing.

Yeah, I expected that reaction from him. "Never mind. I'll handle the problem on my own."

The former sylph passes their toddler to his wife and wipes the tears of laughter from his eyes. "I do apologize, Tris. Which succubus are you having trouble with?"

"Anthea."

Nevan sighs. "She is one of the oldest and most potent succubi in the Unseen. Her skills of seduction are legendary. Males of all species beg for the chance to spend the night with Anthea in her lair. Why would she bother stalking you?"

"We had sex a couple of weeks ago."

"And now you believe she can't do without you. That's rubbish, Tris."

"But somebody's stalking me. I can feel it. And I keep seeing a shadow following me."

"Perhaps you imagined it."

Lindsey walks around the counter to where I stand—and offers me her kid. "Maybe some Liam love will make you feel better."

I take a step backward. "Uh, no offense. But your rug rat smells like poop and vomit."

"No, he doesn't. You have a baby phobia, that's all."

Maybe I do. But I came here to get help from my friends, and they think I'm imagining having a stalker. Well, maybe I am overreacting. But I've had the weirdest feeling that someone or something is tracking me everywhere I go.

"Can I at least get some copper?" I ask. "My stash is getting low."

"Sure thing, sweetie. Grab all you want."

"And then pay for it," Nevan says in what he probably thinks sounds like an authoritative tone. "This is a business, not a food bank for lazy leprechauns."

"Yeah, yeah."

I amble down the aisle that houses wooden bins full of copper ore and conjure a canvas bag. Nevan squints at me, but he knows better than to question where I got the bag from since nobody knows how elementals conjure things. We want something, and poof, there it is.

Now that I've got what I need, I walk back toward the sales counter. And I trip, nearly tumbling headfirst to the floor and coming within a hair's breadth of cracking my skull on a metal shelf.

"What are ye doing?" Nevan asks in an annoyed tone. "Don't damage the merchandise or the displays."

"I tripped. It was an accident. Your precious displays are fine." But when I glance down, I can't see what I tripped over, can't see anything at all on the smooth floor. "That's weird."

"What is, sweetie?" Lindsey asks.

"Seems like I tripped over nothing."

Nevan grunts. "Your own feet is more likely."

I've suddenly become a klutz. Whatever. Maybe I've got bad luck because I'm the thirteenth child in my family, born on the thirteenth day of the thirteenth month in the fae calendar. No, if that were the cause, it would've bitten me in the behind a long time ago, not waited until today.

Approaching the counter, I dig some twenty-dollar bills out of my pocket and hand them to Nevan.

He lifts one brow. "I assumed you would barter for the copper. Where did you get cash?"

"I've become an entrepreneur." That might not be the most accurate description of how I earn money, but Nevan doesn't need to know everything.

"Doing what? Your only skill is eating copper so you can activate the healing vortex."

I try really hard not to snap at him. "My business is none of your business, air fairy."

Nevan isn't a sylph anymore, so the "air fairy" insult isn't accurate. But I couldn't think of a better put-down. Air elementals are all kind of uppity.

I thank Lindsey and Nevan, then head out to the vortex that lies behind the shop, passing through the rock garden and following the dirt path to the bench-shaped rocks that surround the healing vortex. I sit down and pull a chunk of copper out of my bag. Then I start munching on it. Mm, yeah, I needed a snack.

A rustling sound starts up from somewhere near the trees to my left. Sounds like a breeze, but there is no wind right now. And besides, the noise came from a specific spot.

I set my copper down on the bench and move only my eyes to glance in the direction from where the sound originated. Can't see anything. Wait. Was that a flash of movement? I freeze and tap into my ethereal senses, though I've never been great at doing that. Still, I tip my head to the side just a little and listen. My ears detect sounds I hadn't noticed before, clues that a human could never pick up. Soft breathing. Throat swallowing. The faintest hint of feet shuffling.

Anthea. It's got to be her, the psycho succubus.

I zip myself to the spot from where the sounds had seemed to originate. To a human, traveling this way seems like we vanish and reappear like magic. Well, it is magic. But not the way they think. I zip through a dark tunnel and pop back out a nanosecond later, now standing inches away from my stalker.

She's not Anthea.

The girl gaping at me has golden blonde hair and hazel eyes so pale that they seem almost like colored crystal. But whoa, mama, look at that body.

Her shock melts away, and she blinks rapidly. "What are you?"

"Don't you mean who am I?"

"No." She rises onto her tiptoes to peer into my eyes while biting her lip. "Are you an alien?"

"What? No." I should take a step away from her, but I can't do it. She's hot, and I want to kiss her. "Do I look like a little green Martian?"

"Aliens are gray."

I can't stop my brows from cinching up. "I'm not gray either. Who are you, lady?"

"Riley Jordan."

I try to take a step back, but my feet won't cooperate. She smells good. Really good. And her voice has a sultry undertone that's making my manly parts wake up. "What are you doing out here? You're not dressed for a hike."

No, she's wearing shorts that hug her upper thighs and a gauzy shirt that's unbuttoned, revealing the lavender tank top underneath. The low neckline gives me a great view of her cleavage. Hiking boots and lavender socks cover her feet, but I barely notice them. I can't tear my gaze away from the slopes of her breasts. No mortal I've met dresses the way she does, not out here in the woods. Hasn't she met the Michigan mosquitoes? They eat girls like her for lunch.

I'd love to devour her, for sure.

"Um, I'm looking for someone," she says, leaning in just enough that her full breasts graze my chest. "It might be you."

"Lady, we just met. How could you be looking for me?"

"Not you specifically." She bites her lip again and leans back against the tree behind her. "Someone *like* you."

"Uh-huh." I finally manage to override my dick and take a couple of steps backward. "Did you hit your head? You seem kinda dazed."

She giggles. "No, silly. I'm fine."

"How much booze have you had? Or maybe it's marijuana."

"Neither." She takes a deep breath that hoists her tits, then exhales it gradually while her mouth curves into a smile of deep satisfaction. "It smells so good out here."

Yeah, she's got to be on something.

I reach for her arm. "Let me walk you back to the shop."

She shrugs away from my hand, ducking under my arm, and starts twirling around and around.

For a moment, I can't do anything except stare at the sexy little weirdo. Sure, I'd love to get naked with her. But she seems out of it, and even I don't screw chicks who are doped up on…whatever she's taking. So I sling my arms around her waist from behind and whisk us away to the edge of the rock garden, just up the hill from the shop.

I dip my head to murmur in her ear, "Can you get yourself down there to the shop? My friend Lindsey will take care of you."

"What did you do? How did we get here?"

"Uh-uh. I get to ask the questions." I slide my hand up her belly until it bumps into her bosom. "Who are you? And why did you think I'm an alien?"

She wriggles, which makes her ass rub against me. "Let me go, you big dumb…creature."

Her voice has changed. She doesn't sound like a ditz anymore.

"Why were you sneaking around in the woods, Riley?" I demand. "What's your game?"

She wriggles again, trying to get free, and she succeeds only because I decide to let her go. Riley spins around and scuffles away from me, though not far. "What are you?"

"Answer my questions first."

Her gaze narrows, and she puckers her lips slightly. "If I tell you the truth, will you answer my questions?"

"Maybe."

She studies me for several seconds, then blows out a big sigh. "I'm hunting for cryptids."

"For what?" I say, snorting because I'm trying not to laugh. "If you want to see a mausoleum, I can show you one right now."

"Not a crypt." She huffs, then speaks with exaggerated enunciation. "Cryptids."

"Which means what?"

"It means creatures that haven't been proved to exist and that scientists dismiss as nothing but legends. I am a cryptozoologist, which means I study cryptids." She folds her arms over those beautiful breasts. "Do you understand now? Or should I speak in smaller, simpler words?"

"Hey, insulting me is rude."

She rakes her gaze over me from top to bottom, though her attention stalls briefly on my groin. Then she blinks quickly and meets my gaze. "Your turn. What are you?"

No, she won't believe me if I tell her. Mortals have dumb ideas about what my kind looks like and sounds like and acts like. But she wants the truth, so…

"I'm a leprechaun."

Laughter erupts out of her.

Oh yeah, it's my day to be the butt of everyone's jokes, isn't it? My life sucks.

Chapter Two

Riley

Maybe laughing at him is rude, but this man—this creature—is not human. He claims to be a leprechaun. Aren't those little Irish guys who wear green? He can't be one of those. I mean, he towers over me, has bulging muscles, and speaks with an American accent. He dresses in normal clothes too—jeans, a T-shirt, and sneakers. So yeah, I feel justified in laughing because he claimed to be a leprechaun.

But I force myself to stop doing that.

In my defense, he does have red hair and the faintest freckles.

I wipe away the tears in my eyes and struggle to collect myself. "You are not a leprechaun."

"Yes, I am," he growls through his gritted teeth. "How many of my kind have you seen? Zero, I bet."

Okay, yeah, he's right. I've spent years hunting for cryptids, but I hadn't seen one until today. He does have blue eyes that glow like sky-blue topaz lit by a fire inside them. It's eerily beautiful. He has a gorgeous face, and a gorgeous body too. But I don't care how hot he is. My only concern is what information I can learn about his species so I can write an earth-shattering scientific paper that will expose the reality of previously undiscovered creatures that have supernatural abilities.

"Stop smirking at me," he snaps. "You're a rude little ditz, aren't you?"

Maybe I sometimes act like a ditz if it serves my purposes. Until today, I've only done that to keep other scientists from paying attention to my research. Can't let anybody horn in on my big discoveries. Not that I'd made any of those. Until today. Behaving like a dumb blonde is my camouflage.

"Wow, you are so tall," I say in my dumb-blonde voice. "How do you fit inside a car?"

His brows knit together, crinkling his forehead. "You can't really be as stupid as you act. Are you trying to snow me?"

I tip my head back to stare at the sky, then I bite my lip. "I don't see any snow. Isn't it too warm for that?"

He squints at me. "Give it up, lady. You're overdoing the ditz routine."

I study him for a moment while I gauge how best to respond. He could be right. Bumping into him knocked me off balance a bit, so maybe I have overcompensated. But I need to be super careful. A creature who can zip from one place to another in a heartbeat could, I'm sure, rip my throat out if he got too annoyed with me. I need to stay alert and not give away too much.

"Maybe I did go a little too far," I say. "But you surprised me, and I don't understand what you are or why you hang out in a rock shop. I saw you going in there and coming out again."

He folds his arms over his massive chest. "So, you're not as dumb as you pretend to be."

"Nobody's as dumb as they pretend to be."

"What does that mean?"

I shrug. "Whatever you want it to mean. But I'm more interested in why you claim to be a leprechaun."

"Claim to be?" He puckers his lips and squints even harder. "I *am* a leprechaun. Do you get all your info about us from a cereal box? We aren't little dudes who wear green."

"Uh-huh." I shove my hands into the pockets of my shorts. "So tell me what you're like. And by the way, I get my info from books, not cereal boxes."

"Dumb-ass books."

"No. I read stuff written by scientists and scholars, both modern and historical ones. The single best book about supernatural creatures is *The Fairy-Faith in Celtic Countries* by W.Y. Evans-Wentz. He talked to people who claimed to have seen paranormal beings like fairies and leprechauns. They don't look like you."

He makes a derisive noise. "If you believe everything you read, you can't be much of a cryptologist."

"Cryptozoologist. I study previously unknown creatures." I tilt my head to the side. "Weren't you listening? Maybe you're the ditz if you can't remember what I said a minute ago."

He stares at me for a moment. Then his mouth slides into a knowing smile that has a sexy slant to it. "I was right. You're faking the dumb-blonde routine. Why don't we both stop pretending and just be honest with each other?"

"Okay. You go first."

"I've already told you the truth. Do I need to say it more slowly?" He leans forward. "I am a leprechaun."

"But I saw you eating copper."

"Yeah. That's what copper fae do."

I roll my eyes. "Make up your mind. Are you a leprechaun or a copper fae?"

"Both." He steps closer, and I suddenly notice the delicious scent of him. "The word leprechaun is kind of a nickname. Officially, we are the copper fae."

"Okay. I get that."

All I can manage to do is stare at his chest and wonder what his body looks like in the nude. Does he have the supernatural power to make me lust for him? I should've thought about that before I revealed myself to a freaky creature in the woods.

He snaps his fingers in front of my face. "Wake up, lady. It's my turn to ask questions."

I blink rapidly and focus on his face. "Yeah, okay."

"First question. Why did you come to this place to look for elementals?"

"Ele-whats?" I'm not faking it this time. I really am clueless now.

He leans in again, and that yummy scent wafts over me again. "Elementals. Beings who are tied to particular natural elements. For me, it's copper."

"I get it. What other kinds of elementals are there? Where do they live?"

His lip curls into a half smirk, and his blue eyes glitter. Literally. "Uh-uh-uh. Still my turn. You didn't answer my question. Why did you come here to look for elementals?"

"I didn't. I came here to look for cryptids."

"Potato, potahto. You're using a stupid mortal word for something you know nothing about. We are elementals."

"Are all of your kind so grumpy?"

He stalks forward, forcing me to back away until I bump into a large tree. Before I have time to plan my escape, he brackets my shoulders with his big hands and bends his elbows, bringing his body to within a hair's breadth of mine. "I'm only grumpy when you start talking. But I know exactly how to fix that problem."

The leprechaun kisses me.

I hold perfectly still, trying my damnedest not to respond, though his lips feel warm and supple, and my body wants to sag against the tree. Oh yeah, he definitely has superpowers that make me want him. I can't honestly be attracted to a snarky creature from who knows where. But I can't make myself wriggle away from him. Instead, I exhale a soft moan.

He peels his lips away from mine but stays far too close for my sanity. And he smirks. "See? I know how to shut you up."

"That won't work again." Why did I sound so breathless when I told him that? *Ugh.* Definitely supernatural stuff at work here.

"Let's test your theory." He lowers his head toward my mouth again, but I thrust a hand up to shield my lips. He sighs. "You're awfully uptight for a sometimes ditz who walked into the woods half-naked and alone, with no weapons and no clue what she's doing."

"I am not uptight. I don't want to kiss you, that's all. You don't do it for me."

He chuckles. "That's why you moaned. Because I don't 'do it' for you. Come on, you can admit the truth to me. You loved that kiss, and I didn't even use tongue. If I do that, I bet you'll melt like an ice cube in the sun."

I huff. "Please. You aren't that hot."

"Wanna test your theory?"

"No." I duck under his arm and wriggle away from him, staggering several feet before I trip over a rock and almost tumble to the ground. The leprechaun catches my arm, halting my fall. I shake his hand off. "I didn't need your help."

"Sure you didn't. Denial is kinda your favorite thing, eh?"

"No." I tug my tank top down, since it had ridden up when I almost fell. "I told you my name. But do you have one?"

"No, everybody just calls me 'hey, you.' What do you think? Of course I have a name."

"What is it?"

"Tris."

"You don't look like a Tris. Is that short for something?"

He shakes his head. "No way am I sharing that with you. I've given enough info. Time to answer a question. How long have you been stalking me?"

"Stalking? I haven't done that. Only found this place today." I tug my cover-up shirt almost closed, like I can stop him from staring at my tits that way. Because, yeah, he is staring at them. His eyes glow with more intensity while he does that, which makes me tingle in ways I refuse to examine. "I'm here to observe, nothing more. That's not stalking. It's science."

"Bullcrap." Tris pushes a hand into his hair and groans. "Just leave me alone, lady. Okay? Unless you want to have sex."

"Excuse me? I don't even know what freaky powers you have. No way in hell will I get naked with you." My body disagrees, but I've decided that's his fault. Yeah, he's to blame for the fact I wanted him to kiss me with tongue. "I'll find someplace else to hunt for cryptids. Goodbye, Tris."

I whirl around and march down the path through the rock garden that descends toward the rear of the building. When I glance back, Tris is gone. *Oh, thank goodness.* My body gave me disturbing signals back there, but at least now I don't ever again need to think about what that means. I will find a different location for my project and find a different cryptid who doesn't speak or smell so good that I want to rip his clothes off.

But as I reach the shop's rear door, I freeze. *Oh, shoot.* I left my backpack out there in the woods. I'd been about to get out my camera and take pictures of that Tris creature when he found me. I can't go back there. What if he's still hanging around?

Get a grip, girl. You can handle this.

My equipment wasn't cheap, so I can't just let it go.

Taking a deep breath, as if that will protect me, I march back up the path through the rock garden and follow the dirt trail that leads to the so-called healing vortex and the waterfall beyond it. I veer left, bypassing both features, and find my backpack without too much trouble. Well, at least that elemental beast didn't steal my stuff. I shrug into my backpack straps and turn around to go back down the trail.

Tris blocks my way. "Couldn't get enough, huh? I knew you'd want more. No girl can resist a leprechaun's kiss."

"Does that line ever work for you?" I try to push past him, but he grasps my backpack, effectively halting me. "If you came out here to study elementals—what you call cryptids—then you should stay right here."

"I can find a different part of the woods to explore."

"But I can introduce you to other elementals." He keeps hold of my pack even while I try to walk away. Then he hoists it up, lifting my feet off the ground. "Are you serious about wanting to study supernatural beings?"

"Yes, of course." I thrash my legs and manage to kick him hard several times. But he doesn't seem to care. "Are you made of metal under that skin?"

"Uh-uh. I'm not answering questions until after we make a deal."

"I'm listening."

"You want to meet elementals. I know lots of those and can introduce you to them. So here's what I want in return." He sets me down on my feet and spins me toward him, hugging my body to all his muscles. "Another kiss, deeper this time."

A sensuous warmth rushes through me, and I can't deny the truth—to myself. I want that. But no way in hell will I admit it to him.

"Give me your answer," he says. "Right now."

CHAPTER THREE

I CAN'T BELIEVE WHAT I JUST SUGGESTED. A HOT KISS IN EXCHANGE FOR introducing her to my elemental friends? I've gone insane today, or maybe I'm channeling Max. My incubus friend once demanded a woman kiss him in exchange for information, and Harper said yes. Jeez, I'm a copycat now. And I've gone crazy for sure. Nothing else explains what I've offered to Riley. Okay, yeah, I want another, deeper kiss from the semi-ditz who plans on "studying" my kind. The Unseen realm has more varieties of elementals than any human could possibly imagine.

But a lip-lock for information? Not sure how that's going to help anything—other than my dick. Yeah, it loves the idea.

With her body crushed to mine, I'm having trouble with minor things like, oh, thinking clearly. That's my excuse for saying, "Your decision now. Or I'll zip away, and you'll never get so much as a glimpse of an elemental ever again. I can make sure of that."

Can I? Kinda doubt it. But the statement sounded convincing.

Riley puckers her lips and squints her eyes. "Go kiss yourself. I'll find another way to get what I want."

I release her and take a big step backward. Then I shrug like I don't care either way. "Fine. Good luck finding an elemental, much less convincing one to teach you about our kind. I'm sure there are lots of cryptics in the mortal world for you to harass."

"Cryptids, you moron. How many times do I have to say that before the information sinks into your brain?"

I make a derisive noise and wave my hand in a dismissive gesture. Then I turn to walk away.

Riley grabs my arm. "Wait."

"Why should I do that? You called me a moron and a bunch of other insulting stuff."

"Don't be a—" She huffs out a breath. "Fine. I'm sorry, okay? That was rude."

I glance back at her. "Gee whiz, that apology sounded completely believable. What were you about to call me this time? Before you shut your trap, I mean."

"Nothing." She gazes at me with what seems like a genuine lack of nastiness. "I really am sorry. Being rude isn't like me."

"Okay. I accept your apology." I turn around to face her. "And I'm sorry too. For demanding you kiss me in exchange for information."

"So, you're still willing to help me learn about elementals?"

"Yeah." Not like I have anything else to do. The healing vortex doesn't need daily tuning, and I'm only ever called on when someone has a serious injury. Otherwise, the vortex automatically heals minor issues. Most mortals don't even notice the supernatural energies in the air.

"I appreciate your help, Tris. But we need to keep this professional. You are my test subject, and I only want to study you and other elementals in your natural habitat."

My natural habitat? I'm not a raccoon. If she thinks of me as a "test subject," she'll never let me kiss her again. It figures that when I finally meet a cute girl, she's treats me like a firefly in a glass jar.

"Are you okay with me studying you?" Riley asks.

"Yeah, sure." I suddenly remember my little problem. "Uh, you should know something before we move ahead with this."

"What?"

"I kind of have a stalker."

Her brows hike up. "Seriously?"

"Yes. Why do you say that like it's totally ridiculous to think a woman might stalk me?"

She eyes me up and down. "Well, you are hot. I guess it's plausible some girl could have an insane crush on you. Why don't you just disappear whenever she harasses you?"

"What a genius idea. I never thought of that—because I'm incredibly stupid and don't understand my own powers."

"Now who's being nasty?"

"Okay, fair point. But that was an insulting suggestion."

Riley sucks in a big breath, which lifts her breasts, then gusts it out. "Let's both try not to be snarky, okay?"

My middle name is Snarky, according to everyone I've ever met including my family. But for reasons I can't explain, I want to hang out with Riley. So I tell her, "Sure, let's try that. And while we're looking for cryptids together, I can teach you about the Unseen realm."

She stares at me without blinking. "The what realm?"

"Unseen. That's what elementals call the parallel world we come from. It's a lot different from the mortal world."

"Will we go into the Unseen?"

"Not right away." I notice the way she's hunching her shoulders repeatedly as if her giant backpack is too heavy for her. So I teleport it into my hand, gripping the straps. "Let me take this for you."

Her eyes go wide.

"Stop gaping at me," I say, as I hook the backpack straps over my shoulder. "Let's go to the falls."

But she's still gaping.

I lift one brow.

She rolls her shoulders back and shakes off her shock. "Sorry. I've never met a guy who wants to carry my pack for me. Or even carry a little bag of groceries."

"Yeah, I've heard that mortal men are dicks. Elementals can be that way too, so I guess we're all the same in some ways."

I lead Riley back onto the dirt path, heading left toward the falls. Once we get there, I approach the wooden railing that hems in the waterfall and the pool of swirling water below it. A light spray of foam hovers on the surface of the pool, and above us, the sunlight creates a little rainbow at the top of the falls. The cliff consists of red sandstone with a narrow ledge that can only be accessed by jumping onto it from this side of the railing. A sign warns tourists not to do that, but occasionally, some idiot gives it a try. Nobody has ever drowned here, though.

Riley reaches into the backpack I'm carrying for her and brings out a spiral-bound notebook and a mechanical pencil. She roves her gaze over me briefly, then starts jotting things down on her paper.

"Did you even notice what's right in front of you?" I ask.

"Huh?" Riley blinks a few times, then she finally looks up at the obvious thing right in front of her. "What a pretty waterfall. I didn't get this far into the woods before I bumped into you."

"Because you were too busy stalking me."

She veers her gaze to me. "I was observing you, scientifically."

"Acting like a ditz is part of the scientific method, huh?"

Riley studies the swirling waters of the pool. "Who is this woman, your stalker?"

"A succubus."

Without lifting her head, she glances at me sideways. "A sex demon? Why would she need to stalk you? I mean, a succubus must have no trouble getting lucky."

"Anthea is nuts. Which means she's irrational. Which means she would totally stalk me."

"Okay, fine, whatever." Riley faces me, leaning her hip against the railing. "Why are we looking at a pretty waterfall? You said you'd introduce me to elementals."

"Yeah, but first I wanted to explain about the falls."

"What is there to explain?"

I move behind her, with my front flush with her back, so I can point to the falls. Okay, maybe I don't need to stand right behind her to do that. But she hasn't complained—yet. I raise my arm to indicate the rumbling cascade. "The portal to the Unseen lies inside a cave behind the waterfall."

"Oh." She stares at the cliff, her eyes widening just enough to make her look adorably excited. "Can we go through the portal now?"

"Uh-uh. It's too dangerous for a mortal." I might be leaving out some vital details about why it's dangerous, and I'm definitely omitting the part where mortals can enter the portal if they have a touch of the Unseen in them. I need to learn more about her before I reveal that kernel of info. "I wanted you to see this, but right now, we need to find some of my friends so I can introduce you to them."

"Elemental friends?"

"Yeah, duh. Did you think I wanted you to meet a mailman?"

"Mail carrier. That's the correct term."

Great. She's a ditz and an annoying woman, but also a stickler for proper terminology. Maybe I don't want to kiss her again after all. She's too uptight. But my friend Max, the incubus, claims that uptight women are the best "shags" because they go wild when they finally let go. He's screwed more women than just about anyone, so he should know. Of course, these days he's married and only sleeps with his wife.

"Everybody I know calls them mailmen, not carriers," I say. "But I don't care what you call them. Let's move on, okay? I know who I want you to meet first."

"Awesome. Let's go."

I pull her close. Her eyes flare wide, but then I whisk us away. The second we touch down, I release her.

She stumbles backward, glancing around. "Where are we?"

"Not far from the rock shop." I wave to the area behind her. "Take a look."

Riley shuffles around to see what's behind her.

I've set us down a little ways inside the woods, so I wouldn't inadvertently expose my powers. Lindsey has told me over and over that I sometimes get too "cavalier" about when and where I teleport, so I'm trying to do better. My world is called the Unseen, after all, not the In-Your-Face realm. A few hundred feet from where Riley and I stand, a house lies inside a clearing. That house belongs to Nevan and Lindsey, but I know they aren't home right now. Somebody else is, though.

I start walking. As I pass Riley, I say, "Come on. This is where you'll meet your first elemental."

"But I've already met one." She rushes to keep up with my pace, and I slow down since her legs are shorter than mine. "You are an elemental."

"Oh, yeah. I meant you'll meet your first other elemental."

She gets a cute, excited look again and almost skips as we cross the field to reach the house.

I need to kiss her again so badly. But I ignore that impulse and hop up the steps onto the front porch of the house. Then I ring the doorbell.

"Can't you just zip in there?" Riley asks.

"That would be rude. Right? Even elementals have etiquette."

"Good to know."

The door swings open, and Travis grins. He's glamouring to look human right now. "Tris, what are you doing here? We weren't expecting you."

Riley eyes Travis with a skeptical squint. "He's just a normal guy. With huge muscles, but still normal. His eyes don't even glow like yours."

And of course, she scribbles more stuff in her notebook. When I lean over a little bit, I see she made a note about Travis's British accent. Why is that fascinating?

Sighing, I tell Travis, "Show her what you really look like."

"Are you sure?"

"Yeah. My new friend wants to study elementals."

"Ah, I see." Travis holds still for a second, then his image shimmers and shifts to reveal his true salamander nature. His lips twist into a smug smile as he looks at Riley. "There. What do you think, friend of Tris?"

Riley gapes at him. Well, Travis is an incubus with even bigger muscles than I have, coppery skin, and a boatload of supernaturally enhanced pheromones. He could have any woman he wants, but these days, Travis only has eyes for one girl—his wife. Yeah, all my close friends are married.

I can't even get laid.

Well, not with anybody except one succubus, and I don't ever plan on doing the nasty with her again. She's too...weirdly ravenous.

Larissa, Travis's mortal wife, appears beside him. "Didn't you invite them in yet?"

"I was just about to, darling." He and Larissa step aside. "Come in, Tris, and introduce us to your new mate. I will try my best not to overwhelm her with my pheromones and my naturally irresistible sex appeal."

"Too late to worry about that," Larissa says, shaking her head and giving him an exasperated smile. "You're supposed to glamour whenever you answer the door."

"It's okay," I tell them as we all walk into the living room. "She knows about elementals. Well, kind of. Riley, meet Travis and his wife Larissa."

Travis drops into a big armchair, and Larissa settles onto his lap. Riley and I take the sofa but stay an arm's length apart. When our hosts notice that, they exchange confused looks. Yeah, they probably assume Riley is my girlfriend. I don't usually bring mortals to meet my elemental friends, and I'll need to explain why I've done that today.

I drop Riley's backpack on the floor at my feet. "Where's Dani?"

"Visiting with Max and Harper," Travis tells me. "They're at an amusement park. Dani loves to see their baby."

Larissa leans into Travis while she looks at me. "Don't be rude, Tris. Tell us who your friend is."

"This is Riley Jordan," I tell them. "She's a cryptozoologist who wants to study elementals."

"Crypto-what?" Travis says.

His wife slaps his chest. "You remember, honey. We watched those shows about Bigfoot and the chupacabra. The people who study them are called cryptozoologists."

"Oh, yes, of course. The rubbish-headed idiots."

"They aren't rubbish-headed. Well, some are. But most honestly want to understand the unexplainable."

Her husband shakes his head. "If it's unexplainable, they can't understand it."

"Riley wanted to meet you, Travis," I say. "You're the first elemental she's come across."

"Except for you, obviously."

"Yeah. I meant other than me." Why do I keep forgetting that I'm the first elemental she's met? My brain just won't retain that fact. "Do you mind if she asks you some questions?"

"Not at all."

I look at Riley. "Go on. The floor is yours."

CHAPTER FOUR

Riley

I CAN ASK AN ELEMENTAL ANYTHING I WANT, BUT SUDDENLY, MY MIND goes blank. Like, totally blank. Is this amnesia? I finally sit face to face with a creature from another world, and I can't think of a thing to say. The best my brain can come up with is "uh" and "um." So not helpful.

Tris touches my arm. "You awake, Riley?"

"Um, yeah." Technically, yes. I take a deep breath and exhale it slowly in a desperate attempt to calm my nerves. I don't get nervous. I've hunted for cryptids in the swamps of Florida where alligators could eat me at any minute, and I didn't blank out then. *Get hold of yourself, woman.* I take another deep breath and dive in. "What kind of elemental are you, Travis?"

"An incubus."

"Oh. That means you're a sex demon."

Larissa laughs. "Demon? Travis is the sweetest man on earth."

"Don't ruin my image, love," Travis says. "I'm a badass incubus, remember?" He pats her hip. "Now let me explain what that means to Tris's new girlfriend."

"I'm not his girlfriend," I announce with slightly too much volume. I temper my tone when I add, "We just met. And he's helping me with my research, that's all."

"What will you do with your 'research'?"

"Publish it."

He chuckles. "Good luck with that. Mortals are so willing to believe in things they've never seen and don't understand."

"If I had pictures, they might believe it. Well, some of them, at least."

"Pictures?" Travis veers his sharp gaze to Tris. "Did you agree to let her photograph you?"

"No. We haven't talked about that yet." Tris gives me that puckered-lips, narrowed-eyes look I've seen several times just since I met him a little while ago. He speaks in a near whisper. "Pictures? Are you crazy?"

"What's the problem?" I'm whispering too. "I mean, most people won't believe me, anyway."

Travis clears his throat. "I can hear you. Not human, remember?"

"Oh, right. Sorry."

"The problem," he says, "is that elementals prefer not to be seen. That's why our world is called the Unseen realm. Was that title not clear enough for you? Or should we rename it the World Mortals Aren't Supposed to Know About and that Elementals Never Want to Let Them See? Maybe we could put up signs warning that any attempt to photograph us will incur the death penalty."

Larissa kisses his cheek. "Relax, honey. She's new. Give the girl a chance to acclimate before you threaten to murder her."

I do not understand these people. Travis and Tris act like regular humans but have physiques that even the top bodybuilder in the world couldn't hope to achieve. Then there's the way their eyes glow. Travis's seem to be swirling too. Larissa looks like just a normal woman, though.

Travis taps Larissa's nose. "Tell Riley about *you*. Watching her head explode might be entertaining."

Larissa wriggles on her husband's lap and sits up straighter. "I used to be Hathor, the Egyptian goddess of sex, inebriation, and revelry. I was also an evil bitch who ensorcelled my thralls to ensure they would never want to leave me. I'm over that now."

"You aren't, uh, evil anymore?" I ask.

"No. I'm just an average human these days."

"But Travis is an incubus. Does he—Never mind." This conversation is making my head spin, and I think I need to lie down and put a cool cloth over my eyes. Not sure how that will help me deal with the crazy things I'm learning today, but it couldn't hurt. I definitely need a drink. Now. Hard liquor.

"You can ask me anything," Travis declares. "So go on and finish your question."

"Well, um, I was wondering…if you sleep with other women, not just Larissa. Doesn't an incubus need lots and lots of sex?"

"That's true. But I found my fated mate." He slings an arm around Larissa's waist and pulls her close. "I don't need anyone else now. I can't shag other women, not that I want to. Once a salamander finds his fated mate, she is all he ever wants from that day forward. Larissa feeds all my hunger for sex."

"I see." But no, I don't really get it. Fated mates? That can't be a real thing. Then again, I'm conversing with an incubus and a woman who used to be an evil goddess. But I abruptly realize what he said a moment ago. "Salamander? I thought you were an incubus."

Travis chuckles. "I'm both. 'Salamander' is the official term for our kind, but 'incubus' is also acceptable. We use both terms interchangeably."

"That's interesting." I start to scrawl that information in my notebook but hesitate. "I know you don't want me to photograph you, but would it be okay if I take notes?"

Travis and Larissa exchange glances and both shrug. He looks at me. "We don't mind."

I turn to Tris. "What about you?"

"Doesn't bother me."

Maybe I should've asked Tris earlier, but now that I have everyone's official permission, I scribble more notes as quickly as I can. I swear I can feel Tris watching me. When I glance up, I realize I was right. He is watching. The intensity of his gaze sends a shiver tingling up my spine. I can't decide if that's unease or excitement.

"Would you like to know about my pheromones?" Travis asks. "It's an important aspect of being an incubus."

"She doesn't need to hear about that," Tris snaps.

Is he jealous? Does he think I'll want to jump Travis's bones if I hear about his pheromones? Well, I don't care what Tris thinks. "Yeah, I'd love to hear about that, Travis."

"My pheromones are supernaturally enhanced. It's magic, pet. Larissa couldn't resist me when we first met, even though she hated me, because I dosed her with my secret weapon."

"Oh, please," his wife says with a roll of her eyes. "That had nothing to do with it. And I resisted you plenty."

"Yes, of course. When you wrapped yourself around me and tried to shag me with our clothes on in that alley, you were in complete control."

"Could you give me a sample?" I ask. "For the sake of my research."

"A sample of what?" Travis asks.

"Your pheromones." Why did I say that? I don't want to have sex with him, but a strangely alluring scent wafts off that man. "Sorry. I don't know why I said that. It was totally inappropriate."

"No kidding," Tris almost growls.

"Yes, I agree that it's inappropriate," the salamander says. "A married incubus shouldn't share his pheromones with anyone but his wife. I apologize if I accidentally sent a whiff of it your way, Riley."

"Don't worry about it." I still feel a touch lightheaded from that scent, but I'll recover soon, I'm sure. "I have a question for Larissa, if that's okay."

She smiles. "Of course. Go ahead."

"You said you were the goddess Hathor, but she was from ancient Egypt. Thousands of years ago. Did you mean that you were like her, but not actually her?"

"No, I mean I actually was Hathor. The god Eros created me over seventy thousand years ago."

I have no idea how to respond to that statement, so I focus on jotting down a note about it. I guess I assumed elementals should look their age, but

Larissa seems like a relatively young woman, maybe in her thirties. "How old are you, Travis? A hundred thousand years?"

He chuckles. "No, love, I was thirty-five when I died. My elemental age is a few years, though I haven't kept track. Time has very little meaning to an elemental."

Did my head just explode? No, I doubt it. I would've noticed that.

"Travis was forged," Tris explains, though calling that an explanation doesn't make anything clearer. "Basically, forging is how most elementals procreate. I'll tell you all about that later."

Yeah, that sounds like a good plan. My brain needs time to recover from all these revelations. My human mind can't reconcile what these people look like with their true ages. Travis is essentially a toddler? But he called that his "elemental age" and said he was forged, so... I have no idea what any of that means.

But I write it all down in my notebook.

Tris rises. "We should let you guys get back to...whatever you were about to do."

"Shag," Travis says. "That's what we'd been about to do. I'm hungry."

His tone of voice matches the words he spoke. He sounds rough and sensual and thoroughly starved for his wife. No man I've ever met got that excited about having sex with me.

I sling my backpack over my shoulder, and Tris lays a hand on my back as we walk out of the house. Travis and Larissa say goodbye and wave as we hop off the porch. Then the world shifts so abruptly that I feel woozy. But yeah, I've felt that way every time Tris whisked us away to another location. I suppose I'll get used to that, eventually.

How long will I need to stick with him? Only until I get enough information about elementals that I can write a book about them and their world. That might take months. Maybe years. Am I really going to devote my life to this? I wanted to find supposedly mythical creatures, but I never banked on finding out a whole other world exists right alongside the earth. Maybe I should ask Tris if he and his friends mind me publishing the results of my research, but I don't get the chance.

We've landed inside the clearing beside the waterfall behind the rock shop.

Tris takes a step away from me. Then he throws his head back and hollers, "Janus!"

I wince and resist the urge to slap my hands over my ears. "What are you doing?"

"Summoning a god."

"Are you serious?"

"Yeah." He sighs. "You just met Larissa, a former goddess. Why does it shock you that I'm calling a current god so you can meet him? Thought you wanted to learn everything about the Unseen."

"I do. But—"

A man appears beside Tris. He wears a toga and has wide gold bands wrapped around his biceps. His eyes shimmer like molten gold. "Why have you summoned me, leprechaun?"

He speaks with an Italian accent.

"My friend Riley wanted to meet you," Tris says. "Riley, this is Janus, the Roman god of… What is it? Can't remember."

The god flicks his gaze heavenward and shakes his head faintly. "Portals, time, transitions, and beginnings and endings."

"Yeah, that's it. Riley is a mortal who wants to visit the Unseen."

"And you wish for me to determine if she might survive the journey through the portal."

"That's right."

Janus stares intently at me without blinking. His gold eyes shimmer even more, and I feel a strange need to wrap my arms around myself. I don't do it, though. That might seem like a sign of weakness, and I do not want a god to view me as a wuss. Not sure why, but it feels important.

The god shifts his attention to Tris. "She may cross the veil."

He vanishes.

"Not much for saying goodbye, is he?" I say. "Guess a god can afford to be rude."

"The guy is invincible. No one can kill him, so yeah, he's got a free pass for acting high and mighty."

"So, are we going to 'cross the veil'? Whatever that means."

He nods toward the sandstone cliff. "It means going through the waterfall into the cavern behind it, then accessing the portal to the Unseen. Yeah, we're going to do that. But first, you need to understand a few things about crossing the veil."

"I'm listening."

"Once we step through the portal, we will not be in the mortal world anymore."

Can't help it. I roll my eyes. "Gee, really? Thanks for stating the obvious."

He flashes me a scowl. "Let me finish talking before you get snarky. And what happened to not being rude to each other?"

"You're right. We did agree to that." I raise my hands in surrender. "I'll be quiet."

"We won't be in the mortal world, which means the rules of the Unseen take over. The elemental plane is a world dominated by magics where saying the wrong thing can get you ensorcelled, killed, or worse."

What's worse than death? I have a wriggly feeling in my gut that warns me not to ask.

My tour guide to the Unseen grips my upper arms and leans in, his tone and his expression conveying the gravity of the situation. "Listen to me. Once we cross the veil, you cannot ever say the words thank you or please. Never directly express any kind of gratitude. If you do that, you'll be giving the other being immense power over you because you will incur a debt to them. I'm not talking about lending your buddy five bucks. A debt in the Unseen makes you a slave. The person you've indebted yourself to can call that marker in anytime, anywhere, for any reason. And you will have no choice but to obey them."

"You can't be saying an elemental could force me to kill for them."

He leans in more, bending his knees to level our gazes. "*Anything* they want. Get it?"

I nod, biting my lip. Maybe I shouldn't take this risk. Maybe I should run back to my car and forget about cryptids. But I've been the butt of nasty jokes for too long, and I need to prove to the world that creatures of folklore do exist. Vindication has become my obsession.

So I square my shoulders and say, "I get it. And I want to cross the veil."

Chapter Five

Tris

NO MATTER HOW LONG OR HOW HARD I STARE INTO RILEY'S EYES, I CAN'T figure her out. She claims to understand the risks, but I've just told her she might end up magically enslaved or worse if she walks into my world. Still, she wants to do it. I'm starting to think she has hidden motivations, something more than proving "cryptids" are real. I don't feel like a crypto-zoo creature or whatever she calls them. I'm just a leprechaun. I eat copper and oversee the healing vortex.

Way worse beings than me haunt the Unseen.

I'm about to ask Riley again if she's positive she wants to do this when the hairs on my arms and at my nape shiver and stiffen. Out of the corner of my eye, I notice a shadowy shape in the woods.

Riley opens her mouth like she wants to speak.

I seal her lips with my fingers. In a hushed voice, I tell her, "Be quiet. My stalker is back."

Her eyes grow large, but only for a moment.

"Stay here," I hiss under my breath.

Riley nods.

I teleport to the spot where I'd noticed a shadow, but I see nothing there. So I tap into my fae senses and try to listen for any sound that might give me a clue. I can hear Riley's breaths and the beating of her heart, as well as birds chirping in the trees and the rustling of a breeze. Then I detect a different noise—the faint crunching of footsteps. The sound originates from behind me. I zip to the spot.

No one is there.

Crouching, I examine the earth for clues. I'm no tracker, but I've watched enough mortal cop shows to have an idea of what to do. I study the ground and notice the outlines of bare feet. Rising again, I search the woods but see nothing unusual. Whoever had been here must have fled when I zipped over here, but they could still be nearby.

Mortals don't walk around barefoot in these woods.

Whisking myself back to Riley, I frown. "Somebody was there, I know it. Must've been my stalker. Damn sick of waiting for the crazy hag to attack."

"What will you do?"

Instead of answering her question, I throw my head back and holler, "Anthea! Get your ass out here now!"

The air around me shivers with energy. Riley wouldn't feel that, being human, but I can sense it.

"Maybe you scared her off," Riley says.

"Yeah, right." I holler again, "Anthea! Get out here! Anthea!"

A figure materializes at the edge of the woods. Anthea, the salamander stalker, sashays halfway across the clearing, her hips swaying suggestively, and stops to study us. She's naked, of course. Every succubus and incubus I've ever met prefers to walk around naked. Well, except for Travis. He wears pants most of the time, even in the Unseen, since he hasn't been an incubus for long. Both he and Max stay fully clothed whenever they visit the mortal world.

Anthea's toned body is on full display, and her tanned skin bears the hallmarks of a salamander—a coppery sheen dusted with gold flecks. Her swirling red eyes flick from me to Riley and back again, and the silver rims of her irises shimmer. She licks her lips. "Mm, I smell a delicious feast of pleasure. And you brought a friend this time, Triska-licious. I do love a threesome, almost as much as I love an orgy."

"We're not here for sex," I tell her.

Anthea sashays closer and sniffs the air. "Lust is the most potent aroma in any world. Have you not claimed this girl's body yet? The succulent little mortal will be a feast for sure. May I have her if you are not interested?"

"No, you cannot have her." I stalk up to the succubus, towering over her in the hopes I can cow her. "Stop stalking me, you whacked-out sex addict."

"Stalking?" she says like she's never heard the word. Well, she might not have. Elementals generally prefer to stay away from mortals.

"It means you've been following me around, spying on me, who knows what else."

Anthea's brows lift. "Spying? No-no, you are mistaken. I have no need to follow you around. You might be an entertaining lover, Triska-licious, but I have a smörgåsbord to choose from. Why should I waste time haunting you?"

"Stalking. That's the term."

The succubus waves a dismissive hand. "If someone is 'stalking' you, it is not me. Now, if we aren't going to have sex, I must go."

She vanishes.

Riley crinkles her brows as she studies me. "Do you still think she's your stalker?"

"No, I guess not."

"Why did you assume she was the one following you?"

I scrub a hand over my face and groan. "Because we had sex a couple of weeks ago."

"You slept with her once, therefore she's your stalker?"

"No. It was, uh, more than once." I avert my gaze and grimace. "We stayed in her lair for three days."

Even peripherally, I can tell her eyes go wide and her jaw falls open. "You screwed that woman for three days? What, like all the time? Did you take breaks to eat or… whatever?"

"I'm a fae, not a mortal. That means I can go a lot longer without food or water than you can." I force myself to look at her. "So yeah, Anthea and I fucked for three days straight."

Riley's eyes grow so large that I expect they'll pop out any second. Should I cup my hands in case I need to catch them? Nah, they'll dangle from the sockets, I think. Mortal anatomy isn't my strong suit.

But I'd love to become an expert on Riley's anatomy.

"That's a lot of sex," she says. Her eyes aren't bulging anymore, but she sounds baffled. Only for a moment. Then she shakes her head and clears her throat. "If Anthea isn't your stalker, who is?"

"Not a clue."

"Do you have enemies?"

I snort. "Ya think? I mean, I've only helped destroy more evil elementals than I can count. There was Skeiron, then that sorcerer guy, then the harpy Aello. Oh, and let's not forget the vamps created by Eros who somehow became our problem after the Four Winds made Eros, Kamadeva, and Setesh mortal as punishment for being evil bastards. And I've refused to help elemental creeps who wanted to abuse the healing vortex for their own gain."

Riley's brows knit tightly over her nose. "Vamps? Healing vortex?"

I suddenly feel itchy, like ants have crawled inside my jeans. "I oversee a real vortex that can heal mortals and elementals. As for vampires… Yeah, they're real too. Mortals know about vamps, right? I mean, you guys have romance novels about those bloodsuckers. Don't get what's sexy about them."

"Vampires are real?" She blows out a breath. "Wow. The universe is even weirder than I thought."

"No shit. Wait until you cross the veil into the Unseen."

She considers me as if she can't quite grasp anything I've said. "What are the Four Winds?"

"Uh, that's a long story. Let's save it for after you've gotten used to my world."

"Okay." She twists her mouth into the cutest expression of confusion. "What did you mean when you said the vamps have somehow become your problem?"

"Me and my friends, we sort of became nannies for the vampires. Without their god masters, they didn't know what to do with themselves." I wave toward the falls. "Do you want to visit the Unseen or not?"

"Yes."

"Then let's skip the chitchat for now. Okay?"

"Sure."

I wrap my arms around her, bend my knees, and leap over the railing, intending to land on the ledge beside the waterfall. But my foot slips, and we fall backward into the pool below. Riley yelps. We both sink under the water, but I manage to keep my arms around her and kick my feet to surge up out of the pool. With one arm around her, I swim to the edge by the railing and drag us both onto the ground.

"What happened?" she asks, sounding breathless.

"No frigging idea. My targeting slipped or something." I still have my arm around her. So I stand up, hoisting her with me. "Should we try again? This has never happened to me before."

"Is there another way to get into the Unseen?"

"Nope. Only portals, which all involve water."

She sucks in a big breath and exhales it. "Okay. Let's try again."

This time when I leap, we land on the ledge. Before Riley can say anything, I jump through the cascade into the cavern behind it. The roar of the falls is almost deafening outside the cavern, but in here, magics mute the noise. Keeping one arm around her, I thrust the other out toward the rear wall. Then I clench my fist and snap my fingers straight.

The rear wall shimmers, and the portal telescopes open.

Riley stares at the serpentine colors that writhe within the opening amid the roiling obsidian background. "What is that?"

"The portal. We're about to cross the veil."

I jump through the opening, thumping down in the Unseen, just past the boulder that serves as the portal on this side of the veil. Riley's jaw drops. She swings her head left and right, then bends it backward to gape up at the sky. Well, the Unseen does have a sky of deeper blue than anything on earth, and the sun sort of glitters as if it has tiny diamonds embedded in it. Stuff that resembles moss on earth, according to my friend Lindsey, droops from the trees. Mortal ones have leaves or needles. Never seen those in this world.

She doesn't seem to care that our clothes are drenched.

"Holy cow," Riley says, her voice filled with wonder. "This is incredible."

"I've lived here all my life. It doesn't impress me."

"But the sky... It's so beautiful, and scary at the same time." She gives up on staring at the heavens and looks at me. "Do you have a house or something in this world?"

"Or something. We call them lairs here."

"You should give it a friendlier name. 'Lair' sounds like someplace you take people so you can torture them."

"I don't torture anybody."

Riley wriggles in my arms. "You can let go of me now. We already crossed the veil."

"Why should I let go? I love the way you wriggle."

"Do I need to grab your balls and twist them hard?"

I chuckle. "Yeah, that might be fun."

She puckers her lips. "Tris—"

"Okay, okay." I release her, and she stumbles backward a couple of steps. "First, I thought I'd take you to the fae kingdom and introduce you to some people."

"I get to meet other copper fae? Do they prefer to be called fae, not leprechauns?"

"We use both terms interchangeably, but I prefer leprechaun."

"Copper fae sounds sexier."

"Maybe I should start calling myself that, then." I snatch her backpack off her shoulder and sling it over mine. "Let's go."

"Are we walking there?"

"Not unless you want to die of starvation and thirst. The fae kingdom is a long, long ways off." I grab her with my other arm, tucking Riley snugly against my side. "But I think you'd rather travel the elemental way."

Before she can speak, I teleport us away and let the abyssal tunnel dry us off. That doesn't always work, but this time it does. We emerge in a courtyard. The white buildings shimmer with a faint wash of copper imbued with magics that protect the structures from decay. Since the buildings are old, the wash has taken on a slightly green patina.

"What is this place?" Riley asks. "It looks like a spiffier version of a medieval village."

"This is the enclave of the copper fae. We call it Coppertown."

"How original. Must be a thousand places on earth named that."

I step away from Riley and toss the backpack to her. "If you're going to be sarcastic, you can carry your own stuff."

She hooks the pack over her shoulder. "Fine. I don't need your help, anyway."

The bossy woman whirls away from me, takes a few steps, and freezes.

Yeah, she probably just noticed the fae kids who are zipping around, laughing whenever they pop up right behind their friends to surprise them. Teleportation always makes mortals do a double take. But for my kind, traveling that way is normal. We don't even think about it. I'm sure it's more than teleporting that has her flummoxed. Riley must also see the multitude of other magical antics going on around her in the courtyard.

The backpack slides off Riley's shoulder and thumps onto the ground. As I walk up beside her, I see her jaw has gone slack again.

An older man rushes up to Riley and offers her a lump of gold that gives off a glittering aura. "Care to barter this gold for a lock of your hair, child?"

"Um, what?"

I walk up beside her and give the man a light shove. "Back off, pal. She doesn't want your phony gold. At least conjure the real thing for your scam."

He pretends to take offense. "This is the real thing."

"Yeah, right." I grab the rock and take a bite out of the gold, spitting it out as I pretend to gag. "Tastes like garbage, man."

The guy huffs. "Only gold fae eat such rocks. We are copper fae, you silly boy."

"Duh. Thanks for reminding me." I drop the rock on the ground and stomp on it, pulverizing the phony gold. "Don't mess with this girl. She's with me."

The man leaves.

Riley opens her mouth, about to complain, I'm sure. But I grasp her chin and say, "We're in my world now. Follow my lead and my orders. Got it? For your own safety, let everyone believe you belong to me."

"I do not belong to you or anyone."

"You can be liberated all you want back home. But you are not in the mortal world anymore." I bend my head until our noses almost touch. "Do you want to die?"

Chapter Six

Riley

DO I WANT TO DIE? OF COURSE NOT. BUT I REFUSE TO KEEP MY MOUTH shut and let him speak for me. Tris doesn't know me well enough to do that, and I don't know him either. We met earlier today. But as he pointed out, we are in his world now, a place full of magic that can enslave me or kill me or who knows what else. Maybe I should defer to him—for the moment.

"Okay, fine," I say. "I'll do what you say. But if I think you're trying anything sneaky, I will kick your ass."

He turns sideways and pats his bottom. "Go ahead. Try it."

"No thanks. I save my ass-kicking for when it's necessary."

"Good to know." He nods toward my backpack, which still lies on the ground. "Want me to carry that for you? Or would you rather prove how independent you are and carry it yourself?"

"I can carry it. But thank—"

He slaps a hand over my mouth and hisses, "Were you not listening to anything I told you? No T-word, no P-word, no direct expressions of anything resembling gratitude. Got it?"

I nod. When he removes his hand from my mouth, I tell him, "Sor—"

"No S-word either."

"Right. This is harder than it sounded." I hate to admit it, but I can't deny the truth. "Maybe I should let you do most of the talking."

He throws his head back and spreads his arms wide. "A miracle has happened. Riley Jordan agreed to shut her trap."

"You are so not funny. And you're kind of a sexist twerp."

Tris aims a sly smile at me. "Let me kiss you, and I'll prove to you how good I am to the ladies."

"You already assaulted my lips without permission once. I do not give you permission to do it again."

But yeah, I think I'd love it if he did kiss me. Bad idea. For all I know, a kiss qualifies as saying thank you or something, and I'll wind up enslaved to him. Would he lie about what constitutes gratitude? I might find him extremely annoying, but I have trouble believing he would deceive me about something that important.

"Come on," he says as he starts walking. "Let's go meet some other leprechauns. The courtyard is a haven for tricksters, but the rest of the village mostly has nice people."

"Do you have any family here?"

He stops dead but doesn't look at me. "Yeah, I have family here. But we won't see them."

"Why not? Don't they like you? Maybe you got too snarky with them."

"That's not the reason." He shoves a hand through his hair. "Look, maybe I'll introduce you to my parents. Maybe. But you won't meet my siblings."

"Ohhh, so they're the ones who don't like you."

"Yeah. Kinda. It's complicated, and I don't want to discuss it with you."

I raise my hands. "Okay, no problem."

He starts walking again, and I hurry to keep up with his fast pace. I see lots of people with glimmering eyes, though not all of them have blue irises like Tris. I also spot leprechauns doing all kinds of magic, like one guy who throws his hands up to create a semitransparent image of some sort of bird. It doesn't look like any creature I've ever seen in the mortal world. A woman seems to be conjuring jewelry in the palm of her hand, and two leprechauns who look like teenagers are doing sleight-of-hand tricks. Or they might actually be making things appear and disappear.

Tris has started to walk even faster.

I'm breathing hard while I try to keep up with him. "Wait, Tris! I need to go slower."

He ignores me. Or else he didn't hear me because he's now several yards ahead of me.

So I hurl my pack at him. It thumps into his back.

At last, he stops and glances at me. "What did you do that for?"

"To get your attention, obviously."

He picks up my pack, holding the straps in one hand. "You didn't need to whack me with your bag to get my attention."

"Yeah, I did. You're walking way too fast for me, and shouting at you didn't work."

"Oh." He shuffles back to me. "I was lost in thought, I guess."

"You really don't like being in this town, do you?"

He shrugs one shoulder.

"Then why did you bring me here?"

"I thought it'd be okay. But then you asked me about my family, and I got sort of… I don't know."

"Annoyed? That's the word I would use."

He rubs his jaw. "It's more like anxiety."

"Okay. Anxiety about what?" Why do I care? He's been a jerk to me. But he also agreed to introduce me to other elementals. Tris is one confusing guy—er, being.

"It's not my fault. What happened to my brothers and sisters…" He trails off as his gaze shifts past my shoulder. "Oh, crap."

"What's wrong?" I half-turn to see what he's staring at—two people walking toward us. They look a little older than Tris, though not a lot older. Since these people must be fae, I can't gauge how many years they might have under their belts. I mean, Larissa is over seventy thousand years old. How do leprechauns age? Do they age at all? I probably don't want to learn the answer. "Do you know that couple, Tris?"

"Yeah." He winces. "They're my parents."

"I'm guessing you don't get along with them."

"Well…"

The couple reaches us, and the woman seizes Tris's face in both hands. "Where have you been, Triskaideka? It's been months since you've come to dinner at home. You don't visit us, you don't conjure a letter to us, you don't even talk to your brothers and sisters anymore."

"Ma, come on. Don't embarrass me."

She releases his face and kisses his cheek. "We miss you, sweetie."

The man approaches Tris too. "Son, you've made your mother very unhappy. Stop this nonsense. No one cares about what happened anymore."

So this is Tris's dad.

"Nobody cares?" Tris huffs. "Have you asked Ennea how she feels about it? She threw a cauldron at me last time I saw her."

Cauldron? I wonder what his sister was doing with something like that. The only thing I've heard of anybody doing with a cauldron is casting evil spells. And I learned that from the movies.

"Don't be so sensitive," his father says. "Hiding is not the answer. You didn't even try to apologize to the others."

"Apologize?" Tris seems flummoxed by that suggestion. "I didn't do anything. The frigging Unseen made it happen, not me."

I can't follow this conversation at all. The Unseen made what happen? Then there's the cauldron throwing. Jeez, this world is totally bizarre.

Tris's mom swerves her attention to me. "Are you Triskaideka's girlfriend?"

"No. I'm just a friend." That's quite some first name Tris has. I understand why he prefers the shorter version. "He offered to introduce me to other elementals to help with my research."

Tris's face goes blank, then he scrunches it up so tightly that he almost looks like a cartoon character.

What did I say? I was just being friendly.

His mom glances from Tris to me and back to him. "Dear, what does your friend mean? Research?"

"Don't listen to Riley. She's a ditz."

"But you brought her home with you. She must be important to my son if he does that." His mom comes up to me and grasps my upper arms. "We should get to know each other, dear. I'm Nyara, Triskaideka's mother. And that frowning man over there is Frimis, his father."

"I'm Riley Jordan. It's, um, nice to meet you both."

She kisses both my cheeks. "You must stay for the midday feast."

Feast? Not sure I can eat that much. But I don't want to be rude to Tris's parents.

Nyara looks at Tris. "While we feast, my son can explain what sort of 'research' you are doing, Riley."

While his mother leads me away, I glance back at Tris and hunch my shoulders, trying for a contrite expression. I can't say "sorry," so I have to show my regret in another way.

He shakes his head and follows us ladies, with his dad bringing up the rear.

I honestly did not mean to get him in trouble with his family. Whatever happened between Tris and his siblings, it's none of my business. But okay, I am dying to know the details. I also wonder what kind of food will be served during our "midday feast." I hope it's nothing too bizarre, like the roasted innards of a freaky bird.

While we head for what I assume will be his parents' house, Nyara chatters about Tris's childhood and how he used to be a "slip of a thing, with no strength at all" and she used to worry he would die in one of those "crazy battles" that he and his friends keep starting.

"Come on, Ma," Tris complains. "We don't start the battles. It's evil jerks who do the instigating."

"No, it's that Lindsey woman you insist on fraternizing with."

"You've never even met her. Lindsey is a good person."

"She married a former sylph. They are the most arrogant beings in the Unseen."

Maybe I should change the subject. Tris looks frazzled. "Nyara, why are all the buildings here painted a light shade of green?"

"They aren't painted that color, dear. Every building has been washed with a copper glaze, which develops a green patina over time." She's walking beside me, and she casts me a sidelong glance. "Doesn't copper do that in the mortal world?"

"Oh, yeah. I guess it does. But I thought it must be different here." I hesitate before asking another question, because it seems too personal. "Um, Tris mentioned he eats copper. So isn't covering your buildings with that metal kind of like wallpapering your house with food?"

Nyara laughs. "Yes, I suppose it is. But not all leprechauns eat copper. The ones like Tris, who serve as guardians of the healing vortexes, must eat copper to keep every vortex working properly. The rest of us eat it only as a treat."

"So we won't be consuming rocks during the midday feast."

"No, dear. You can't eat copper ore, and we don't wish to at the moment."

"What kind of food will we have?"

"Oh, it's very much like what mortals enjoy on earth. In fact, we often buy meats and vegetables imported from your world." She hooks her arm around mine. "And you are in luck, dear. We have T-bone steaks, green beans, and even russet potatoes. Oh, and Granny Smith apples that I've made into a delicious dessert."

"Wow, that sounds amazing. I'm hungry enough to eat all of that."

"Good. We don't call it the midday feast for nothing."

I glance back at Tris, and he lifts his brows. Not sure what that means. But he seems more relaxed now. After the strange mishap he had earlier when he missed the waterfall's ledge, I wonder if he needs more copper. But he looks strong and virile right now, so maybe his mishap was just a freak accident.

Oh yeah, he looks *very* virile.

"How long have you known my son?" Nyara asks.

"We met today."

"But you look at him like a woman who sees exactly what she wants." Nyara nudges me with her elbow. "Have you slept with him yet?"

I think my eyes might be bulging. Are all elementals this direct about intimate matters? "Well, um, we just met. I think it's too early for that."

"Nonsense. The multiverse is a dangerous place, and you never know what might happen next. Don't hold back with your feelings or your desires." She winks. "I made love with Frimis two hours after we met. And we were married eight days later."

Eight days? I'd need to know a guy for longer than that before I'd tie the knot. As for sex… Well, maybe I would love to find out what it's like to be with an elemental. But no, that's a bad idea. What happens to a mortal who sleeps with a copper fae? I need a lot more info before I'll get naked with Tris.

The home where Tris's parents live, and where he grew up, looks relatively normal. The outside walls have that green patina, but inside, it looks a lot like an average house in the mortal world. Our midday meal tastes delicious and fills my tummy. I love listening to Tris and his parents joking with each other and sharing stories about Tris's childhood antics. But I get a little confused by the way they keep implying he was a scrawny kid until recently. When I ask about that, Frimis responds.

"You don't understand our kind," he says. "When a copper fae reaches puberty, he remains in a state of suspended growth for many hundreds of years. His brain matures, but his body does not. Only when the transmutation begins does he become his true self. Of course, that also applies to females."

"What is the transmutation?" I ask.

"Something like puberty, but far more excruciating." Frimis looks at his son. "Perhaps you should explain it to Riley."

Tris pinches up his face. "Not now, Pa."

"You should tell her about it before you make love to the girl. Your fated mate should understand what you went through."

"She's not my fated mate. That's bullshit, anyway."

Nyara smiles, her cheeks dimpling. "That's what your friend Max thought—until he met Harper."

"Only salamanders have fated mates."

Frimis raises his brows. "No one knows when or how or why any elemental will discover that they are destined to be with one person. Don't resist what the Unseen wants."

Nyara clasps her hands on the table and gazes at me. "Tell me, Riley, what sort of research are you conducting?"

"I want to learn more about elementals and other supernatural beings. I'd been using the term cryptid for anything that modern science claims can't exist, but now I'm thinking I should adjust my terminology."

"What is the goal of your research?"

"To uncover the truth and find proof that supernatural beings do exist."

Nyara lifts her brows. "How would you prove that?"

"By gathering evidence. Photos, videos, hair samples, whatever. I met Travis the salamander, Tris's friend, and he prefers not to be photographed or recorded on video."

"Of course he feels that way. It would expose us. We live in the Unseen because we wish to remain in hiding. If one of us enters the mortal world, we glamour to hide our true nature."

"I don't want to expose you. I just want to understand the supernatural and show everyone that it does exist."

Nyara opens her mouth, but she doesn't get the chance to speak again.

Tris tosses his fork onto his now-empty plate, and it clatters loudly. "It's time to go. Riley wants to meet other kinds of elementals too, not just leprechauns."

He gets up and urges me to do the same. But as we head for the door, Nyara rushes up to us and grasps her son's arm.

"Oh, Tris," she says. "Speak to your brothers and sisters. It hurts my heart to see you at odds with them. And also convince Riley not to expose us."

He takes my hand, leading me away.

CHAPTER SEVEN

Tris

WHY DID MY MOTHER HAVE TO HARASS RILEY ABOUT HER RESEARCH? And why did she need to harass me about my brothers and sisters? Riley just wants to understand the Unseen, and I've tried to talk to my siblings. They won't listen. What happened to them is my fault, they say. And Ma shouldn't have gotten annoyed about Riley wanting to take pictures of our kind since mortals wouldn't believe what the photos show, anyway. This is why I rarely come home anymore. I don't feel welcome here in the kingdom of the copper fae. Don't think I belong anywhere these days.

Once we've left the village behind, I stop and turn toward Riley. "What kind of elementals would you like to meet next?"

"I have no idea. You know more about them than I do."

"Okay. Let's try the silver fae. They make awesome jewelry, and they also know how to party."

"Sure. Sounds like fun."

I lash an arm around her waist.

But before I can whisk us away, a giant bolt of lightning slams down a dozen feet from us. The flash blinds me, the electricity arcs out to sizzle on my skin, and the shock of it makes me lose my grip on Riley. We tumble to the ground with me on top of her. I scramble to get out from under her while black spots obscure my vision and my ears ring so loudly that I can't hear it if she's screaming or crying. Once I get to my knees, I feel around to find Riley.

She's still on the ground. Not moving.

I pat her legs and hips but can't feel any injuries. Since I'm still blinded, I need to keep exploring her body with my hands, making my way up to her breasts and higher to her throat and face. She doesn't react at all. No, she can't be dead. I remember what Lindsey told me once about how to check for a mortal's pulse, and I do that. She's still alive.

My vision finally returns to normal.

Her eyes are closed. I consider performing mouth-to-mouth, which Lindsey also explained to me. But Riley's eyelids begin to flutter. Do mortals perform mouth-to-mouth on someone who's breathing? I have no idea. So I tip her head back, which makes her mouth fall open a touch, then I seal my lips over hers and blow.

She coughs. Her eyes flutter open, and she gazes at me with a dazed expression. "Did you save me?"

Yeah, she sounds dazed too.

I scratch my neck. "Uh, well…"

"Thank you, Tris."

A thread of magic snaps taut between us and releases a zing of power. *Oh, no.* She just indebted herself to me. Well, all I need to do is absolve her of that debt. But I don't get the chance. The ground shudders so hard that I almost fall over even though I'm kneeling. If I'd been standing, I would've toppled over for sure. What in the worlds is going on?

I grab Riley and zip us to the portal where burbling water cascades over the boulder that marks the entrance. Then I grasp Riley's shoulders and give her a gentle shake, hoping to knock her out of her stupor. It doesn't work, so I decide to do this without her consent.

Taking her face in my hands, I stare into her bleary eyes. "I absolve you of your debt to me."

Nothing happens. I should feel a zing like what I experienced when she said the T-word. Why didn't it work? I try again, speaking in a more fervent tone and concentrating all my mental power on freeing her.

"I absolve you of your debt to me, Riley."

Still nothing. It makes no sense. Speaking those words should release her, but it hasn't. I think back on the events of today and suddenly realize something vital. I've had multiple accidents today. I tripped in the rock shop, though the floor was level and free of debris. Then I missed the mark when I tried to jump onto the ledge beside the waterfall. When I tried to teleport us to the silver fae village, we wound up in the woods—and then lightning struck and the earth shook.

Now I can't release Riley from her debt.

Though I really, really don't want to do it, I realize I have no choice. I need help. And I can think of only one person who has the power to give me that assistance. So I whisk us straight into the laboratory of the smartest, most competent fae witch in the Unseen.

Ennea stands behind a table, gazing down into a simmering cauldron. She lifts her head, and her attention zeroes in on me as her bright green eyes begin to swirl. My sister straightens and squints at me. "What are you doing here, Tris? I told you to stay away."

"I need your help. Well, it's really my new friend who needs you."

Riley slumps against me, still dazed. Dammit, shouldn't she be back to normal now? The lightning hadn't left me in a stupor, but I have no idea how something like that might affect a human.

Ennea marches over to us and grasps Riley's head with both hands. "What did you do to her?"

"Nothing. A bolt of lightning hit right next to us and knocked her out. When she woke up, she was like this."

My sister waves a hand, conjuring a small sofa that has no back. I think that's called a settee or something. Max used to have one of those. "Put her down on that."

I pick Riley up and set her on the sofa. Her eyes are open, but she still acts like she's semi-comatose.

Ennea snares my arm and drags me back to the table where her cauldron still boils away. "Who is that girl? And what happened to her?"

"Riley is a mortal who wants to learn about the Unseen. I met her this morning." I hunch my shoulders as I glance at the girl in question. "I've had some weird accidents today. The last one involved lightning and an earthquake."

"Are you telling me everything?"

"Yeah, of course I am. Can you help Riley?"

"Only if you're a hundred percent sure there's nothing else I need to know. Magics are finicky, Tris. The slightest error can turn a good spell into a nasty one."

I shove my hands into my pants pockets and bow my head. "Well, she, uh, kind of indebted herself to me."

"What?" Ennea virtually shrieks. She slugs my arm. "You've turned into a real scumbag, haven't you? What you did to me and our siblings was bad enough. But this is beyond the pale even for you."

"I didn't make Riley do anything. She mumbled the T-word when she woke up. I tried to absolve her, but it wouldn't work."

"Yeah, 'cause you suck at magics."

"Can you rip me a new one later?" I glance at Riley. "Just help her, okay?"

"All right. But first, we need to figure out why you can't release her debt."

Ennea bustles around hunting for who knows what, then comes back to me. She holds a small vial. "Drink this. Then try again to absolve her."

I take the vial. It's full of neon orange liquid. "Uh, what is this crap?"

"You don't want to know. Just swallow it." She smacks the back of my head. "It's your fault she's bound to you, so make it right."

Okay, she has a point. My mishaps today led to this problem, and I need to suck it up and make things right. So I pop the cork on the vial and swig its contents. The gunk burns down my throat and makes me gag, then the gagging mutates into hacking. I'm bent over, sure I'll vomit any second, when the torture ends.

I straighten and tromp over to the settee where Riley still lies dazed. Kneeling, I brush hair away from her eyes. "I absolve you of your debt to me, Riley Jordan."

Nothing.

Ennea rushes over to crouch beside me. "That should've worked."

"Well, it didn't."

She eyes me with a strange expression. "Maybe you do have something hinky going on with you today."

"Oh, so now I'm not a scumbag anymore."

"I'm still ticked at you, but I won't shirk my responsibility to the family. Ma and Pa would be heartbroken if you got destroyed or turned into a gnome or something."

No, I don't expect her to forgive me yet. But at least she'll help me and Riley. Honestly, I don't care about myself right now. I only worry about the mortal girl lying limp on a little sofa.

"You like this girl a lot," Ennea says. "Don't you?"

"I barely know her. But yeah, I think I do like her even though she can be annoying."

My sister smiles. "Harper hated Max at first. She even tried to kill him. So don't give up because Riley rubs you the wrong way sometimes. Maybe she's your—"

"Don't even say it. Ma already gave me the speech when we had midday feast at home."

"You saw Ma and Pa?"

"That's right." I lean toward her. "And they didn't smack me or call me a scumbag."

Ennea studies me for a moment, then rises and sighs. "I'm doing this for the girl. Our issues can wait until another time."

"I appreciate that." And yeah, I can say the word appreciate without incurring a debt. The rules of debts and bargains are kinda vague sometimes.

"Come on," Ennea says, waving for me to get up. "Let's figure out why you're having accidents today."

I follow her back to the cauldron and eye it with a hint of suspicion. "Are you planning to throw this thing at me again?"

"Not unless you get snarky." She bustles around the lab again, hunting for whatever ingredients she thinks she needs to sort me out. Then she comes back with several items in each hand, dumping them on the table beside the cauldron. "Give me your hand, Tris."

I offer it to her.

She grasps my wrist, turning my palm up, and holds my hand over the bubbling cauldron. The humid air wafting out of it carries a weird scent, and I can't help wrinkling my nose. Ennea rolls her eyes at me. "Don't move, okay? Keep your hand right there or it might foul up my spell."

"Too late. It already smells like a dead gnome."

She ignores me and goes about opening the vials and little cloth bags she'd gathered, pouring potions into the cauldron and then adding dashes of dried who-knows-what. Herbs? I have no clue. Ennea doesn't share her secrets with anyone, not even the guy she's dating. He's a gold fae, and that tribe has the snootiest attitude. I guess my sister likes him because he's "hot," according to every woman I know.

Every time Ennea dumps a new ingredient into the cauldron, sparkling flames erupt. Each flame has a different color. My arm is starting to ache and quiver from holding my hand out for so long, but I won't complain about that.

Finally, she dips an eyedropper into the fetid mixture and collects some of the liquid. Then she grasps my wrist again and deposits three drops of brownish gunk onto my palm.

"Ow, that's hot," I hiss. "Are you done yet?"

"Uh-huh." She stares down at my palm, her eyes half-closed and her lips puckered. Suddenly, her eyes flare wide. She releases my hand and swerves her attention to me. "Tris, you…"

"What is it? Will Riley never come out of her coma?"

"That's not it." My sister stares at me with her lips parted. "Tris, you are cursed."

"What? No, that can't be." I shake my head as coldness spreads across my skin and sinks deep inside me. "I thought I had a stalker, but this is just crazy. Who would curse me? Are you sure that's what I've got?"

She nods slowly. "I'm sorry, Tris. This is as bad as bad gets."

"You can fix it, right? De-curse me?"

Now she shakes her head slowly. "The only way to remove a curse is to find the one who cast it. But that kind of spell is degenerative. It will only get worse, progressively, until it infects your body and mind too."

"I have to find the jerk who cursed me. I can do that." No idea how to do that, but I have no choice. Maybe I annoyed a few people when I took little trips into the mortal world. That's no reason to clobber me with dark magics.

Ennea punches my arm. "What did you do to make somebody want to hate you this much?"

"Nothing. I mean, I tick people off sometimes, but elementals are always harassing each other. It's our way. That's no reason to throw a curse on me."

My sister sets her palms on the table and leans into them, her head bowed. "This is seriously bad, Tris."

"Yeah, I get it. I need to find the jerk who did this to me."

"I'll stay here and work on the magic end of things. You need to scour the Unseen for whoever did this." She raises her head to look at me sideways. "You need help, Tris."

"The gang will pitch in. We always help each other out."

"Be careful." She grips my face in both hands and gives me her Stern Big Sister stare. "I've seen what a curse can do. If we can't stop this, you are going to die."

Aw, shit. I should've stayed in bed today.

Chapter Eight

Riley

I FELL INTO A TRANCE OR SOMETHING A LITTLE WHILE AGO, AND ONLY now do I feel it lifting. My eyes have been open, but I couldn't understand what I was seeing or hearing, not until a minute ago. That's when I saw Tris standing on the other side of this weird underground room while he talked to a woman who kind of resembles him. One of his siblings? The answer hardly matters. The look on Tris's face tells me something very bad has happened.

Little by little, I sit up and swing my legs off the sofa I'm lying on, then I yawn. Kind of loudly.

Tris veers his attention to me. "Riley. How are you feeling?"

"Okay. A little weird, like I just woke up from a freaky dream that lasted for days." I rise from the sofa and stretch. "But basically fine."

Tris blows out a breath as if he'd been holding it. Was he worried about me?

I walk over to the long table where he stands beside a pretty, petite woman who has luminous green eyes. A cauldron sits on the table, steam rising from its depths. I can hear the contents bubbling away. As I get closer, I wave a hand in front of my nose. "Pew. What is that?"

"A potion to aid my spellcasting," the woman says. She reaches around Tris to offer me her hand. "I'm Ennea, by the way. Tris's big sister."

"Nice to meet you." I shake her hand. "I'm Riley Jordan."

"Yeah, hon, I know. Tris said your name while he was trying to absolve you of your debt to him."

"My debt? I don't owe him any money."

Ennea laughs softly. "No, hon, not that kind of debt. You said the T-word while you were dazed, and that sealed a debt with Tris. To his credit, he feels awful about it. But the curse somebody cast on him seems to be blocking his ability to absolve you."

I think my head is spinning again. Or else the room actually does whirl round and round like a carnival ride. The sensation passes quickly, thank goodness. "I don't remember speaking the T-word. But if you say I'm indebted to him, I believe you." I suddenly realize what Ennea said a moment ago. "Wait. He's cursed?"

"Yeah. It's wicked evil mojo. Curses are some of the blackest dark magics in the Unseen."

"But we can save him, right?"

Tris's brows hike up. But then he glances away, almost as if he's embarrassed. Why? Because I suggested I might want to help him remove his curse? Maybe we don't know each other very well, but I could never stand by and watch someone suffer.

"I should take you home," Tris tells me. "It's not safe to be around me right now."

"Are you reneging on our deal? You're supposed to introduce me to more elementals." I can't explain why I want to stay with him. Well, he does look so miserable, and I've always been a sucker for an underdog. "Let me help you, Tris."

"You don't have magics. Not sure what you can do other than get hit by lightning again."

"It didn't hit me. The bolt kind of sideswiped me and left me stunned. I'm fine now."

Ennea has been watching us while we talked, and now her lips curl up at the corners. "Take Riley with you, Tris. She's a spitfire. I like her."

He squints at his sister. "You met her thirty seconds ago. She's a mortal, which means my curse could kill her. It almost did already."

"I have a good feeling about Riley. Trust her."

"Get your nose out of my business."

She plants her hands on her hips and lifts her chin. "Listen to your big sister, Triskaideka."

"You guys have cool names," I say. "But something about them seems familiar."

"They're Greek numbers," Ennea says. "Our parents decided it would be more expedient to name their kids numerically to make it easier to remember our birth order. Fae are weird that way."

"So which numbers are you two?"

"I'm Ennea, which makes me the ninth child. Triskaideka is the thirteenth."

Her statement makes me curious, and though I shouldn't poke my nose into their business any further, I can't help myself. "Is Tris the last child in your family?"

"No. Our parents didn't stop until fifteen."

I study Tris, and something occurs to me. "Do you think somebody cursed Tris because he's the thirteenth child? In the mortal world, thirteen is usually considered to be a bad omen."

"Not so much in the Unseen," Ennea says. "But maybe whoever cursed him has been to the mortal world and adopted some human traditions. It's worth exploring."

Tris scrubs his hands over his cheeks and groans. "It's worse than you think. I'm the thirteenth child born on the thirteenth day of the thirteenth month in the fae calendar."

"You guys have your own calendar?" I say. "Do all elemental races create their own versions? That must get confusing."

"Not really. We're used to it."

Ennea's cheeks dimple when she looks at me. "You're a smart cookie, Riley. And I'm starting to think you're onto something here." She punches her brother's arm. "Take her with you, Tris."

He rolls his eyes. "Fine. She can come with me."

"Good. Now go investigate."

"How? I can't go around asking everyone I run into whether they know who cursed me."

Ennea taps his head with one finger. "Use your brain. Or better yet, use Riley's."

He glances at me, then returns his attention to Ennea. And he winces. "Aren't you still mad at me? It wasn't my fault, but you did throw a cauldron at me the last time we saw each other."

"What you did doesn't matter right now. Go, find your curse-caster."

He kisses his sister's cheek, then grabs my hand and whisks us away. We wind up inside a small cavern carved out of solid rock, much like Ennea's cave but without the bubbling cauldron and other paraphernalia. But the space we stand inside now has rough-hewn walls, a rough dirt floor, and only two pieces of rickety furniture—a wooden chair and a matching footrest. And oh yeah, it also features a musty odor, as if mildew has infiltrated the space.

"Um, what is this place?" I ask.

Tris grimaces while avoiding my gaze. "It's kind of my, uh, lair. Temporary lair, that is. I haven't found a good home base yet."

"How long have you been looking for one?"

Scratching his neck, he grimaces even more. "About eight hundred years."

I freeze for a moment, and I'm pretty sure my eyes must be bulging. The air drying them suggests that is the case. Though I open my mouth, I can't make any words come out.

Tris flashes me a scowl. "What's your problem now?"

Did he seriously just ask me that? Like it's not obvious to anyone with a brain that what he said is insane. I might've learned that one of his friends is over seventy thousand years old, but the revelation about his age still floors me. I flap my arms, but the only sound I can make is a series of sharp huffs. When I finally manage to speak, I can't help sounding shocked and annoyed in equal measure. "Eight hundred years? You can't drop that bomb and expect me to act like it's normal. I mean, if you've searched for a 'lair' for eight hundred years, that must mean you are… um…"

"Older than eight hundred. Yeah, duh."

I get why I'm freaking out. But why should he get so upset about it? Ohhhh, wait. I get it. "You're embarrassed to tell me your age."

"Ya think?" He stalks over to the rickety chair and flops his butt onto it. "Mortals don't like to hear that kind of thing. 'I'm eight hundred and seventy-two years old' isn't a great conversation starter."

"*How* old are you?" Okay, I'm probably gaping at him again with my eyes bulging. "But you look—You can't be—I'm only twenty-eight."

I cannot form words anymore. What are words? Something that involves letters and syllables…

Tris flattens his lips and narrows his gaze. "How can you be shocked? You met Larissa, the former goddess who told you she was created more than seventy thousand years ago."

Once again, I make only sharp huffing sounds.

A loud crack reverberates through the cave. His chair wobbles, then shatters. His butt hits the floor. The leprechaun now sits on a pile of broken sticks. He thumps his fists on the floor and snarls, "Dammit!"

Tris bends his knees, rests his elbows on them, and cradles his head in his raised hands. Then he moans pitifully.

Okay, it's time for me to suck it up and act like a mature adult. He's upset. I need to comfort him, somehow. Why do I need to do that? Because he's being pitiful again. Yeah, I'm a pushover. So I kneel in front of him and kiss the top of his head. Then I give him a quick hug.

He lifts his head a teeny bit, spreading his fingers so he can peek at me through them. "What are you doing?"

"Trying to make you feel better."

"Why?"

"Do I need a reason? You look miserable, and I can't just stand by while anyone suffers."

He removes his hands from his face and regards me with a strange expression. "You met me this morning. Now you're indebted to me, and I'm cursed. Being nice doesn't make sense in this situation."

"Of course it does." I stand up, gesturing for him to do the same. "Time to get off your ancient ass and stop feeling sorry for yourself."

He gives me a lopsided smirk. "You're hot when you get bossy. Actually, you're hot all the time, even when you act like a ditz."

"Th—" *Rats.* I almost spoke the T-word. "I'm glad you feel that way."

He hops to his feet and grins. "I think you're getting the hang of life in the Unseen. Almost said the word that shall not be spoken, didn't you? But you stopped yourself."

"I'm getting a crash course in how not to accidentally indebt yourself to an elemental." I bump my shoulder into his upper arm. He's too dang tall for me to reach his shoulder. "And for the record, I think you're hot too."

"Don't you worry I might abuse your debt to me?

"Nope."

He shakes his head slowly. "You are the weirdest mortal I've ever met." His mouth slides into a sensual smirk. "You're also the sexiest."

Warmth blossoms inside me, and a delicious wetness gathers between my thighs. I'm attracted to a leprechaun. That's too bizarre for words but also incredibly erotic. I can't resist skimming my gaze over his entire body while my pulse revs up and that wetness grows, instigating a tingle down there.

"Damn, Riley," Tris growls. "You're turned on. I can smell it, and the scent is driving me crazy."

The rough tone of his voice must be turning me into a crazy person because I have no other excuse for the words that tumble from my lips. "Does my debt to you give you the power to order me to do anything you want?"

"I guess so. Never thought about that."

"So, if you wanted to order me to have an orgasm, I'd have to do it."

"Uh…" He stares at my breasts, his chest rising and falling as his breathing grows heavier. His voice gets even rougher too. "I guess that might work."

"Why don't you try it?" Is that my voice? I suddenly sound like a sex kitten.

He pulls me into his arms, gazing down at me with his blue eyes burning from a fire within. "Come, Riley. Come like I'm inside you right now, fucking you hard."

For a second or two, nothing happens. Then I go off, my inner muscles pulsating and my entire body snapping taut while I cry out, squeezing my eyes shut to ride out the orgasm. It wasn't a mind-blowing climax, but the mere fact that he could tell me to come, and I did… Wow, that's simultaneously the hottest thing in history and the most terrifying thing I've ever experienced in my life.

I tip my head back to look into his eyes. "Do that again."

A rumbling noise originates from overhead. The floor begins to shudder, and bits of earth break off from the ceiling to splat down around us.

Then the roof collapses.

Chapter Nine

I SPIRIT US AWAY A SPLIT SECOND BEFORE THE CEILING CRASHES DOWN, and we fall into a heap on the grass, coughing from the debris that enveloped us right before we got the heck out of there. Has my curse struck again? Jeez, I can't imagine who would have this much of a grudge against me. Sure, sometimes I annoy other elementals. It's usually because they want me to use the healing vortex to bring their dead evil-bastard friends back to life. I can't resurrect a destroyed elemental, though. Once they're gone, they turn to dust and blow away on the wind.

Why would anybody want to curse me?

I push up into a sitting position and help Riley get up too. She's coughing, but not too much. We stand and brush the debris off our clothes and out of our hair.

"Are you okay?" I ask.

"Fine, yeah." She bends over at the waist and shakes her head, making dust pour down from her hair. Then she straightens and sighs. "That was… weird."

"My temporary lair might seem like a dump, but I swear it was solid. No way should it have collapsed." I stare down at the ground for a moment, then force myself to look at her. "This was my fault, Riley. Whoever cursed me triggered the collapse. You should go home and forget about the Unseen. It's too dangerous for you to be here, especially with me."

"No way. I am not leaving you to deal with this alone."

"Why do you care? We just met, and so far, all I've done is get you into trouble."

She moves closer, bending her head back to meet my gaze. "You introduced me to elementals. I appreciate that. But mostly, I want to stay with you because I like you. Maybe you annoy me sometimes, and maybe I don't understand your world, but I'm not the kind of person who can just walk away from someone who needs help."

"Helping me might get you killed. You aren't immortal, Riley. I am. That means I can't die. I can only be destroyed, which requires a boatload of dark magics."

"Oh, you mean like the magics that somebody used to curse you." She shakes her head. "I am not leaving you until we vanquish that curse."

"How can you ever be sure you're doing this because you actually want to help me? You owe me a debt."

"But you haven't abused that. I think I'd know if you forced me to do something."

A few minutes ago, she asked me to command her to have an orgasm. And it worked. That must be the most bizarre thing any woman has asked of me. She looked so beautiful when she came, and I want to see that look again when we're both naked. But I should never, never do that. What if sex transfers my curse to her? I can't risk it.

Not that she suggested she wants to have sex with me, the cursed leprechaun. Telling me to make her come doesn't mean she wants me.

"I'm taking you home," I tell her. "Right now."

"No."

"Stop being so pigheaded. This is for your own safety."

Riley straps her arms over her chest. "No."

"I could order you to go home."

Her lips twitch in an almost smile. "You won't. Nice guys don't do things like that."

She thinks I'm a nice guy. Isn't that what women say when they aren't at all attracted to a man?

Though I could force her to leave, I don't want to do it. If that makes me a wuss or a jerk or whatever, so what. She knows the risks, and she wants to stay with me. Even if this turns out to be just another way to study elementals, at least I'll have gotten to spend more time with her. She's kind of awesome.

"Okay," I tell her. "You can stay. But you have to listen to me and trust what I say. I know this world. You don't. It's more dangerous than you could possibly imagine."

"Tris, you can stop trying to scare me. I get that this world is a scary place, and I will listen to your advice." She gives me a teasing smile. "Besides, I have to listen. The debt makes it impossible for me not to."

"I wish you cared more about the fact that you're bound to me by magic."

She raises onto her tiptoes to kiss my cheek. "Relax. I might act like a ditz when it serves my purposes, but I have a brain and use it often. I'm fully informed about the risks."

I really can't talk her out of staying, so I might as well give in. "Okay, I won't try to convince you to leave anymore. But I need to focus on finding a way to get rid of this curse, which means I need to figure out who might've done this to me."

"Do you think it might be your succubus friend? You thought she was stalking you."

"Not sure about Anthea. Cursing me seems like a dumb thing for her to do if she just wants to screw me again." I shove my hands into my jeans pockets and stare down at the ground as if that will make my brain work better. "A curse is degenerative, that's what Ennea said. Making me weaker and weaker wouldn't get Anthea the sexual energy she needs to survive."

"Good point. But I still think we should keep her on the list of potential suspects."

I snort as I try not to laugh. "Suspects? This isn't a TV show. Have you suddenly become a detective?"

She shrugs. "We both need to be detectives, don't you think? Two heads are better than one."

"Yeah, okay. You've got a point." I shut my eyes for a moment and try to brainstorm ideas for who might want to curse me. That leads me to an uncomfortable revelation. "Truth is, I kind of annoy everybody. Being snarky doesn't make a leprechaun lots of friends. I also control a healing vortex, which ticks off even more elementals. They want its power."

"I doubt you're sarcastic enough to make someone want to curse you for that. But the vortex could be a solid lead."

Solid lead? I chuckle. "You're the cutest fake detective I've ever seen."

"Flirting doesn't get us any closer to finding out who did this to you."

"So, asking me to make you come does get us closer to the truth?"

Riley wags a finger at me. "There you go again, getting sarcastic."

"You just pronounced that my snarky attitude isn't enough to make somebody want to curse me."

I need to get her naked soon. But not until we find a safe place where we can do that. Since no such place exists, for a cursed man like me, I will never get to have sex with Riley.

She bites her upper lip, which I think means she's racking her brain for ideas. That expression is adorable too. Maybe I can't seduce her, but I could kiss her senseless. If she'll let me. Yeah, I've become a pathetic wuss.

"Let's go visit more of my friends," I say. "We've all been sort of babysitting those vampires I told you about. Not sure if Max is back from the amusement park yet, but maybe somebody else will be there."

"You babysit the vampires?"

"It's a long story."

"Better tell me before we go there. What if I accidentally flirt with a bloodsucker?"

She's teasing me, which I love, but it's not appropriate right now. Since I realize she won't give up until I explain, I might as well do that now and save some time.

"Do you remember Larissa mentioned the god Eros?" I ask. "He created Hathor, aka Larissa, and ensorcelled her so she'd adore him and do whatever he wanted. Ensorcellment is like brainwashing on steroids. The being who casts the spell turns the other person into their slave, taking total control over them."

"What does this have to do with vampires?"

"I'm getting there, Little Miss Impatience." I rub my neck as I consider how to explain the rest. "Eventually, Hathor got away from Eros and the two other gods who wanted to control her. So Eros came groveling back to her with a gift. One she didn't appreciate."

"Did he give her vampires?"

"Yep. You're one smart cookie, Riley."

"I accept your compliment."

She's catching on to the rules of this world faster than I expected.

"Back when Eros created the vamps, they were hideous monsters with pale, greasy skin and creepy red eyes. Hathor rejected the gift." I rock back on my heels as I remember the events that happened not long ago. "Then Travis met Larissa. I'll skip over most of the story. The part you need to know is that those three gods tried to get control of Larissa, the human who used to be Hathor. And to convince her to go with him, Eros offered her the vamps again—but this time, he transformed them into what Larissa calls 'drop-dead sexy but mentally unbalanced hotties.' They're attractive now, but they're not exactly sociable."

"Ooh, hot vampires. This is sounding better and better."

"I don't get the appeal of the bloodsuckers. But all the women I know think those weirdos are hot. There's one in particular, Cyneric, who isn't like the others. I get the willies every time he looks at me. Feels like he's always plotting something, like he might go rogue anytime."

"Are you warning me to stay away from him? Will he be wherever you're taking me?"

"Yes. It's the camp we created for the vampires, to keep them contained while we try to retrain them. You know, stop them from wanting to rip everybody's throats out and somehow make them trustworthy allies." I grunt because the idea is insane. "I don't think I'll ever trust them, though. I was the one who had to heal Travis and Larissa after Cyneric attacked them. As an elemental, Travis couldn't die. But Larissa is human, and she got way too close to going into the light. So yeah, that's why I don't trust the vamps."

"Wow, that's one terrifying story. But your friends wouldn't be working with the vampires if they didn't understand the risks. They must think it's relatively safe."

"Are you trying to convince me to take you there?"

"You said you need your friends' help. And they're all at the camp, right? So we need to go there."

"True. But maybe I should send you back to Ennea while I go to the vamp haven."

"No. Take me with you. I would say the P-word, but I know you don't want me to do that."

I can't talk her out of this. Might as well stop wasting time and just take her with me. "Fine. Let's go. But do not approach a vampire or look one in the eye. Got it?"

"Yes, sir." She salutes.

Slinging my arms around her, I teleport us to the camp. It lies inside a large clearing surrounded by some of the scariest woods in the Unseen. That's why we set up the camp here. Nobody will want to breach the perimeter, which means we have another layer of security. But no, there's never enough security when we're dealing with creatures who need to drink blood to survive. I don't ever want to meet a starved vampire. Max was one scary dude when he let himself starve, but he didn't want to drink blood. The vamps, and especially Cyneric, are so much more dangerous than a sex-starved incubus.

"Hey, why do I see sunshine in the woods," Riley asks, "but not in this camp? It should be the other way around. Besides, it was daytime when we left Ennea's place."

We've landed near a tent that serves as the headquarters for our mission to help the poor bloodsuckers. This is as good a spot as any to stop and explain. "Ennea cast a spell to plunge this clearing into permanent darkness—to accommodate the vamps. The rest of the Unseen still goes by the regular rules for sunrise and sunset."

"Right, I get it. Makes sense to do that for the vampires."

I make a slightly rude noise. "Yeah, it makes sense for the evil fang boys. But it's extremely dangerous for the rest of us."

Releasing Riley's hand, I walk into the tent. She follows. But nobody is in here. They must've gone out to the training ground or the tent next to that where we try to teach the bloodsuckers manners. *Yeah, good luck with that.* My opinion of the vamps might be colored by what I saw Cyneric do to Larissa and Travis, but I can't help that. They are my friends. Cyneric is...spooky.

"Did we come here to stare at an empty tent?" Riley asks. "Or are your friends invisible?"

"No, of course not. Everybody must be outside." I grab her hand. "Let's go find them."

We tromp outside and pass by the other tents, but when I peek inside each one, I don't see anybody there either. Continuing through the camp, I discover the mind-your-manners tent is also vacant. That just leaves the training ground. I lead Riley toward that area, where a series of tarps have been attached to metal poles, creating an enclosed arena. The vamps could break out of that if they wanted, but so far, they haven't tried to escape. Before we can glimpse anything inside the arena, we catch sight of the lights attached to even taller poles.

And we walk straight into the vampire's den.

CHAPTER TEN

Riley

THIS MAKESHIFT ARENA MUST MEASURE AT LEAST A HUNDRED FEET WIDE and slightly more than that in length, since it has an oblong shape. The floodlights cast a sterile white glow on the training ground. I can see a number of people—um, make that individuals milling around inside the space. Some of them are talking, though I can't understand their words yet. We're still too far away.

One of the individuals resembles Travis, though only in his skin tone and dark hair. Still, it's clear he's a salamander. But I don't recognize anyone else, not their species or their faces. Tris keeps hold of my hand while we approach the nearest group, which is much smaller than the gathering of beings that stand on the other side of the training ground.

"Hey," Tris says as we halt near the smaller group. "Quin, when did you join the Save the Vamps Coalition?"

Tris is speaking to a tall, slender man who has a young-looking face. His features remind me of Tris, but he doesn't look exactly like him.

"I was here a couple of weeks ago," the man Tris had called Quin says. "Filled in while you were, uh, otherwise engaged."

"And you're speaking to me? I thought all you guys wanted to kick my ass."

Quin shrugs one shoulder. "Nah. I was annoyed at first, but now I'm glad you did it."

Is this guy Tris's brother? Before I can ask, the other man offers me his hand. "I'm Quindecim, the fifteenth and final child of Nyara and Frimis. But everybody calls me Quin."

The man who resembles Travis glances at me, then Tris, then me again. His brows rise, and his lips kink into a playfully knowing smile. The salamander punches Tris's arm. "You got yourself a girl. About bloody time."

His British accent confirms it for me. This man must be an incubus like Travis, though I don't know for sure that every creature of their kind speaks with the same accent. Probably not. I want to ask Tris about that, but he and the incubus have started talking.

"She's not my girl," Tris informs his friend. "We just met today. This is Riley Jordan. She's a cryptozoologist who wants to study elementals."

"A crypto-zoo...what? I don't understand."

"Never mind." Tris hooks an arm around my shoulders. "Riley, this is Max. He's an incubus like Travis, but he's way more annoying and totally full of himself. He's also one of three people who volunteered to help the bloodsuckers."

People? I'm not sure that's the right word to use when we're talking about elementals. But if he wants to say "people," I'll go along with it.

"Who are the other two?" I ask Tris.

"Me and Harper. But Max won't let his wife come here anymore, since she just had a baby a few months ago. He banned her from coming within half a world of the vamps." Tris chuckles. "Harper agreed, but she threatened to cut off Max's favorite body part if he issued another command without talking to her first."

No, I will not ask what Max's favorite body part is.

The salamander smiles in an almost wistful way. "Ah, yes, the love of my life is a murderous beauty."

Tris rolls his eyes. "She only ever tried to kill you."

Max approaches me and clasps my hand, bending over to kiss it and wink at me. "It's a pleasure to meet you, Riley."

Tris waves a hand in front of Max's face. "Dial back the pheromones, Romeo."

"Afraid I can't do that. It's an innate instinct." Max releases my hand. "But I have no interest in seducing your girl, Tris. The only woman I want is Harper, my fated mate."

Quin smirks at his brother. "Hey, maybe Riley's your fated mate."

"No, she is not." Tris flashes Quin a scowl, then turns to Max. "Why did you invite sylphs to come here?"

I had noticed two other males, but they've been hanging back while we talked to Max and Quin. Now the two males approach us.

Max claps a hand on each sylph's shoulder. "These blokes have agreed to fill in while Harper is unavailable. Travis will take over for one of them once he's done shagging his wife."

"How long could that possibly take?" Tris asks. "He ought to be here soon."

Max chuckles. "Travis is an incubus, mate. He might not turn up for days."

"What about Dani? She needs her parents."

"The child will stay with Lindsey and Nevan."

Quin seems confused. "I thought Dani was adopted. But you called Larissa and Travis her parents."

"It's the mortal way," Tris tells him. "Humans like to call their adoptive parents Mom and Dad."

"Oh, I get it." Quin glances at the other two men. "I thought the sylphs hated us."

"No. They're jealous, but they'll work with us when it's necessary. Nobody wants to leave these vamps alone."

I can't keep up with all these people and the things they say. Sylphs? Vampire trainees? This is all so weird.

Max tells the sylphs to go help the "fiendish bloodsuckers" figure out "how not to drain anyone dry." He says that in a light, almost joking tone. Jeez, I hope he's kidding about the vamps draining people dry. Tris did mention that Cyneric had almost killed Larissa and Travis. Maybe we shouldn't be here, but Tris thought he could get some help from his friends.

He glances at me, almost as if he's waiting for my approval. For what? I don't care if he talks to his friend and his brother.

I give him a tight smile, hoping that conveys whatever permission he's waiting to receive.

Tris faces the other two men. "Look, I've got a problem. I was hoping you guys could help."

Max's lips twitch like he's trying not to smirk. "You want my help? Blimey. It must be a terrible problem."

"Actually, it is." Tris hesitates, but only for a couple of seconds. "I'm cursed."

"You're what?" Quin says. "Do you mean you're having a bad day? Or that you are literally cursed?"

"Both. I'm having a horrible day because some jerk has actually cursed me."

No one speaks. We all just stand here like we have no idea what to say or do. Well, I guess we don't have a clue. Ennea couldn't de-curse him, and Tris can't even absolve my debt.

"I think he's embarrassed," I say. "Tris seems to feel like it's his fault he can't remove the curse."

"Did I say that?" Tris asks. "No, I did not. If you're going to speak for me, at least don't make it sound like I'm a useless coward."

"You really shouldn't interpret my words. I said what I meant." I lean closer to whisper, "Don't pretend you aren't feeling guilty about doing you-know-what to me, even though it wasn't your fault. I'm the one who said the you-know-what word."

"We can hear you," Max says in a very sarcastic tone. "Elementals have excellent hearing. Might as well share with the class. What did Tris do to you?"

"Nothing," Tris says. "It just happened."

"Do tell me we're talking about something naughty."

"Afraid not," I say. Well, okay, I did tell Tris to command me to have an orgasm, but I won't share that with Max. "We got sideswiped by some freaky-powerful lightning, and I accidentally said the T-word."

"I see." Max eyes me with a curious expression. "Has he released you from your debt?"

"He can't. It won't work. Tris has tried, but something keeps blocking him from absolving me. We think it's because of the curse."

Quin clears his throat. "Did you talk to Ennea?"

"Yes, we did," I say. "She couldn't figure out how to absolve me either or how to de-curse Tris. She's working on it, but we need to find answers fast. Ennea warned us that the curse is degenerative."

"Bloody hell," Max says in a hushed tone. "This is bad. I assumed Tris was being melodramatic."

"He's not exaggerating. It's bad. He keeps having weird accidents, and it seems like each is worse than the one before."

Movement draws my attention to the sylphs, who are just now reaching the congregation of vampires. Swords appear in their hands—gleaming obsidian blades laced with shimmering crimson bands. The two sylphs walk straight into a crowd of vampires that must include at least two dozen individuals.

"Should those guys be out there alone?" I ask. "I mean, the vamps aren't quite housebroken yet, right?"

"Housebroken?" Max laughs. "I love that. I'll need to use it whenever Travis complains about the vampires. 'They aren't housebroken yet, mate.' That's hilarious."

"This isn't a joke. Why aren't you worried about letting the sylphs walk into a horde of vampires?"

Max abruptly turns serious. "I'm always concerned when anyone approaches the vampires. But those two blokes have endued swords, which means they can slice the heads off those bloodsuckers."

"Endued swords?"

Tris pulls me closer to his side. "It means the blades have been imbued with magics that make it possible for the swords to kill an elemental. Otherwise, we're basically unkillable."

"Basically? That's not super comforting."

"Relax. The only things that can kill an elemental are endued weapons, magically enhanced poisons, and powerful dark magics."

"What about a curse? Ennea implied that could kill you."

"I know. That's why I was hoping these guys could help." He glances at his brother and Max. "So, got any ideas?"

Both men shake their heads.

Great. We came here for help, but we've gotten zilch.

While Tris, Quin, and Max start spitballing ideas, more movement draws my attention. I can see the sylphs are talking to the vampires, and most of the vamps listen and watch the sword-wielding duo. But one figure separates from the crowd surreptitiously, sidling away while the others are focused on the sylphs who in turn focus their attention on the vamps.

The male being skulking this way keeps glancing around as if he's making sure no one noticed his escape.

I should point that out to Tris or Max, but I can't tear my gaze away from the vampire. The way he moves reminds me of a panther, graceful and purposeful, stealthy and self-assured. The vamp fascinates me, though I can't explain why. As he comes up behind Max and Quin, still the men haven't noticed him. I can't make my voice work. There's something mesmerizing and sensual about his movements and his single-minded focus.

He halts behind and to the right of Quin. Now I can see the vamp has dark hair brushed back from his beautiful face and shockingly pale blue eyes that stare into mine with such intensity that a chill shimmies up my spine.

"Riley," Tris snaps. "What are you doing?"

I blink swiftly but can't stop staring at the vampire. "Who is that?"

Tris leans around me to see the vamp. Then he pushes me behind him as he speaks in a harsh tone. "Cyneric. What the hell do you think you're doing? Get back to the group. Now."

Cyneric ignores him and keeps watching me. His tongue snakes out to moisten his lips, and his gaze drops to my throat.

Max leaps in front of the vampire. He jabs a finger toward the area behind Cyneric. "Back to the group. Right now. Unless you want me to behead you."

He conjures a sword.

Cyneric's gaze flicks to Max, then to Tris, and finally to me again.

The salamander slaps a hand on the vamp's chest and shoves. "Go. Now."

The vampire vanishes, only to reappear inside the group at the other end of the arena.

"What was he doing?" Tris asks.

"Not a bloody clue," Max tells him. "No one can figure out Cyneric."

I raise my hand like a kid in school. It's a dumb thing to do, but I still feel weirded out by Cyneric. "How do you feed the vampires? They need blood, right?"

Tris responds. "Yeah, they need blood. The vamps don't enjoy drinking it, though. That's a fail-safe measure Eros included when he created their kind. We get donations, from our group of friends and from other elementals who volunteer to feed them. We realized pretty fast that bottles of blood only keep a vamp going for so long. They need it straight from a living body too. But we do not let humans donate."

"Why not?"

"Elementals are essentially invincible. Humans aren't. If a vamp got overeager, he could kill someone."

"Right." I can't help crinkling my nose. "Do elementals really volunteer to have a vamp sink their teeth into their veins?"

"Arteries are best. That's the freshest blood. But yeah, some freaks actually enjoy a good bloodsucking."

"Freaks like who?"

He grunts. "Salamanders."

"But not me," Max announces. "Not Travis either. Only some of the kinkier salamanders enjoy that."

"I'm curious. Why are you guys called salamanders?"

Max grins. "I love it when mortals ask me that. Paracelsus, a human, introduced the names of four elemental species into the mortal vernacular in the sixteenth century. But a fetching succubus whispered them into his ear. As for why we're called salamanders, allow me to demonstrate."

He bursts into flames, and his body vanishes.

"Look down," Tris tells me. "He won't shift back until you see him."

I glance down—and see a small red lizard on the ground where Max had stood seconds ago.

With another burst of fire, he resumes his usual form and bows. "Now you see, darling."

"You actually turn into a lizard?"

"That's right. We're shapeshifters, pet. Women think it's adorable when I turn into a red salamander." He flicks his finger, and a small flame shoots out of it. "We are fire elementals, which is appropriate since we're scorching hot in bed. Or out of bed. We don't care about the location, only that we can get a leg over."

"That's so interesting. I'd love to hear more about—"

"We've got serious problems," Tris says. "You can learn all about the amazing Max later. I'm cursed, remember? That's kind of an important thing to discuss right now."

"Of course. My curiosity got the better of me."

Max folds his enormous arms over his enormous chest. "I know exactly what you need to do."

Tris makes a face that suggests he's not convinced. "What is it?"

"You need to see an oracle."

CHAPTER ELEVEN

Tris

"A N ORACLE?" I GROAN AND THROW MY HEAD BACK TO STARE UP AT THE sky. "Those guys are never helpful. That's what everybody says. They issue vague pronouncements and act all high-and-mighty, then they kick you out the door. I don't see how talking to an oracle is going to do any good. Ken hates me, and Bob thinks I'm annoying, though I've never pestered them for advice or a prophecy."

Max snorts as if he's trying not to laugh. "Everyone thinks you're annoying, mate."

"Who are Ken and Bob?" Riley asks me.

"Oracles. That means holier-than-though asshats who are supposed to have deep insights into…everything." I rub my neck. "We need to find another way."

"There isn't one," Quin says. "Bro, you need to see an oracle. Ken doesn't hate you, anyway. He just doesn't want to see you ever again."

"How is that different?"

"Because he doesn't have any animosity toward you." My brother gives me a long-suffering look. "It's your own fault he won't speak to you. I mean, you did call him a useless mook. He's kinda sensitive about his usefulness."

"Whatever." Does anybody like oracles? I don't think so. Well, maybe Lindsey likes Bob. Absolutely no one could like Mr. Sensitive aka Ken.

Riley looks at me, her forehead crinkled in the cutest way. "I've been meaning to ask. What did you do to your siblings? Most of them won't speak to you, right?"

Quin chuckles. "Oh yeah, especially not Pendi."

"Pendi? That doesn't sound like a Greek number."

"Her birth name is Pente, the number five. But after her transmutation, she changed the spelling to Pendi. She thinks it's sexier or something." Quin sighs with way too much sarcasm. "But you wanted to know what Tris did that ticked off all his brothers and sisters."

"Yes."

"He changed his accent and forced us to go along with it."

Riley stares at him blankly as a sweet little dimple forms between her eyebrows. "I don't get it. How did he force you to change your accent? What did you sound like before?"

"We all talked like… What do you call it, Tris?" Quin doesn't give me a chance to respond. He raises one finger. "Oh, yeah. It was like Chicago and the Bronx had a love child. I don't know where those places are, but apparently that's what we sounded like."

"Lindsey said that," I correct, "not me."

"Doesn't matter. When your accent changed during your transmutation, it affected all of us. Not right away, but soon after."

"Fascinating," Riley says, and she sounds fascinated too. Her eyes light up. She honestly does love researching elementals. She even reaches into her backpack and brings out her notebook and pencil to start scribbling. "Did anything else change?"

Quin smirks. "You betcha. Tris used to be a scrawny twerp. Now he's a big, musclebound twerp."

"Hey!" I snap. "I didn't change you. The Unseen did. And calling me a twerp doesn't help anything. I'm still cursed. Or have you forgotten because you're having too much fun harassing me?"

"Now who's sensitive?" Quin says. "Little Tris got bigger, but he didn't grow up any."

"Shut your trap, Quindecim."

"Ooh, you called me by my full name. Must be mad now."

Max exhales a loud sigh. "Enough. Tris, you need to visit Bob. End of story."

The incubus disappears, then reemerges near the gathering of vampires.

My brother notices Riley furiously writing in her notebook. "Hey, what are you doing there? Writing your will?"

"I'm documenting what you said about Tris's accent changing and how it affected the rest of you. Tris agreed to help me learn all about elementals and document it all." She shuts her notebook with the pencil trapped inside it. "But I won't photograph or videotape you."

"Why not? I'm very photogenic."

"Your parents didn't like the idea, and neither did Travis."

I clear my throat. "We should get going."

Quin hugs Riley. "Good luck. If you're with my brother, you'll need it."

He teleports to the vamps, joining Max and the sylphs.

I turn to Riley. "Ignore Quin. He says he's not mad about the accent thing, but he clearly has issues related to that."

"So do you. If you were cool with it, you wouldn't have gotten so upset."

"Maybe I do have issues." I study her for a moment. "You know all about my family, but I know nothing about yours."

"What would you like to know?"

"Anything you want to tell me."

"Okay." She stares at my left pectoral muscle for a moment, then lifts her gaze to mine. "My parents are veterinarians. They used to work at a zoo and take care of the animals, but they also liked to take vacations to places like Africa and Australia to see the wildlife in their natural habitats. Eventually, they got curious about all the stories of supposedly mythical creatures that have circulated for centuries."

"Is that where your interest in cryptozoology came from?"

"Yes. I'm an only child, and the three of us traveled to so many fascinating places. But we never saw a cryptid. We found evidence that convinced us, but it wasn't enough to convince anyone else. Those trips were amazing, though." She hugs herself and stares at my chest again. "Then when I was away at college, Mom and Dad agreed to go on a TV show about cryptids and share their experiences. The show was well done, and lots of people saw it. Including the head of the zoo where my parents worked. He fired them."

"Because they were on a TV show?"

She nods. "They had embarrassed the zoo and tarnished its reputation. That's what the jerk said. Mom and Dad were devastated, and ever since, they've refused to talk about anything to do with mysterious animals. They stopped talking to me when I told them I wanted to study cryptids in my spare time."

"Riley, that's awful. I can kind of relate, since my siblings are mad at me. But for parents to shut their daughter out… That's terrible."

"We reconciled when I promised I wouldn't investigate cryptids anymore. Secretly, I kept searching for proof. I know it was wrong to lie, but…" She lifts her head just enough to roll her gaze up to mine. "Want to know a secret?"

"If you want to tell me, yeah. I'll listen."

"Part of the reason I've been obsessed with cryptozoology is because I'm hoping someday I'll find proof that vindicates my parents or at least makes them proud of me."

She rubs her arms, which she still has wrapped around herself, and stares at the ground.

I can't stop myself. She looks so forlorn that I need to pull her into my arms and cradle her to my body. She rests her head on my chest, sighs, and relaxes into me. I caress her hair. We just stand here like this for a long time, while I watch my allies and my brother trying to teach vampires how to behave like normal people. Well, normal elementals. Not sure such a thing exists, though. Normal elementals? Yeah, that's a bigger myth than cryptids.

Riley raises her head to gaze up at me. Her lips form the barest of smiles. "I'd like to say the T-word, but I don't want to get us in even more trouble. So I'll settle for this. You are a good man, Tris, and I'm glad I had the chance to meet you."

"I'm glad I met you too."

"Should we visit that oracle now?"

"Yeah." I wave my arm in the air until Max notices, then shout, "We're heading out to see the oracle."

Max gives me a thumbs-up sign and goes back to housebreaking the vamps.

I could've zipped us over there to tell Max without needing to shout, but I do not want Riley to get anywhere near Cyneric ever again. I don't like the way that bloodsucker looks at her. I might not have seen what he did to Larissa, but I was there for the aftermath. The bastard ran a sword straight through her heart. He used to have a fixation on Larissa, but now he seems to have shifted his obsession to Riley.

No, I don't trust Cyneric.

I lash my arms around Riley more firmly and transport us to the edge of the creepy woods that hide the lair of Bob the oracle. Bob is rather paranoid. He protects his domain with magics and monkey-like creatures who have a hard to pronounce Greek name. Those creatures can fly and wield wickedly sharp talons, but the river we'll need to cross is filled with toxic substances. Though it's still daylight behind us, we're about to walk into a precinct where night always reigns, no matter the time, and eerie stars hover overhead.

"Stick right by me," I tell Riley. "These woods and the things in them can kill you."

"Okay. I'll be glued to you."

"Good. Remember not to say the T-word or the P-word. Doing that is even more dangerous in an oracle's lair."

"I understand." Her lips quirk into a little smile that makes me want to do things to her we can't do here. "Before we go in, I'd like you to do something for me."

"What?"

"Kiss me. Make it a hot one."

I can't restrain my grin. "You got it, baby."

Grasping her bottom with one hand, I hoist her up until her toes barely touch the ground. Then I push my other hand into her hair and mold my mouth to hers. She latches her arms around my neck and exhales, her breath whispering over my skin. I slip my tongue between her lips, and she relaxes her jaw in the best invitation I've ever received. I thrust deeper while I squeeze her ass and tip her head back just enough to give me even better access. She sags into me and moans softly. Riley tastes incredible, but I could never describe the flavor of her mouth. It's intoxicating and exciting, and I feel like

I'm high on that flavor. Her breasts are crushed to my chest, the taut nipples rubbing against me, which makes my dick wake up.

She hooks one leg around my hip and wraps her arms even more tightly around my neck, her fingers diving into my hair.

The way she kisses drives me crazy, and I can't stop myself from grinding my hardening dick into her. The way I'm holding her up means that I'm rubbing my length into her cleft with only our clothes between us. I want to take her right now, here on the edge of a dark and creepy forest.

But I force myself to peel her away from my body and set her on her feet.

She fake pouts. "Why did you stop?"

"Gee, I don't know. Why shouldn't I rip your clothes off and make you scream? It's not like we're about to walk into a demonic forest."

Riley throws her head back and moans. "I want to do that."

"You're excited about the demonic forest?"

She gives me an exasperated look. "No. I want to have sex."

"Me too. But this isn't the time or the place."

"You're right. But I thought we were seeing an oracle, not a demon."

I wave toward the black, oozing trees a few feet away from us. "Bob defends his lair with demonic-looking garbage like that. But everything inside that forest can kill you."

"You already told me that. Let's get this over with."

I grasp her hand and lead us into the oracle's domain. Viscous black stuff oozes from the bark on the trees, and the faint stench of caustic chemicals and rotting flesh pervades the woods. Riley wrinkles her nose at first, but then gives up on trying not to smell the odors. Yeah, it's pointless to fight it. Might as well get used to the nauseating stink. Soon, we reach the river that separates the outer forest from the much smaller area around the oracle's hideout.

Riley raises one leg like she wants to jump over the river.

I grab her around the waist to stop her. "That water is full of acid. Unless you want your skin to melt off your body, don't take another step."

When I release her, she backs away from the river. "I won't make a move without asking you first."

"Smart girl." I pick her up and jump across the water, whumping down on the opposite bank. Then I set her down. "We're almost there."

Riley lays her palms on my chest and glides them up and down. "I want you so bad right now."

"Because I jumped over the river? Any elemental could do that." I reclaim her hand. "Let's get moving."

I do love that what I did got her hot and bothered. Everything about her gets me that way.

Riley glances every which way during our hike to the oracle's lair, even tipping her head back so far that I need to lay a hand on the small of her back to keep her from falling over backward. She honestly does love seeing new and strange things. The Unseen doesn't scare her. She wants to learn all about my world and understand how elementals live.

Her insatiable curiosity turns me on.

"Why couldn't we teleport to the oracle's place?" she asks.

"Because this whole precinct is warded. Nobody can get in unless they walk through the woods."

"What about your stalker?"

"I guess that person could walk in here if they wanted. Nothing I can do about that. Not sure if the wards will stop my curse from striking again while we're inside this precinct."

"Seems like we have a ways to go yet," she says. "May I ask you a question in the meantime?"

"Yeah, okay."

"What exactly is the transmutation? Your dad said it's like puberty but much worse. And Quin mentioned that your accent changed after the transmutation."

Up ahead, I notice the sloping mound that represents the oracle's lair. "Answering your question will have to wait. We're here."

CHAPTER TWELVE

Riley

WHILE WE TRUDGED THROUGH THE DARK AND SMELLY FOREST, I'D watched as the trees closed in and formed a canopy above us, one so thick that no light whatsoever could penetrate it. Now, as we approach the oracle's lair, a pale green glow suffuses the air. I can't see any visible source for the glow. It just…is. The earth squishes under my boots as if it's composed of wet sponges.

I still want to know more about the transmutation, but Tris is right. We have bigger issues.

As we enter the clearing, the trees open their boughs to reveal strange stars that shimmer in the sky. Just like the vampire training ground, here it seems to always be night. I suppose that's another safety measure to make it hard for anyone to reach the oracle's home. At the center of the clearing hunkers a sloping hill that stands a little taller than Tris.

High above us, creatures shriek.

"That's the kerkopes," Tris tells me. "Basically, they're the flying monkeys from *The Wizard of Oz*. Except the kerkopes are bigger and more humanoid."

"Oh." I can't manage to say anything else. Toxic woods. Night in the daytime. Now screaming monkeys that fly. A girl needs time to adjust to all of that, but I won't get any leeway.

Tris approaches the hill and raps his fist on it three times.

Seriously? We're knocking on dirt? He must be pulling my leg.

A section of the hill ripples, transforms into a semitransparent barrier, and finally melts away into nothing. It has become a doorway. Beyond the opening, I see nothing but the blackest darkness, and a chill stiffens every hair on my body and tingles down my spine. Tris grips my hand as he guides us down a pitch-black corridor. Can he see in the dark? He must, since he walks at a brisk pace. I'm trusting him not to lead me straight into an abyss.

We turn left—into another corridor, I assume—then round another corner. Now I notice a faint yellow glow up ahead, where the passageway dead-ends at a doorway that has no door. The glow emanates from whatever room lies beyond the threshold. Since it's shorter than Tris, he needs to crouch to cross into the space. But he keeps hold of my hand while we enter the chamber beyond.

"Can you see in the dark?" I whisper.

"Not really. My eyes adjust to the dark a lot faster than yours, and I can see better under any conditions than you can."

Of course he can. He's not human.

Maybe that explains why he can kiss like no other man I've ever met.

We halt in the center of a chamber carved out of solid rock that has a dirt floor and rough-hewn walls that have been gilded with a semi-translucent coating of something like pale gold. Maybe it is gold. Directly in front of us, a huge bronze bowl squats on its four metal feet that resemble a cat's paws. Amber flames lick up from the depths of the container, flicking back and forth in the faint current of air that wafts through the space.

A figure saunters out of the gloom on the other side of the chamber and stops near the bronze bowl. The flames leap higher briefly, almost as if they're greeting him. He does not meet my preconceived expectations of an oracle. No flowing robes. No long white hair. The guy wears a navy-blue suit, and his short gray hair has been slicked back. His face does sport quite a few wrinkles, though.

When he smiles, the wrinkles around his eyes deepen. "Welcome, young lovers."

I open my mouth to inform him Tris and I are not lovers, but I clap my mouth shut instead. Something about this chamber, about this oracle, makes me uneasy.

"Do you know why we're here?" Tris asks.

The oracle sighs. "You haven't even introduced me to your girl. Allow me to do the honors." He faces me. "You are Riley Jordan. It's a pleasure to meet you, dear. I am the oracle Bobanzhistilanovitz, but you can call me Bob."

"Hi, Bob. It's, um, nice to meet you too."

The oracle waves toward Tris. "I already know the leprechaun. Let's move on to the reason for your visit."

"I'm cursed," Tris tells him. "I need to know who did that and why."

Bob bows his head, shaking it slightly. Then he aims his glittering, bright green eyes at Tris. "I cannot give you the name of the one who cursed you, but I can provide some insight."

Maybe I should keep my mouth shut, but I can't. "Aren't you supposed to know everything? I mean, you're an oracle."

"How kind of you to remind me, dear." He smirks. "I'd almost forgotten what I am."

"I'm sor—I didn't mean to offend you." I almost said the S-word. Not saying that or the P-word is really hard. "I'm just confused about why we came here if you can't help us."

"Did I say I can't help? No, I did not." He raises an arm over the bronze bowl and wriggles his fingers. The flames jump and writhe. "I can give you guidance. The one you seek is both closer than you think and further away."

"What does that mean?" Tris asks.

"Enemies often have allies. I suggest you seek out the individual who does his bidding, for that elemental is closer than you think."

"Can you tell us," I ask, "whether that person is a man or a woman?"

"Neither. The individual is an elemental. Try phrasing your question differently."

"Okay. Is the elemental who's helping the curse-maker male or female?"

Bob smiles and winks. "Very good, Riley. Now I can answer your query. She shouldn't be difficult to find, though you must exercise caution when approaching her because she has been ensorcelled by the one who wants to destroy Triskaideka."

Out of the corner of my eye, I see Tris clenching his fists. But he manages to sound reasonably calm when he speaks to the oracle. "Can't you give us any more clues? If the female who's helping my enemy is ensorcelled, she won't be able to tell us anything even if we find her."

"I'm afraid even I have limitations. Though I can see the identities of both elementals, I can't share that information. You need to discover it on your own." Bob pulls his hand away from the spooky fire. "Remember, she is closer than you think."

He backs away from the bowl, into the shadows, and vanishes.

"That's all we get?" I say. "What a rip-off."

"No, it's not a rip-off." Tris clasps my hand. "I think I know what he meant. The one who's helping the jerk who cursed me, she must be Anthea."

"But you said you believed her when she claimed she hasn't been stalking you."

"Maybe that was semantics. It's the literal truth, but not the actual truth."

I'm probably gaping at him like a moron. "What's the difference? Literal is actual."

"No, it's not. Literal means the exact, word-for-word intent. But actual means the straight-up truth."

I sort of growl. Frustration will do that to me. "There's no difference between those two words."

He half scowls and hauls me out of the oracle's chamber.

I wait until we exit the pitch-black passageway and step out into the yellowish glow in the clearing before I speak up again. "Are we going to find Anthea and question her?"

"Seems like my only option at this point."

"Not *your* only option. *Our* only option. We're doing this together, right?"

He moves only his eyes to glance at me while we traverse the clearing. "Are you absolutely sure you want to be in this with me? I have no idea what might happen if we find Anthea. Ensorcellment is one of the blackest forms of dark magics. She won't be able to fight it. If her master orders her to kill us, she will have no choice but to do it. If it were a debt binding her, we could probably break that. But not ensorcellment."

"Why not? There must be a way."

"I appreciate your determination, but we could both wind up dead. Even if you survive, would you want to date a cloud of scattered particles? That's what destruction means for an elemental."

"We aren't dating yet. Because that kind of requires going on an actual date."

He makes a growly noise. "Are you planning to argue semantics with me all day?"

"No. I'm just trying to help."

"I get that. But right now, we need to focus on finding Anthea."

As we leave the clearing, journeying through the creepy forest again, I remember something. "This morning, you shouted for Anthea—and she came. Maybe you should try that again. Can't hurt, right?"

"Yeah, I'll try that. Once we leave this warded precinct."

I decide to stay quiet for the rest of our journey through the oracle's domain, and I don't even speak when Tris scoops me up and jumps over the sulfuric river. I'd hoped an oracle might provide more specific insight, but like Bob said, even a seer has limitations. I believe he gave us all the information he's allowed to provide. Not sure why I believe it, but I do. On a visceral level, I trust the oracle. I trust my leprechaun companion too, in the same way. There's no rational reason for it, but reason flew away the moment I met Tris.

The second we finally exit the creepy woods, Tris grabs me and whisks us away. We emerge near the small boulder that I'd seen when we first entered this world. It's the portal.

"Are we going back to the mortal world?" I ask.

"I saw Anthea there this morning, so I figure that's our best bet."

"Good idea."

Keeping one arm around me, he stretches his other arm straight out and flourishes his fingers. The portal telescopes open, and he jumps through it. We've landed inside the cave behind the waterfall, where the rumbling of the cascade is muted. But he wastes no time, hugging me tightly to him while he leaps across the cavern and steps out onto the rock ledge. Then we soar through the air to whump down on the other side of the wooden railing that encompasses the pool. We're both soaked.

Tris releases me and takes a few steps backward. Then he throws his head back and hollers, "Anthea! Get your ass over here now!"

The succubus appears almost instantly. She's naked, of course, and showing off her perfect body. I can't help glancing down at my wet clothes and my figure. I like my body, but I can't compete with a supernatural bomb-shell. Not that I need to compete. Tris likes me just the way I am, otherwise he wouldn't be so hot to have sex with me. I'm hot for him too.

"What do you want?" Anthea asks. "I still have many lovers to enjoy today."

That's all she has to do? Screw people? Jeez, the succubus should get a job and do something useful.

I glance at Tris just as he looks at me. I guess neither of knows how to handle the situation. Interrogating an ensorcelled succubus? I have no clue where to start.

"Where did you come from just now?" Tris asks. "You live in the Unseen. And you told me you never visit the mortal world because it's boring."

"It is quite depressingly mundane." She sashays closer to Tris, then glances at me. "Come with me to my lair, and the three of us will enjoy intense pleasure for hours, even days. I would love to defile your sweet little mortal."

Defile? Yeah, that sounds like loads of fun.

The succubus is staring at me with a weird kind of hunger. It makes my skin crawl, so I sidle up to Tris. He slips an arm around me. Does he sense the weirdness too?

"You're ensorcelled, Anthea," he says. "We want to help you free yourself."

"Free me?" She laughs. "I have not been ensorcelled."

"Which is exactly what a brainwashed elemental would say." He twists his mouth into a frustrated expression. "This is pointless. We need to find another way."

Anthea's lips stretch into the evilest smile I've ever seen, one full of ravenous lust.

While the trees begin to shiver, a stiff breeze mutates into a gale force wind. Limbs crack and tumble to the ground. The earth itself rolls like waves on an ocean, knocking us down. My hair flies in my face, plastered to my eyes and mouth, but I can still see it when Tris scrambles to get on all fours and crawl toward me.

The crack of a tree snapping reverberates through the clearing, and the entire trunk of a six-foot-wide pine begins to tip toward us. Tris shoves me out of the way. The tree smacks down on him.

"You saved my life," I say. "Are you all right, Tris?"

He gazes at me with bleary eyes, clearly dazed.

I try to crawl toward him, but powerful hands seize me.

Anthea clutches me to her nude body and hisses into my ear, "You are coming with me, sweet child. I have many plans for your body."

She whisks us away.

CHAPTER THIRTEEN

Tris

I CAN'T MOVE. CAN'T THINK. CAN'T UNDERSTAND WHAT THE HELL JUST happened. Anthea kidnapped Riley? This is my curse, not hers. I need to get up and…do something. But the blasted tree is still on top of me, and it feels like every muscle in my body has turned to jelly. So, what, I'm going to lie here feeling sorry for myself? Screw that. My transmutation gave me all these ridiculous muscles, and it's about time I used them.

So I take a deep breath—well, as deep a breath as I can take with a frigging tree on top of me—and push up with both my arms and my legs too. I let out a primal roar as I slowly rise onto my hands and knees, every muscle screaming and my head throbbing. Christ, how big is this tree? Feels like a million pounds bearing down on me. But I suck in another breath and exhale it with another roar while I shove the fucking tree off my back. It slams down on the opposite side from the waterfall.

The entire clearing shudders from the concussion.

Sweat streams down my temples and soaks my shirt and my hair too. My body feels weak. My head still throbs too, which doesn't seem like a good sign. I try to zip myself away, but it doesn't work. All I accomplish is to make my head pound even more. I feel like I might vomit, and the world has started to tilt and whirl around me. *Oh, great.* I need to rescue the girl, but instead of doing that, I'm waiting to upchuck.

Yeah, some hero I am.

I doubt it's a coincidence that I had another "accident" right after Anthea showed up. She must be working with whoever cursed me, but I still have no idea who that person is or why they hate me. All I have the brainpower to worry about now is how I can find Riley. So I try again to teleport. And

I get zilch. Well, I do accomplish something. My headache gets even worse, and so do the nausea and weakness.

At least I'm close to the rock shop. If I can make it there, my friends could help me or at least suggest someone else I can contact for assistance.

When I try to walk, I realize I must've injured my left leg. It doesn't want to move properly, and I wind up limping down the trail, which takes forever. I'm a frigging elemental, an unkillable copper fae. Only an endued weapon or a magically enhanced poison can destroy me. But Ennea said the curse will only worsen the longer I have it, and it will infect my body and my mind too. Is that why I couldn't get that tree off me? Is it why I feel so crummy now?

I take a break at the healing vortex and lie down inside it. The energies gather around me, invisible and ethereal, but they manage only to make my leg hurt less. Now the vortex isn't obeying me? What the hell? After waiting a few more minutes and getting nothing more from the vortex, I finally hobble to the shop and shuffle through the back door. A few feet from the sales counter, I collapse onto the floor.

"Tris!" Lindsey shouts.

Her footsteps clap on the concrete floor as she approaches me, but I'm having trouble keeping my eyes open. I notice it when she kneels beside me, but only because her shadow falls over me. My lids feel as heavy as iron, and I give up the fight to keep them open. The second my eyes close, I pass out.

When I rouse a while later, I realize I'm lying on something soft. A bed? Not sure. I hear a gentle whirring sound, but I can't place that either. I've heard it before somewhere… A throat-clearing ends that thought. Not my throat doing the clearing, though.

"I can tell you're awake," Lindsey says. "Open your eyes, Tris. Can you do that?"

"Not sure," I mumble.

"Give it a try, sweetie."

I take a few slow breaths, then open my eyes. Wow, that didn't feel like I was peeling iron blankets away from my face. I rotate my eyes to look at Lindsey. "What happened?"

"You fainted."

"No, I passed out. Only girls faint."

She smiles and laughs. "You must be feeling better if you're arguing about my wording."

I push up on my elbows and wait a minute to see how that feels. No spinning. No gonna-vomit sensation. *Awesome.* I push up all the way into a sitting position. This feels pretty good too. So I swing my legs over the edge, my feet landing flat on the floor. Then I stretch and yawn. "Yeah, I'm feeling a lot better now."

Guess the healing energies of the vortex finally kicked in.

Lindsey studies me for a moment. "What happened to you, Tris?"

The memory of everything that went down in the clearing by the water-fall rushes through my mind, and my shoulders slump. "I lost Riley."

"You lost who?"

"Riley. The girl I met this morning." I rub my eyes and groan. "It's a long story."

"Better tell me everything. Then maybe we can work out a plan to help you."

Well, it can't hurt. So I tell Lindsey everything that's happened since I saw her this morning. She doesn't comment or make any funny faces. Like a good friend, she just listens. When I'm done talking, she moves onto the bed to sit beside me.

She lays her hand over mine. "You really like this girl, don't you?"

"I just met her today. Don't start thinking it's fate or love at first sight or whatever."

"Why not? I fell for Nevan so fast my head spun. Max and Harper had the same experience, and so did Travis and Larissa." She squeezes my hand. "Don't fight it because you think you can't possibly feel that way yet. Just let yourself enjoy the fall."

"That's a nice idea, but I've got bigger problems. I'm cursed, and an ensorcelled succubus abducted Riley."

"I know. But the answer is obvious."

"How do you figure that?"

She pats my hand, then clasps both of hers on her lap. "Riley owes you a debt. Tap into the power of that bond. Nevan once owed me his life, and that debt gave me the power to free him from Skeiron. Maybe you can free Riley from the succubus."

"But Riley doesn't owe me her life."

"Are you sure about that? She was almost struck by lightning, then you pushed her out of the way of a huge tree. She thanked you for that. You just told me so."

"No, I told you she said I saved her life. There was no use of the T-word."

"But she expressed gratitude. Didn't you feel the debt when it took effect?"

"Well, maybe I felt something. But we were in the mortal world at the time. No debts here."

Lindsey gives me a look that implies I'm a dumb-dumb. "You were right beside the falls, right beside the portal. Your curse might've allowed a bit of the Unseen to leech into this world. You know better than anyone how that can happen."

She's talking about the time when Skeiron punched a sword through Nevan's chest, and Lindsey hunted me down to beg me to heal him. But the situations aren't the same. "You could seal a debt to me then because I had to bring a sliver of the Unseen into this world to heal Nevan. I didn't do that this time."

"Are you sure? Your curse follows you into the mortal world, after all."

I wish it were true. I want that to be the case more than I've ever wanted anything because it would mean I can bring Riley to me. Even if her debt to me should give me that power, I have my doubts about whether this damn curse will allow it. I couldn't absolve Riley of her debt to me. Why would the curse let me rescue her?

Lindsey hugs me and kisses my cheek. "Might as well give it a try, hey? You can do it, Tris."

I close my eyes and picture Riley, then focus all my mental energy on one thought—*come to me, Riley, you owe me*. I keep sending out that single thought, channeling every ounce of magic inside me to make it happen.

A bolt of pain slams through my head.

My entire body cramps up, and I scream. No, scratch that. I didn't just scream because men don't do that. I shouted at high volume and at an elevated pitch. Yeah, it takes a leprechaun to get sarcastic while writhing in agony. I fall off the bed, thumping down on the floor, and lie here for a minute or two until the pain subsides.

What the hell happened? Now I can't even summon Riley? If she owes me a life debt, the power of that bond should override everything else.

Lindsey kneels beside me. "Tris? Are you okay?"

"Uh…" That's the only sound I can make. Sure, the pain has lessened. But I still feel wrecked.

"Nevan!" Lindsey hollers. "Get in here! Emergency!"

I try to tell her it's not that bad, but I end up mumbling incoherently. Even I can't understand what I just said.

The former sylph king halts on the threshold of this room, gazing down at me with wrinkled brows. "What did you do this time, Tris?"

I moan, then finally manage to speak. "Me? I didn't do a thing. Somebody cursed me."

"Well, that does explain your condition."

Groaning, I lever myself up into a sitting position and rub my forehead. "Getting really sick of this. I can't use my own powers or invoke Riley's debt. I'm useless."

Nevan kneels beside his wife. "You are not useless. Someone put a powerful hex on you, and it will take a great deal of magics to override that. Remember, you are not just a copper fae. You are the guardian of the healing vortex, and that means you hold great power inside you. Don't give up yet. Search for the one who cursed you and look for ways to work around the hex."

I stare at him. Might be gaping. Did Nevan just give me a pep talk? He's never liked me, so I need a minute to process the fact that he tried to boost my morale.

Lindsey smiles at her husband and kisses him. "That was a great speech, honey."

I draw my knees to my chest and rest my arms on them. "You're right, Nevan. I know that. But I fought in actual battles with you guys, and now

I can't even invoke a debt. It's, uh, kinda demoralizing. Your speech helped, though."

"Glad to hear it." Nevan rises, helping his wife up too. "Perhaps you should return to the Unseen and seek answers there."

"I'll do that." I spring to my feet. "But first, I need a hell of a lot of copper." I raise a hand when Nevan opens his mouth. "Don't worry, I'll pay for it."

He folds his arms over his chest. "I was going to say don't worry about the cost. This time, it's on the house."

"Oh. That's really nice of you, Nevan."

Lindsey tips her head to the side as she regards me. "Are you ever going to tell us how you're earning mortal money?"

"Maybe later. I need to save the girl first."

"Good luck, Tris."

She kisses my cheek, and Nevan slaps my arm.

Then I whisk myself away to the shop. I find Lindsey's parents holding down the fort there, but they know all about elementals, which means I don't need to come up with an excuse for taking a boatload of copper ore. They wish me good luck, though they have no idea why I need the copper or what I plan to do with it. They trust me.

I head for the healing vortex and drop onto one of the stone benches, then start chowing down. The more I eat, the better I feel—but it's more than physical strength I get from the copper. I feel more centered and confident now, like I can actually do this. I can hunt down the curse-maker and rescue Riley.

What is Anthea doing to Riley right now?

Don't think about that. My only job right now is to get answers and come up with a plan. I've powered myself up. Time to cross the veil and get things done. The curse has hindered me so far, but I will not let it drag me down anymore. I might have no clue how I'll accomplish anything, but I have something vital on my side.

I'm an annoying, sarcastic shit.

Once I reach the Unseen, I zip straight to the vampire training camp, straight into the arena. Max and Travis are both here now, along with the two sylphs. My brother seems to have left. Well, that makes sense. Travis took his place. We all take turns babysitting the bloodsuckers.

The sylphs are hanging out with the vamps on the other side of the arena. But Max and Travis rush over to me.

"Houston, we have a problem," Travis announces.

"Who is Houston?" I ask. "Have you forgotten what my name is?"

"It's a mortal saying." Travis waves away my impending question. "Forget about that. The point is that we've lost one of the vampires."

"Excuse me? You swore the vamps couldn't escape. After the incidents with some of them running into the woods to destroy themselves with sunlight, you guys had Ennea create a containment spell."

Max rubs his jaw. "Yes, but we, ah…didn't count on Cyneric."

An icy coldness floods through me, and I feel my hands curling into fists. I clench my teeth too and squeeze words out between them. "You let Cyneric get away? How many times have you morons told me he's the most dangerous one of all? And you just… What? Waved goodbye when he took off?"

"Don't get shirty with us," Travis says. "He teleported away. The containment spell failed. Maybe your curse is to blame for that."

"Oh, sure, lay it all on me."

Max sets a hand on my shoulder. "We didn't mean it that way, Tris. We're upset because we know where he's going. Or rather, to whom he's going."

"What does that mean? He told you?"

"No. But his intense interest in Riley is a clue."

Travis nods like he agrees with Max's assessment. "I zipped back to the mortal world to check on Larissa, and Max checked on Harper. They're both fine, and neither of them has seen Cyneric."

"How can I find him?"

The two salamanders exchange glances I can't interpret. Then Travis tells me, "The oracle."

I zip straight to the edge of the oracle's domain. This time, Bob will answer my questions.

Or I'll throttle him with my bare hands.

CHAPTER FOURTEEN

Riley

HOW DID I END UP HERE? LYING STRAPPED TO A HUGE BED THAT HAS PUR-ple sheets, a purple blanket, and purple pillowcases. I can't deny the bedding is unbelievably soft, better than even the most expensive silk on earth. I'm not on the earth anymore, though. Anthea spirited me away to the Unseen, through the portal near the rock shop, and then dumped me in this room. At least I've dried out now.

Anthea brought me to her lair, I assume. It's a cave decked out like a porno queen's den of sex. Well, I guess that's what she is. I mean, the succubus needs sexual energy to survive. But if she thinks she'll get that from me, she will find out just how hard I can fight.

Anthea bound me to the bedposts with silky strips of fabric that seem way stronger than any silk I've heard of in the mortal world. Still, I tug on the bindings as hard as I can. Nothing happens. I try the bindings around my ankles, which are tied to the foot of the bed, but I have no better luck with those. *Come on, girl, think of something.* I refuse to just lie here waiting for an ensorcelled succubus to do who knows what to me.

At least she didn't strip me naked. I'll be grateful for small mercies.

I owe Tris a debt. Two debts, actually. I expressed my gratitude for the way he threw himself on top of me when the lightning almost hit us, then I sort of expressed gratitude for him saving my life when he shoved me away from that falling tree. I didn't say the exact words—"thank you—" but I felt them in my heart when I spoke the words "you saved my life." Somehow, I know that cemented another, stronger debt. So yeah, I owe him a lot. Can't I leverage that? Or does he have to invoke the debt? Not sure how all this magic stuff works. One thing I know for sure is that Tris would have invoked the debt already if he could, because he wants to help me. The fact that he hasn't done that makes me worry. A lot.

Has the curse destroyed him? Or can he simply not take control of my debts to him?

I test my bindings a bit more, looking for any sign of weakness. But I still can't find any way out of them.

The wooden door to this rock-walled room swings open, and the succubus sashays up to the foot of the bed. "I hope you are comfortable, darling. The pleasure of all my lovers is of paramount importance to me."

"Lovers? I'm not having sex with you."

"You constrain yourself to only men, don't you? What a shame."

"I'm not attracted to you. No offense."

"You do not offend me." She climbs onto the bed, crawling up it on all fours until she kneels beside my shoulder. "Don't worry. I will ensorcell you, which will strip away all your inhibitions. You will experience more pleasure than you could possibly imagine, then you'll beg me for more."

Oh no, no, no. Ensorcellment? Tris told me that's one of the blackest forms of dark magic. I do not want to become the plaything of a succubus who obeys her master's commands. Since the puppet master has a hard-on for punishing Tris, I can't help thinking that torturing me will be an integral part of the plan to destroy him.

My brain can't seem to generate any ideas, much less a plan.

Anthea lays a hand on my calf, sliding it up my bare leg until her fingers brush the hem of my shorts. "You will enjoy your time with me. I will make certain of that. Why not relinquish your body to me willingly? That will be much easier on you than the ensorcellment process."

Those are my only choices? Oh, hell no.

Maybe I should rely on my secret weapon.

"Wow, this bed is sooo soft," I say like a true ditz, while I writhe around just enough to establish my dumb-blonde image in Anthea's mind. That's the plan, anyway. "I'd love to just roll around on this mattress for hours and rub myself all over the silky goodness."

The succubus licks her lips, and her eyes begin to burn with a reddish gold fire.

"Mm," I moan. "Too bad I can't do that. I mean, these bindings are super silky too, and I love the way they feel on my skin. But I'm desperate to get the full experience."

I writhe a bit more, as much as I can when I'm tied to the bed. My ditz act seems to impress Anthea. She lays a hand on her chest, petting her skin with her own fingers while she watches me.

What the heck. Might as well go all the way.

Pushing my head back into the pillow, I lift my hips as much as possible, which isn't that much, and hoist my tits. Oh yeah, that gets her attention. I still do not want to have sex with her, but at least now I'm in control of the situation. She's getting too turned on to be in command.

The salamander chick purrs like a cat.

I thought she could shape-shift into a red lizard, not a feline. Whatever. I need to focus on my plan and keep acting like a brainless bimbo. So I giggle. "Oh wow, wow, wow. I bet I could orgasm from how good this bedding feels, if I could just rub my body all over it."

For good measure, I hoist my tits again.

Anthea's mouth falls open, and her eyes burn with a red-hot fire that seems to be imbued with crackling sparks. Her chest heaves. Her purring turns into a long, low, ravenous growl.

I swear I've never been a tease. But I can't be shy while I'm trying to break free of the succubus and escape from her lair.

My bindings vanish.

Anthea poises on all fours, like she wants to pounce on me.

Great plan, Riley. Get the ensorcelled succubus dangerously aroused. But I just thought of something. Ooh, this could work. So I bend one knee and drag my hand up and down my thigh. "You know what would be super-hot? If you shifted into salamander form. I've heard that's the sexiest thing any incubus or succubus can do for a woman."

She stares at me for a moment, her tongue almost hanging out of her mouth. Then poof, she shifts.

I'm now gazing at a small red lizard.

Okay, I got what I wanted. Now what? My idea has fizzled out, since I can't think of a way to leverage this.

A figure appears halfway between the door and the foot of the bed. Eerily pale blue eyes fixate on me, and the vampire Cyneric inches closer like a panther hunting his prey.

But who is he hunting? Me or the succubus?

He halts at the foot of the bed and sniffs the air. His lip curls. "Salamander."

I point to the lizard. "Yep. There she is. Did you come here to, um, have sex with Anthea? She'd probably love for you to bite her neck."

The vampire glances at the lizard, then veers his attention back to me. "I came for you."

"Oh. Well, that's…sweet." Every hair on my body has gone stiff, and a tingle of fear spreads across every inch of my skin. I think I'd rather screw the salamander chick than become a meal for a vampire. But a girl has to work with what she's got. "Can you get me out of here?"

Cyneric nods.

"Okay, that would be awesome." I slide off the side of the bed to avoid getting too close to the vampire. "But no sucking my blood without my express permission. Got it?"

Cyneric nods again.

Anthea shifts back into humanoid form.

The vampire growls at her, baring his glistening fangs. "Stay away from her, succubus. A filthy creature like you does not deserve to lie with such a woman."

He's rather eloquent. The way Tris and his friends described the vamps, I assumed they couldn't do anything more than grunt like cavemen. But Cyneric speaks—with a slight German accent.

Anthea shrieks and hurls her body at him, biting and clawing at his flesh.

Cyneric slams her to the floor, crouching over the succubus on his hands and knees with one fist clamped around her throat.

"Let's get out of here," I say. "Forget about her. Just take me somewhere else."

I almost added the P-word at the end but realized at the last second that I do not want to indebt myself to a vampire.

Cyneric freezes and slowly rotates his head to glance back at me. "You wish for her to live?"

"Yes. She's ensorcelled, so it's not her fault she's acting like a lunatic."

He peels his hand away from Anthea's throat and rises to his full height, towering over both the succubus lying prone on the floor and me, the mortal standing on her feet. He is huge, though not quite as enormous as Max or Travis.

Cyneric rushes at me so fast that I barely have time to process the movement. He lashes his arms around me and teleports us away.

We touch down inside a small clearing. Two moons glow in the sky above us. Night had fallen while I was trapped in Anthea's lair, but that hardly matters now. I'm more concerned with what Cyneric will do next. He hasn't let go of me.

"I'm glad you got me out of there," I say. "But how did you find me?"

"Your scent permeates the Unseen."

I smell? Did I forget to use deodorant this morning? "Would you mind letting go of me? I'm kind of getting squished."

He lets go and takes two big steps away from me. His fingers twitch, but his gaze remains steadily on me. That's disconcerting, to say the least.

I try for a casual smile and a casual tone. "Since you found me, do you think you could find Tris too?"

The vampire shakes his head. "Only you."

Oh yeah, this gets creepier by the second. I back away slowly, feigning a relaxed attitude. "Well, maybe I should go look for him. He's been cursed, you know, and I promised to help him out with that."

I carefully turn partway, not wanting to upset the twitchy vamp but needing to get the heck out of here.

Cyneric winks out, then winks in again, standing right in front of me. "Not safe. I must protect you."

"That's nice of you, but I need to check on Tris. Why don't we, um, go to the oracle's precinct? Bob might be able to help me."

"No oracle."

I open my mouth but shut it again a split second later. I'd been about to say the dreaded P-word. I take a moment to consider how to phrase my request. "I would appreciate it if you could teleport me to the edge of the oracle's forest. I can take it from there."

Cyneric studies me again in that unnervingly intense way.

My pulse is beating so fast that I feel a touch woozy, but I will not let the vamp see that. Fear is the root cause. I've been terrified ever since Anthea kidnapped me and announced she'd really love to screw me, whether I like it or not.

The vampire clamps a hand on my upper arm, and he whisks us away. We now stand on the periphery of the creepy, oozing forest.

"Good job," I tell Cyneric, strictly because I can't think of a better way to safely thank him without speaking those words. I slap his arm. "You're really good at teleporting."

His brows crinkle. "Tel-ah-por-ting?"

"That's what we call it when elementals disappear and then reappear in a different place. It's also called whisking or zipping or...other stuff like that." Yeah, I'm suddenly an expert on the subject after less than a day in the Unseen.

"I see," Cyneric says, though he doesn't sound sure of that.

Turning toward the woods, I throw Cyneric a tight smile over my shoulder. "See you later."

And I march into the woods. I've traveled no more than a hundred feet when something whizzes past me. The figure halts, then whirls around to stand in my path.

Cyneric is back.

Damn, I thought I gave that lost puppy the brush-off already. Guess I didn't get brushy enough. So I plant my hands on my hips. "What are you doing, Cyneric?"

"Protecting you."

"No magics can get through the wards here. You don't need to protect me anymore. Okay?"

He shakes his head.

I veer around him and continue down the path at a brisker pace, though I don't hold out much hope that will discourage him. The vamp has developed a sudden and bizarre fixation with protecting me, though he only saw me once before he came to my rescue in Anthea's lair. I might be slightly grateful for that, but I do not appreciate the stalking that followed.

When I glance back, I realize that Cyneric is maintaining a discreet distance behind me.

At least he's got a smidgen of common courtesy.

I walk faster than I had the first time I came to this forest, but when I reach the toxic river, I need to do something I really don't want to do. I ask for help from the vampire. "Cyneric, I can't jump across the water. Could you—"

He sweeps me up in his arms and flies across the river, at least twenty feet above its surface. We land gently on the opposite shore. Then he sets me down.

"That was impressive," I say. "You're one awesome jumper."

Cyneric lifts his chin a touch, and his lips form the teeniest of smug smiles.

Well, at least I can make a bloodsucker feel better about himself. That was always one of my goals in life. No, not really. Of all the cryptids I'd like to meet, vampires are not among them. Maybe Cyneric isn't totally evil, but I suspect he's not entirely stable either.

The closer we get to the oracle's lair, the more convinced I become that I will find Tris there. No idea why. But if I've learned one thing today, it's this.

The universe is so much weirder than I ever imagined.

CHAPTER FIFTEEN

Tris

COME ON, BOB, LET ME IN!" I SHOUT WHILE POUNDING MY FISTS ON THE big mound. The oracle won't open the doorway for me. What's his problem? I need help finding Riley, and this twit won't even show himself. "I'm not leaving until you open up. You know I'm very, very annoying, and I won't give up until I've driven you insane with pounding and hollering."

"There's no need to be rude."

Riley's voice makes me spin around and grin like an idiot.

She grins at me too.

And then I notice who stands behind her. Cyneric the bloodsucking vampire hovers a little further down the trail, just at the edge of the clearing.

I hurry to Riley and jab a finger in the vamp's direction. "What's that creep doing? Has he hurt you?"

"No. He rescued me from Anthea's lair."

The vamp did what? All Cyneric ever does is stare blankly at everybody and sometimes tip his head to the side. Yeah, we all think he's creepy. Because he is. But if he helped Riley, well, I guess I have to thank him. Not out loud. Indebting myself to a bloodsucking weirdo is not on my to-do list.

So I tell Cyneric, "Glad you were there to help out."

The vamp's brows lift the slightest bit, but he just keeps staring.

"Did Bob help you?" Riley asks me.

I shake my head. "He wouldn't even open the door. Bob might be kind of full of himself, but I can't believe he'd refuse to even let me into his lair."

"Of course I would not."

Riley didn't say that. Someone behind me did, and I know exactly who it is.

I turn around to face Bob. "So you finally decided to show yourself. About time."

"Mind your manners, leprechaun, or I might toss you out of my precinct."

"Go on. My day can't get much worse."

Bob's lips tick up at one corner. "Yes, I heard a tree had fallen on you. Tough luck, eh? But you are immortal, so pity isn't appropriate."

Gee, sympathy might be nice. But the oracle doesn't really do that sort of thing.

I finally notice his clothing, and I can't help smirking. "You look like you just got bowled over by a tornado, Bob."

Yeah, his hair is mussed, he lost his suit jacket, his shirt is half unbuttoned and hanging out on one side, his pants are wrinkled, and he's only got one shoe. The other foot is naked. Then I spot a solid clue—lipstick on his chest, like somebody has been kissing his pecs. He has lipstick on his neck and mouth too.

I can't resist chuckling. "You got laid, didn't you, Bob? Did you and Miriella kiss and make up?"

He tries to stuff his shirt back inside his waistband but doesn't quite accomplish that. The oracle clears his throat and shoves a hand through his hair. "That is none of your concern, leprechaun."

Oh yeah, he got laid for sure. Didn't do a great job of putting his clothes back on, though. I would've thought an oracle might see company coming and just whoosh his clothes back onto his body in perfect order. But no, he looks like he got caught in the act and scrambled to cover up.

"Do you require sanctuary or not?" Bob asks in an annoyed tone.

"Yes, we do." I glance back at Cyneric. "Not sure what to do with him, though."

"He may remain outside to guard. That's what he wants to do, anyway."

"Whatever you say."

Bob turns and flourishes a hand in front of the mound. The doorway opens. "Come with me, Tris and Riley. Cyneric will remain in the clearing."

I take Riley's hand as we follow Bob into the dark passageway and the door seals itself behind us. We turn several corners, heading down corridors I'd never known existed, until we finally march into a passageway that has torches on the walls. Their flickering amber light reminds me of Bob's giant metal fire bowl.

He stops halfway down the corridor and flourishes his hand toward the wall. A doorway opens, revealing a bedroom inside. "You may stay here until you are ready to continue your journey."

"What are we supposed to do? I need advice on how to find the person who cursed me."

"No, that is not what you need the most." He steps away from the door. "Go inside. You will soon realize what you really need right now." He leans toward me. "Here's a hint. It is not advice from me."

A flash of movement draws my attention to the opposite end of the corridor where a woman has just exited a doorway that hadn't been there a second ago. She has a sheet wrapped around her like a shroud, with only her hand holding it up. Miriella's hair is just as messy as Bob's, and she looks exactly like she's been screwing the oracle.

Well, good for them.

I smirk again. "You horny old goat, Bob. Don't keep your girl waiting."

He scowls at me, then he and Miriella both vanish. So does the doorway she'd come out of a moment ago.

Bob might've been suggesting I should have sex with Riley, but I don't know if that's a good idea. I'm cursed, after all. But I can't see the corridor we'd come down right before we turned into this one, which means we might as well go inside this bedroom to sit down and rest.

"Oh, Bob, yes!"

That's Miriella for sure. Jeez, Bob doesn't waste time with foreplay, does he?

"Yes, Bob, yes!"

I glance at Riley sideways, feeling a tad uncomfortable all of a sudden. She bites her lip and looks at me sideways too. I shrug. She shrugs. Then we shuffle into the bedroom.

The door vanishes behind us.

Riley and I are alone. In a fancy bedroom inside an oracle's lair. While two powerful beings are getting it on down the hall. Miriella keeps shouting Bob's name over and over and over.

I sit on the edge of the huge bed.

Riley sits on the other side of the mattress.

Bob roars, and Miriella screams. Then they finally cut out all the racket.

Now I feel kind of…horny.

Riley gets up and starts pacing the width of the room while staring down at the floor.

"Are you okay?" I ask.

"Uh-huh, sure."

"Then why are you pacing like a caged animal?"

She stops but keeps her attention aimed at the floor. "I feel a little weird after hearing…"

"Bob and Miriella screwing each other's brains out?"

Riley nods.

I get up and walk over to her, grasping her upper arms. "Relax. I don't expect you to get naked with me."

She lifts her head to look at me, her eyes luminous and darker than usual, thanks to her pupils dilating. "What if I do want that?"

For a few seconds, all I can do is stare at her. "I want that too. I want you, period. You're the sexiest woman I've ever met, and the smartest too."

"Meeting you has been the most amazing thing that's ever happened to me." She wraps her arms around herself. "I don't really have friends anymore, and I even lost my job because of my mission to prove cryptids exist."

"You got fired? What did you do for a living?"

"I was a flight attendant. It was a great job. I got to fly all over the world and see new places, plus I had time to look for cryptids too. I never told anybody about that."

"Why did you lose your job, then? If nobody knew about your secret passion, I mean."

She shrugs. "Somebody told the higher-ups about my parents and the documentary they took part in years earlier. It's not hard to find that online, though I never imagined anyone would go looking for that video. But someone did, and I got fired for not behaving in a professional manner because I talked to a passenger about Bigfoot. That was the excuse. I know I got fired because my bosses think I'm crazy."

"What jackasses. That's horrible, Riley."

"Actually, I don't mind so much anymore. Not since I met you." She shuffles a little closer. "Now I've met honest-to-goodness supernatural beings, and I know I was right—and my parents were too. Don't care what anybody else thinks."

"Good for you." I tug her into me. "You are one amazing woman, Riley. And I want to make love to you right here, right now."

"I'd love that."

"Are you sure? I'm not human, and I can't swear my curse won't infect you too if we, ah, get intimate."

She rests her palms on my chest and gazes up at me with the sweetest expression. "I want this, with you, right now."

My dick is getting stiff already, just from the sultry way she spoke those words. I fold my arms around her. "Just so you know, I can't get you pregnant unless I consciously try to do that. I don't have any diseases either. Well, other than a curse."

She smiles. "I trust you, Tris. You don't need to give me all the fine print."

"You want to get naked, right? Here, now, in the oracle's lair."

"Oh, yes, absolutely."

"All right, then." I snap my fingers, strictly for dramatic effect, and our clothes vanish. "Your wish is my command."

She grins. But that expression turns sensual as she skims her gaze over my body. "Wow, you are so amazingly hot." She roves her hands over my chest and down to my hips. Her focus shifts to my dick. "Holy cow. Do all elementals have equipment like yours?"

"No idea. I don't like to look at naked men, though Max loves to prance around au naturel. But I try really hard not to accidentally see his manly parts."

"I'd love to admire your manly parts for hours."

"Later, baby." I pick her up and leap onto the bed, landing on my feet. Then I drop her onto the mattress. "It's my turn to admire your body."

She writhes on the blanket while biting her lip and clasping her hands above her head on the pillow.

I make the covers disappear. Now she lies on a sheet that's so silky smooth it seems almost iridescent. She looks beautiful lying there, her naked body on display, her expression full of hunger. I hunger for her too, so much that I need to summon all my willpower to give her what she deserves before I fuck her like crazy.

Lying down beside her, I skate my palm over her belly and tease her navel with my thumb. She grips the pillow harder. I drag my palm down to her hip, pausing there to massage the hollow before I move on. My hand glides down her leg, then I shift it to run my palm up her inner thigh. She spreads her legs for me, and the scent of her cream inundates my senses. As an elemental, I have senses far more heightened than any mortal, which means I can detect every minute aroma hidden within the musky, sweet scent of her desire. It's intoxicating.

I place my mouth on her belly and kiss a trail down to her mound, nuzzling the hairs while I pull in a deeper draft of her scent. A low growl rumbles in my throat. I've never growled like that before, not even when I had sex with Anthea. The succubus couldn't turn me on half as much as Riley does. I move between her thighs, and she bends her knees as if she's begging me to make her come.

There's nothing I want more right now.

So I push my head between her thighs and latch on to her clit. She gasps and arches her back. My powers always ramp up a little during sex, but here with Riley, those healing energies become something else, something I've never experienced before. They heat up, transforming from healing to arousing, the magics permeating me and Riley. I can feel that happening to her. My dick is rock-hard and throbbing, and the second I start suckling her nub, she starts thrashing beneath me.

I need to be inside her. But not yet.

While my powers flow through me into her and back again in a never-ending loop of heat and sensual energy, I push a finger inside her and keep devouring her clit. She thrashes even more, gasping and whimpering, crying out every time I thrust into her. When I add another finger, then another, she jerks and cries out. I pump my fingers faster and faster, nipping her nub and groaning at the incredible flavor of her.

And she comes. Her entire body goes rigid, then curls in on itself. While the spasms of her climax grip my fingers, she clutches my head and screams.

I can't wait any longer. Even as her orgasm keeps going, I rise to my knees and lift her hips off the mattress, then thrust into her slick, hot flesh. A deep groan resonates in my chest. She feels so good, better than any woman I've been with before, better even than a succubus. I haul in a deep breath and exhale it as I pump into her hard and fast. Her cream glistens on my cock and dribbles onto my balls, and I can tell she's heading toward another climax already. I haul in a breath every time I pull back and blow it out with every inward lunge. Her body fits me like a glove, so hot and wet and silky.

"Oh yes, Tris, yes," Riley shouts. "Harder, faster, yes, yes, yes!"

"Fuck, Riley."

A strange sensation sweeps over my skin and dives inside my body, energizing me with the most incredible burst of…something. But suddenly, I can't hold back. I need to punch into her so deeply and take her so thoroughly that it will become more than sex. I drop onto my elbows, my face hovering above Riley's, and thrust wildly. Her second orgasm strikes with such ferocity that her screams turn hoarse, and her eyes roll back in her head. I pound into her a few more times and come deep inside her, unleashing a powerful jet that goes on and on and on while I hold perfectly still, frozen in that last thrust.

When it finally ends, I collapse on top of her. Can't speak. Can hardly breathe.

Riley struggles to catch her breath too. She lashes her arms around me and whispers into my ear, "Best sex ever."

I can't help chuckling. "I appreciate the compliment, but it's never been like this before. Did you feel that?"

"Feel what? Oh, you must mean the energy burst or whatever that was."

I rub her back, which soothes us both. "Yeah, I meant that. What was it?"

"No idea." She spreads her thighs and wraps her legs around me. "Give me some food, and then we can try that again."

Again? Hell yeah, I want that.

CHAPTER SIXTEEN

Riley

OH, WOW. I HAVE NEVER EXPERIENCED ANYTHING LIKE THE SEX I JUST had with Tris. No words can describe it. When I came, my heart pounded so hard and fast that I felt sure I was about to go into the light. Dying while Tris is inside me would be the perfect way to go, but I don't want to kick the bucket just yet. No, I need a lot more time with him, in and out of bed.

Who knew a leprechaun would give me the best sex in the history of the universe?

Tris conjures food for us, and I don't ask where he got that from because I trust him. He wouldn't feed me leftovers from some other fae's garbage can. The luscious foods he offers me replenish my energy, but after we're done eating, we just lie here in each other's arms for a while. He strokes my hair. I draw circles on his chest with my fingertip. He caresses my back. I snuggle up to him with my face buried against his neck and revel in the delicious but completely indescribable way he smells.

Eventually, I sit up and announce, "I want to eat you up, Tris."

"More food?" he says with a smirk. "Maybe donuts this time?"

"Uh-uh." I swing my leg over him to straddle his hips. "I want to swallow you whole."

His breathing grows heavier, and I feel his dick swelling against my bottom. "You don't have to do that."

"I want to." With my hands on his lower belly, I rock my hips to rub myself against his hardening cock. "You're ready for action already, aren't you?"

"Yeah. I'm an elemental, not a mortal. That means I can get rock-hard in a second flat if I want." He sucks in a sharp breath. "Kinda loving this, though. Taking it slow while you rub yourself all over me."

"Mm, I love it too." Scooting backward, I lie down between his legs and set my hands on his hips. The unbelievable length and breadth of his erection waves in front of my face. I had that inside me earlier. He filled me up like no man on earth ever could. "Are you ready?"

"Hell yeah."

I grasp the base of his cock and gently lick the head.

He jerks and grunts.

The look on his face, full of hunger and intense need, makes my clit throb. I close my mouth around the crown of his erection and pump my hand while I lick voraciously, like I can't get enough of him. I can't. No way. I'll still be starved for him when the universe finally explodes. God, he tastes incredible. I could get addicted to the salty yet sweet flavor of his dick. I've given men head before, but none of them tasted anything like Tris. I lick and suck, swallowing more of him, pumping with my mouth in time with the rhythm of my hand's movements.

He groans and grunts, gasps and splutters. His hands fist in the sheets, and I hear fabric ripping. "Riley, ah!"

I speed up my movements, devouring him while moaning and grunting, my pulse throbbing in my ears and slickness flooding my cleft.

Tris comes with a hoarse bellow that echoes inside the room. The strength of his release stuns me, but I need to consume every last bit of him. When it finally ends, he lies limp and gasping on the bed.

I roll over onto the mattress beside him, my head near his hip, and lay a palm on my chest. "Wow. I have never enjoyed giving a man head that much. I almost came again just from making you go off."

Tris gets a sneaky look on his face. "I can alleviate that problem."

"What? There's no problem."

"Sure there is. You didn't get to climax." He folds his hands over his belly. "Come for me, Riley. Do it now, and make it explosive."

The second he speaks those words, the muscles inside my sex begin to pulsate hard and fast. My entire body curls in on itself from the sheer power of the orgasm rushing through me. I scream and gasp and finally whimper, and I think my eyes even roll back in my head. Oh. My. God. I've never experienced a climax like this. By the time it subsides, I'm breathless and lying limp on the bed with my head lolling onto Tris's belly.

He grasps me under my arms and hauls me up the bed to lie beside him. He hugs me to him, kissing the top of my head. "That's how I express my gratitude. What you did for me was incredible. *You* are incredible, Riley."

I snuggle up to him. "Mm, it was mind-blowingly fantastic. But I'd rather have you inside me when I come."

"We probably have time to do that again."

"Let's do it."

He suddenly stiffens.

Pushing up on my elbow, I gaze down at him. "What's wrong? You've tensed up."

"Well, I was just thinking..." He winces. "Never mind."

"Now you have to tell me."

He exhales a heavy sigh. "I couldn't help wondering if your debts to me forced you to love having sex with me."

"Baloney. You didn't invoke the debt in any way. I did this because I wanted to do it, because I wanted you."

He opens his mouth, and I just know he wants to tell me it might be the debt.

But I seal his lips with my fingers. "No way. It had nothing to do with my debts. I made the decision to be with you, and magic had no say in it."

Someone knocks on the door. "Are you two done yet? Your vampire friend is growing restless."

"Out in a minute, Bob," Tris shouts.

We both climb off the bed, then he makes our clothes magically reappear. I could get used to this. Poof, and my clothes not only appear on my body, but they're in perfect order, not a spot or wrinkle on them. How does he do that? It's such a time-saver. Even my socks and shoes poofed back onto my feet.

As for my hair... Well, I'm pretty sure I've got sex hair. It feels tangled and frizzy.

Tris squints at my head. "Wish I could help you with that, but I've never been able to fix a girl's hairdo. Tried it a few times. The results were, ah, less than optimal." He winces. "It involved some hair loss."

"Don't try to fix my hair. I'd rather have a rat's nest on my head than go instantly bald."

His eyes light up, and he smiles with his mouth closed. Then he holds his closed hand out to me, palm up, and flicks his fingers straight. "Here ya go."

Tris has just given me a hairbrush.

I kiss his cheek. "That was such a sweet thing to do."

"Nice avoidance of the T-word."

Using the brush, which is not mine, I detangle my hair. Tris clasps my hand as we walk out of the bedroom into the corridor beyond, where Bob waits for us.

Tris waggles his eyebrows. "Miriella went home already, huh? Glad you two crazy kids patched things up."

"Your vampire has been irritating me," the oracle says. "Make him stop."

"Stop what?" I ask.

Then I hear it—a pounding noise coming from somewhere else inside the oracle's lair, or maybe from the outside.

Bob stalks off down the corridor at a swift clip, and the torches on the walls snuff out one by one in the oracle's wake. Tris and I hurry to keep up with him or risk being left in the dark. That didn't seem to bother Tris the first time we came here. He had traversed the dark passageways as if he had night vision eyes. Maybe he does. I hadn't thought to ask.

The pounding grows louder and louder as we draw closer to the invisible doorway of Bob's lair. He stops ten feet away from it and gestures wildly with one arm. "Make him stop. I will go insane if that howling bloodsucker does not cease rattling my home with his fists."

"So open the door for us," Tris tells him. "We can't do it ourselves, Bob."

The oracle makes a huffing-growling noise, then flings a hand out toward the invisible doorway. It shimmers, and the center of the rock wall fades into nothing, leaving a perfectly oval hole. I hadn't noticed its shape before. It might not have been a perfect oval last time I was here. Who knows?

Tris and I exit the hill, and the doorway seals itself shut.

Cyneric stands a couple of yards away, staring intently at the boulder, his chest heaving and his skin sheathed with sweat.

I whisper to Tris, "Let me handle him."

My fae lover raises his brows, but then screws up his mouth and nods.

The vampire keeps his gaze nailed to me as I approach him. "Cyneric, what are you so upset about?"

"You were gone."

"We went inside the oracle's lair for a while. That's all."

"But you were gone for a long time."

How long had we been in there? I have no idea, but it couldn't have been as long as he seems to think. Maybe he has a screwed-up sense of time. Considering how the god Eros changed him so drastically and suddenly, I imagine it would have mental side-effects.

"It's okay," I tell Cyneric. "I'm okay. Tris and Bob wouldn't let anything happen to me."

"But I heard—" He swerves his eyes to glance at Tris, then veers them back to me. "I heard noises. Someone in pain."

Did he hear us having sex? Jeez, Bob needs to invest in more insulation for his lair. "No one was hurt. I'm fine, and so is Tris."

"You are unharmed?"

I pat his arm. "Yes, I'm unharmed. Okay?"

His jaw works, but then he relaxes visibly.

Tris comes up beside me. "We need to head out."

Cyneric whirls around and starts off down the trail through the woods.

I hustle after him but trip over something, about to fall flat on my face.

Tris flings an arm around my waist to lift me up and onto my feet. He releases me, then studies the ground. "Damn. It must've been my curse. It's infected you now too."

"Don't panic." I point at a tree root that sticks up out of the ground. "I tripped on that."

"You can't be sure."

"Let's not assume the worst when there's a simple explanation right in front of us." I kiss his cheek. "At least I have you to catch me before I hit the ground."

"Okay, I'll accept your tree root theory. For now."

Up ahead, I see the vampire watching us and waiting.

Hand in hand, Tris and I march down the path.

When we reach the toxic river, Cyneric tries to grab me to carry me over it, but Tris bats his hand away. "I've got it covered. Worry about yourself."

Cyneric leaps across the river like he had earlier, springing twenty feet into the air, only to whump down on the other side with stunning grace and dexterity. Tris picks me up and jumps over the river, thumping down near the vampire. He didn't accomplish the feat with as much finesse as Cyneric had, but I would much rather be ferried across the sulfuric river by my favorite leprechaun.

The vampire stalks off down the path.

We follow him, and soon I spy the edge of the oracle's domain up ahead, maybe fifty feet away.

A figure leaps out of the woods, flying straight toward me.

Tris throws himself in front of me. Just as Anthea bares her teeth and shrieks, barreling toward Tris, she gets yanked backward—into Cyneric. He clamps one arm around the salamander's midsection, effectively shackling her arms. Then he lays his free hand on her face, forcing her to tip her head to the side, exposing her throat. He growls and bares his teeth.

And he sinks his fangs into Anthea's neck.

"Cyneric, no!" I shout.

Her eyes go wide, but only for a second. Then her lids drift half-closed, and her body slackens. Her lips curve into a blissful smile even as blood trickles down her skin. Since she's naked, I can see her nipples hardening. She moans as if she's about to have an orgasm. Despite the fact she seems to enjoy getting bitten by a vampire, I feel like I should stop this.

I lean around Tris to shout, "Let her go, Cyneric!"

He lifts his head, fangs stained with blood, and gazes at me without expression. After a few seconds, he lets go of Anthea. She slumps onto the ground, still dazed and almost blissful.

The succubus looks up at the vampire. "Do that again, darling."

Cyneric glances at Anthea, and his lip curls in disgust.

She rolls around, moaning. "Come on, baby, bite me."

Tris marches over there and hoists Anthea onto her feet, leaning her against an oozing tree. "Stay put. Understand?"

She nods and smiles dreamily.

Getting bitten by a vamp must be erotic to the extreme. Sure, that's what romance novels tell everybody. But I never imagined it would be true. Of course, Tris told me how Cyneric attacked Travis and Larissa, so maybe a vampire's bite isn't always hot. Anthea sure loved it, though. Maybe salamanders are the only ones who like it.

"Why did you do that?" I ask as I approach Cyneric. I stop an arm's length away, but honestly, if he wants to grab me, he can do it no matter how far away I am.

He cants his head, almost like he's analyzing me. "She wanted you. I stopped her."

"You could've just grabbed her. The bloodsucking wasn't necessary."

The vamp eyes the succubus sideways, his lip curling again. "She is vile."

Well, I can't argue with that.

Tris throws an arm around me. "Stay here, Cyneric. Riley and I need to discuss a few things. Your job is to stop Anthea from running away." He glances at the moaning succubus and smirks. "Not that she seems likely to go anywhere. But keep her here anyway. Got it?"

Cyneric nods crisply.

And Tris ushers me back down the trail until we're out of earshot of the vamp and the salamander. He takes hold of my upper arms, leaning in until his face hovers inches from mine. "I've got a plan. And it involves your vampire groupie."

CHAPTER SEVENTEEN

Tris

RILEY SEEMS CONFUSED. I DON'T BLAME HER. MY IDEA WILL SOUND EVEN crazier once I explain the whole plan, especially since we're relying on a vampire who isn't entirely stable and whose moods and motives we can't gauge. But I can't go on stumbling around in the dark, trying to hunt down a phantom. Bob hadn't given me much in the way of clues, but I get that he's not allowed to just offer me a road map to solve my problems. It would be awesome if he could. That's not how the Unseen works, though.

"My groupie?" Riley says. "He's more like a lost vampire puppy."

"Only if that puppy is a deranged hell hound."

"Cyneric isn't deranged. He's analytical."

I hope she's not about to suggest we adopt him. "Think whatever you like about Cyneric, but the fact is, he tore Travis's throat out. Even if he didn't mean to punch a sword through Larissa's chest, that's only because he meant to stab Travis. Forgive me for not having warm, fuzzy feelings about the bloodsucker."

"He's dangerous. I get that. But we shouldn't treat him like a monster with no heart or brain."

"Do you want to hear my plan or not?"

Riley sighs. "Yeah, tell me."

Gee, she could probably sound less excited if she really, really tried. "We let Anthea go, but Cyneric goes with her. She, uh, likes him. So she'll allow him to tag along with her."

"How does that help us?"

"She knows who cursed me, right? She must, since she's ensorcelled to do that person's bidding. Your vampire groupie wants to help you, so if you tell him to report back to you once he finds the curse-maker, he'll do it."

"Can't we just follow Anthea ourselves?"

"Sure. But whoever cursed me must be tracking me too. How else would they know when to drop a tree on me? I don't believe Anthea did that herself. She's a succubus, not a gnome."

Riley's forehead crinkles in the cutest way. "What does that mean? She's a succubus, not a gnome. I mean, duh, obviously she's not a little guy with a beard."

"What are you talking about?" I realize why she said that and shake my head. "Here in the Unseen, a gnome is not a garden ornament. They're huge, hulking, tree-like monsters who love to cause earthquakes by stomping their feet."

Her eyes widen. "Oh. I didn't know that."

"Of course you didn't. Mortals aren't supposed to know about the Unseen." I kiss her forehead. "It's okay. What do you think of my plan? We just let Anthea go, and the vamp follows."

"It could work. If I can convince Cyneric to stick to the plan. He tends to do his own thing, especially if he thinks I'm in danger."

"He listens to you. That means you can convince him." I peer around her to see the vampire, who's guarding Anthea while she rolls around on the ground and moans with intense pleasure. What a nutcase that succubus is. "Anthea can't teleport inside these woods. But once she recovers from that bite, she'll try to run, I'm sure. You need to talk to Cyneric right now. I'll guard the ensorcelled salamander chick."

"Okay."

"My plan also involves letting Anthea believe she escaped from us."

We walk back to Cyneric and Anthea. I grab the succubus by her arm and drag her back down the trail, out of earshot but not eyesight. Do vamps have enhanced hearing? I've got no idea. I keep hold of Anthea's arm while I watch Riley and Cyneric. I wish I could hear what they're saying, but I couldn't risk the succubus overhearing our plan. Standing way over here while my girlfriend chats with a vampire is not my favorite thing to do.

Riley looks at me, smiling and making the thumbs-up sign.

I drag Anthea back over there, then let go of her. "Let's get moving. No point in hanging around in these woods."

The four of us start walking, and soon we exit the creepy woods. Anthea just keeps following us as we cross a large clearing. The sun is starting to rise, though I didn't feel like we spent enough time in Bob's lair that night should be over now. Time can move differently here. Maybe Riley and I had sex for longer than it seemed like we did, or maybe Bob manipulated time. Certain things in the Unseen will always remain a mystery.

Suddenly, Anthea rushes past us and whirls around, cackling like a maniac. She races up to Cyneric, seizes his hand, and whisks them both away.

That's not exactly how I pictured my plan unfolding, but it'll work. Assuming the vamp holds up his end of the deal.

"What do we do now?" Riley asks. "Stand here waiting?"

"No. We're going to shop for my new lair."

"Are you kidding? You're cursed, and we're relying on an unstable vampire to find out who did that to you. We should... I don't know. Hunker down somewhere."

"Like that will help. My enemy can find me anywhere."

"Good point." She chews on her bottom lip for a moment, thinking hard enough that I swear I can hear the gears turning in her brain. "Take me to your favorite place."

I need to consider that request. Where is my favorite place? The answer is obvious and kind of embarrassing. But I pull Riley into my arms and take us straight to the portal and through the veil to the other side—the mortal world. We step out of the cave, and I jump down to the clearing near the wooden railing around the falls.

Yeah, my favorite place in the multiverse is the rock shop.

"This is it?" Riley asks. "You could've gone anywhere, and you chose this place. That's not what I expected."

"Where did you think I'd take you?"

She shrugs. "Maybe the copper fae village."

"Nah. That's boring. The mortal world is way more fun."

I take her hand, leading Riley past the healing vortex and through the rock garden, to the back door of the shop. As the door shuts behind us, we find ourselves abruptly severed from the bright sunshine. Our eyes need a minute to adjust.

"Tris, you're back!" Lindsey calls out from behind the sales counter. "How are you feeling? You weren't at your best the last time we saw you."

"Yeah, but I'm fine now." I guide Riley toward the counter. "This is Riley Jordan. We're, uh..."

"I'm his girlfriend," Riley says.

Did I hallucinate? No, I'm pretty sure she actually said that.

Lindsey grins. "That's wonderful. Tris is such a sweetie-pie."

"Yes, he is," my girlfriend announces. "And he's smart too."

"I know. Tris doesn't always believe it, though." Lindsey twists her head around to holler toward the back room. "Nevan! Get out here. Tris brought his girlfriend."

Nevan races out of the back room, halting beside his wife. He grins at Riley. "You must be the woman in question."

"Don't get weird about this," I say. "We're a couple, end of story. No need to go on and on about it. Besides, we're here for a reason, not just to entertain you."

Lindsey rests her arms on the counter, and she studies me briefly. "What's wrong, Tris? You seem anxious."

"You know I'm cursed. But things have gotten weirder since the last time we talked. The vampire Cyneric has a crush on Riley, and we convinced him to go with the succubus Anthea to find out who has cursed me." I pause when a baby-like noise emerges from under the sales counter. "Have you locked your baby in the safe?"

Lindsey laughs. "No. We moved that into the back room, so we could fit Liam's cradle under the counter."

"Oh. Makes sense, I guess."

"Tell us more about your plan. How did Anthea get involved?"

I work very hard not to sound smug when I tell her, "Because she's in league with whoever cursed me. That person ensorcelled her, so she does whatever her master commands. We're hoping Cyneric will discover that person's identity, then report back to us."

Nevan eyes me askance. "Your plan depends on a vampire? That doesn't sound promising."

"Relax, Nev. I don't expect you to let Cyneric sleep in your house and tuck him in at bedtime. But I hoped Riley and I could find a place to hang out while we wait for the vamp to report back."

"You cannot wait in our home, not if you're expecting a vampire for lunch." Nevan makes a disgusted face. "Or he's expecting you for lunch."

Lindsey elbows her husband in the side. "Cut it out, honey."

Her husband doesn't want us here, and I get why, but that means we need to find another place to wait for Cyneric. "We'll go hang out in the woods. Just wish I knew why somebody cursed me."

Nevan snorts. "That's hardly a mystery. You annoy everyone."

"Not true," Lindsey says. "I love Tris."

Can't help smirking. "Hear that, Nev? Your wife loves me."

He gives me a hard stare that doesn't impress me. Then he sighs. "Be careful, Tris. Vampires and curses are not a desirable combination."

Did he just express a modicum of concern for me? Don't think that's ever happened before. "We'll be careful. Come on, Riley, we need to scoot."

Nevan lifts his brows. "Scoot? You've spent too much time with Lindsey and Larissa."

"Zip it, air fairy."

I lead Riley out of the shop and up the hill, past the vortex and the falls, down a narrow trail that nobody ever bothers to explore because it looks like nothing much. Overgrown weeds. Dense pine trees. A few maples and aspens. The canopy above our heads blocks out most of the sunlight, and even hikers don't find much of interest in this area. I've always loved it, though. This place is tranquil.

And it has a house. Well, kinda.

Riley's brows draw together while she studies the little abode that hunkers inside a small clearing barely big enough to accommodate the house. "Did you bring me out here to see a dilapidated trailer?"

"No. I'm showing you my little hideaway." I grasp the knob on the trailer's door and tug several times until it finally pops open. Then I offer Riley my hand. "Let me escort you into your castle, milady."

She tries not to laugh but winds up sputtering. "Not exactly the fairy-tale castle I dreamed about when I was a little girl."

"It looks better on the inside."

"Only if you ensorcell me to think so."

"Hmm." I pretend I'm considering her idea. "Maybe I should try that."

She smacks my arm.

I grin and grasp her around the waist, then lift her up to set her down inside the trailer. "Should've conjured a crimson carpet for you to walk on."

Stepping inside, I shut the door. Then I raise my hand palm up, fingers curled as if I'm holding a ball inside it. A glittering orb of blue and white materializes.

"What is that?" Riley asks, her voice full of awe. "It's beautiful."

"This is a fairy light. Fae use them, but so do other elemental races. It's an easy way to light things up." I toss the orb toward the ceiling, where it hovers about six inches from the roof. Then I toss up a few more fairy lights. "How's that for a romantic atmosphere?"

"Nice." She turns in a circle. "Can you do anything about the decor?"

"Can I do it?" I make a sarcastic huffing sound. "You don't understand what a fae can do."

The worn furnishings disappear, replaced by lush new stuff—a cushy bed with silky sheets and plush pillows, plus soft carpeting and new curtains. I also made sure to stock the new mini fridge with plenty of sensual foods and drinks.

Oh yeah, I want to seduce my girlfriend.

"Wow, Tris," she says while surveying the new digs. "This is incredible."

"Glad you like it."

She bites her lip. "Not to sound ungrateful, but, um…where did you get this stuff?"

"I conjured it."

"That means you stole it."

"No, it doesn't." I clasp her hands. "Relax, I conjured all of this from a friend of mine who won't care. He lets me pay later."

"How do you pay? Do elementals have money?"

"No, we barter. Well, I have money. But I didn't get it from elementals."

"How did you get it?"

"I, uh…" Hunching my shoulders, I try for a sheepish but cute smile. Women love that kind of thing. "The truth is, I've been going into the mortal world to earn money. So I can take mortal girls out on dates."

"What do you do to earn money?"

"Can we talk about that later?" I nod toward the bed. "Let's get comfortable, then I'll answer any other questions you want to ask."

"Any questions? Wow, that's an offer I can't refuse."

Chapter Eighteen

Riley

WE CLIMB ONTO THE BED AND CUDDLE UP TOGETHER. IT WAS TRIS'S IDEA. Not many guys I've dated felt like wasting time on just snuggling with me, which is yet another reason I love being with the hot leprechaun. I met him yesterday, but I already feel closer to him than I have with anyone else in the universe. He makes me feel good in so many ways. But I've got questions that he promised to answer.

"Do you like snuggling with me?" I ask. "Or are you just doing what you think I want?"

"I like it. A lot." He rubs my back in slow, gentle circles that relax me even more. "I've never done this with any other women, elemental or human. I dated, sure, but it was always a casual thing. This feels like more."

"Feels that way for me too." I rest my chin on his chest. "Would you tell me about your transmutation? How did it change you?"

"You wouldn't believe what I used to look like. I was shorter and skinnier—like a teenager, stuck in puberty until the Unseen decided it was my time to mature. Like my dad told you, copper fae stay in a state of suspended growth for hundreds of years." He rubs his eyes, clearly uncomfortable with sharing that part of his life with me. "The transmutation made me bigger and stronger, but it came with a hefty price in pain. Can't even describe how excruciating it was. The process also changed my voice, and later my accent. Lindsey described my original accent as 'like Chicago and the Bronx had a love child.' But I don't sound that way anymore. I have no idea why my new accent affected my brothers and sisters too."

"I'm sure they'll get over it. Quin doesn't seem to care."

"Maybe this curse will convince them to stop hating me. Not sure I want them to change their minds because they pity me, though."

"They don't hate you."

"You've only met two of my siblings. You don't know how they feel."

"I've met your parents, and they're wonderful. That's all I need to know." I slide one leg over his thigh and stretch an arm across his broad, unbelievably muscular chest. I love the warmth and firmness of his body. "Your dad also mentioned that a copper fae becomes his true self after the transmutation."

"Not sure I've accomplished that yet."

"You have. Trust me."

He gives me a lopsided smile, not quite a smirk. "You didn't know me before the transmutation. How can you be sure I've become my true self?"

"I just can."

"Well, if you say so, I believe it. You are the smartest person I've ever met, in either world." He slides a hand down to cup my bottom. "What should we do while we wait for the vamp to report back? I have an idea, but I don't want to wear you out."

"If you mean that you want to have sex, my answer is yes. I want that too."

"Are you sure? Elemental sex can be hard on a mortal. Did you get sore from what we did last night?"

"Only a little. I can handle it." As I shift the rest of me onto his body, I already feel his dick stiffening. "Besides, you own a healing vortex. Can't you heal my soreness for me?"

He grins. "Yeah, I can do that. Anything for you."

"Problem solved."

Maybe I should question him about how he makes money in the mortal world. But for now, I want only one thing—to make love with the man who has come to mean more to me than seems possible after so little time together. I've given up worrying about that. So I sit up, straddling his hips, and whip my cover-up shirt off, then peel my tank top away too. "Let's make this trailer rock."

And we do exactly that. For the better part of the day, we give each other incredible climaxes, talk about our families and our lives, and play silly games like go fish and naked tag. I think Tris let me win our three rounds of tag. After that, he zips us over to the waterfall while we're both still naked, and we cool off while engaging in more silly antics. I've never had this much fun in my life. He takes us back to the trailer and conjures food to replenish our energy. I don't bother asking where the food came from because I trust him not to steal it from starving people. Tris insists on taking me to the vortex to make sure I won't get sore, using the healing energies as a prophylactic. I feel fantastic, but I let him do that anyway, strictly to ease his worries.

The day has whizzed by like it's on fast forward.

In the later afternoon, Travis texts Tris to invite both of us to his and Larissa's house for dinner. That turns out to be a hoot, with our hosts sharing stories about how they met and everything they've experienced as elementals, while Travis entertains us with tales of his days as a cop. Their daughter Dani knows all about who they were and who they are now, but amazingly, the seven-year-old has no problem with any of it and, according to Larissa, the girl never forgets to keep the secret. She's one smart kid. Since Dani doesn't know what cryptozoology is, I explain it to her. I also share the story of how I met Tris in the woods. She loves that.

At dusk, we prepare to say good night to our hosts.

Then Tris suddenly smacks his forehead and winces. "Oh, no. I forgot the vamps can't cross the veil. We need to go back to the Unseen and look for Cyneric."

Travis chuckles. "You only just now remembered that?"

"Hey, I've had some stress. Cursed, remember?"

"I don't like knowing Cyneric is on the loose. Especially if he's become obsessed with Riley." Travis raises his arm, and a sword appears in his hand. "Take my endued sword. You need some sort of protection beyond your abrasive personality."

Based on the upward tick of his lips, I know Travis is only teasing my boyfriend. But I also realize he's serious about Tris needing a deadly weapon in case the vampire decides to go rogue. Well, I guess he already has. He escaped from the training camp, then hunted me down. Knowing he can sniff me out whenever and wherever he wants does not make me feel any better. I might believe he wants to help, in his weird way, but I still can't trust Cyneric—because I can't figure him out.

Tris decides to stash the sword in the trailer, hidden under the bed's mattress. He can retrieve it anytime he wants from anywhere we might be. With the weapon safely tucked away, he rushes us back to the falls and jumps through the cascade with me in his arms. We've just touched down on the pockmarked rock floor of the cavern when the portal opens.

"What the..." Tris's question trails off as he stares at the unfurling gateway to the Unseen.

"Did you do that?" I ask, as I hug myself because my wet clothes make me feel cold inside this cavern.

"No. It wasn't me."

The vampire Cyneric jumps out of the portal.

"How the..." Tris doesn't finish that question either.

Since he seems stunned and confused, I take the initiative. I wriggle out of his arms and face the vamp. "You came through the portal. That's not supposed to be possible."

He tilts his head to the side, those spooky eyes nailed to mine. "It is possible, for I have done it."

Something about his voice sounds different now. He seems more centered too, if that's even the right word for it. And suddenly I get it. "You're British now."

"I am British?" Cyneric says, like he doesn't quite know what the word means. He touches his fangs. "I am still a vampire, not a British."

"Just British," I say. "Not *a* British. It means your accent has changed, but the rest of you is the same." I glance at Tris. "Isn't that right?"

"Yeah, pretty much." Tris comes up beside me. "Not sure how I feel about the fact he traipsed through the portal. Did Janus grant you access, Captain Fang? I can't believe he'd do that."

Cyneric stares at me as if Tris hadn't spoken. "Do you like the way I sound now?"

"Sure. You sound good. Not that you didn't before. I just meant—" I freeze, my focus trained on the vamp as a realization hits me. "You're not acting awkward anymore."

No, he seems entirely too self-assured now.

Tris eyes the vampire with suspicion. "Did you know you'd be able to cross the veil?"

Since the vamp continues to ignore Tris, I ask the question. "Did you know you could do that?"

"Perhaps I did, perhaps I did not."

I don't like his new evasive streak. It makes me uneasy, to say the least. "You were supposed to tail Anthea and ID whoever cursed Tris. Did you get that information?"

"The succubus vanished soon after you left. I tracked her scent, though, and found her." Cyneric finally turns his attention to Tris. "The one who cursed you was not there. I engaged in sexual intercourse with Anthea until she shared the information." He glides his tongue over his fangs. "She enjoyed the way I feasted on her."

"I thought you didn't even like her."

The vampire tips his head to the side. "I do not need to like a female in order to take pleasure from her body."

"You better not have bled her dry," Tris growls.

"Even if I did, she will not die."

"It's not cool to put somebody in a coma, even if they'll wake up later feeling fine."

"I did no such thing." Cyneric angles his head to the side. "Do you wish me to share the information I obtained?"

Tris rolls his eyes. "Duh. Yes, share the info. Why do you think we sent you on that mission? So you could get laid? I thought you didn't like Anthea, anyway."

"She served a purpose." The vampire narrows his gaze on Tris and just stares at him for a moment. "Anthea did not know his name, but the one who cursed you is a shifter. He lives among mortals."

"Are you kidding me? I've been searching the whole Unseen, and this jackass lives in the mortal world?"

"Do you know exactly where in this world the shifter lives?" I ask.

The vamp swerves his gaze my way, watching me with that unnerving intensity he often employs. "He resides in a place called London, England, and owns a 'nightclub' known as The Dragon's Den."

Cyneric sounds like he has no idea what a nightclub might be or where London is located.

"Do dragons live in the 'nightclub'?" Cyneric asks, and he's talking to me, of course.

"I doubt it." I glance at Tris. "You're the expert."

"They're shifters," he says. "They could stay in human form and glamour to look normal, which means they use a magical screen to disguise their true nature. That might let them live it up in a club without causing a scene. But that's kind of irrelevant. We need to head for London to find the shifter."

"What about—" I sidle up to Tris and hop up on my toes to whisper in his ear, "What about him?"

Then I move my eyes to indicate Cyneric.

"Screw him," Tris whispers.

I wrap my arms around him—and Cyneric moves closer to us.

Tris raises a hand. "Hold up, Captain Fang. You need to go back to the training camp."

"No."

A defiant vampire is exactly what we need right now.

Tris grits his teeth. "You are not coming with us."

Before the vamp can argue, Tris teleports the two of us to London. We touch down in an alley behind a big stone building.

"Do you know where we are?" I ask.

"London, I hope. I've never been here before."

"Neither have I."

He screws up his mouth as he surveys our surroundings. "I had to guess about where to drop us, and my main concern had been to avoid getting creamed by a car or landing inside a crypt."

Cyneric materializes right in front of us.

Oh, great. My vampire stalker has tracked us down. We're about to walk into a mysterious club owned by a mysterious shifter who probably wants Tris dead. That would be the end result of the curse, apparently. I haven't had a chance to ask Tris about that.

"Go home, Cyneric," I tell the stubborn vampire who has decided to tag along with us on our mission to un-curse Tris. Who invited Cyneric? Not me. Tris told him to go back to the training camp, but naturally, he ignored that strong suggestion. Do we have to de-fang him to get the vampire to stop following us around like a lost puppy? *Ugh.* I did not sign on for that.

The vampire does not move except to lift his chin slightly.

I wave my hands at him. "Go on, shoo. Scram. Vamoose."

"Maybe he doesn't understand," Tris tells me. "After all, the guy didn't know what the word British meant."

Cyneric closes his fists and keeps his attention solely on me. "I will protect you."

"But not me, right?" Tris says. "You couldn't care less if I die."

"I care only because your curse might harm Riley."

"She's not your girlfriend, pal. Riley is with me." Tris stalks closer to Cyneric and stabs a finger into the vamp's chest. "You will never get in her pants or in her veins."

"If I wish to feed on her, you cannot stop me."

"Like hell I can't."

"Enough!" I holler. Then I wave my arms in the air. "Remember me? The girl you're fighting over? Maybe you should, I don't know, give a hoot what I think."

Both men swerve their attention to me.

Okay, I got myself in this mess. Time to crawl out of it. "Listen, maybe you should both come to the club. Before you bitch about that, Tris, remember that Cyneric stopped Anthea from grabbing me again. He also helped me escape from her lair."

The vampire smirks. I've never seen him do that before.

"Don't get cocky, Cyneric," I say. "Tris saved my life—twice. He trusted me and showed me his world when he didn't have to do that. He nearly died protecting me."

Now Tris is smirking. *Ugh, men.*

"Since you two are just going to argue for the next ten years," I say, "I will make the decision for the three of us. Tris and Cyneric, you are both coming to the club. No arguments. Decision made."

CHAPTER NINETEEN

Tris

RILEY IS HOT WHEN SHE PUTS HER FOOT DOWN AND ORDERS TWO POWerful elementals to shut up and do what she says. I want to whisk her back to that trailer and let her boss me around in bed. But I do not like the fact that she proclaimed Cyneric will come with us to the club. I don't trust that vamp. The way he looks at Riley makes me itchy deep under my skin. From the moment I first met Cyneric, I knew he wasn't like the other vampires.

He's too smart. Too analytical. Too self-contained.

I can't gauge his reactions to anything. And that's never a good situation to be in, particularly with a vampire who just drank blood from a living being and, for the first time in his entire existence, relished doing that. If I see him so much as look at Riley's neck, I'll conjure Travis's endued sword and turn Cyneric into a cloud of shattered molecules.

Riley stands between me and the vamp with her hands on her hips and the sexiest look of stubborn determination on her face.

I love her shorts and tank top, but I'm wondering whether we need a change of clothes to blend in at the club. Maybe I should ask Riley before I conjure an outfit for her, but I'm letting her decide whether Cyneric goes with us. So I'll make the clothing decision on my own.

Riley yelps and jumps, then glances down at her body. She plants her hands on her hips again and shakes her head at me. "What did you do, Tris? Looks like you shopped at Slut Central."

"You don't look slutty. You're hot."

Okay, I dressed her in a skintight leather dress with spaghetti straps and matching stiletto heels. She has big silver earrings too. I also removed the elastic thing that held her hair back and released a puff of air to give those locks a fluffy, flowing style that makes her look even hotter. I'm not an air elemental, but even I can summon a minor disturbance. Riley also has red lipstick and smoky eye makeup. I know very little about women's clothes and cosmetics, but all I had to do was visualize what I wanted, and poof, it happened.

"We want to blend in, right?" I say. "You know I love your sexy hiker duds, but we're about to walk into a nightclub."

She drums her fingers on her hips, but her puckered lips relax into a reluctant smile. "Okay, fine. You have a point."

"Glad you approve."

She roves her gaze over me. "Gotta admit, I love your outfit."

I'm wearing a gray suit and a dark-blue shirt with the top three buttons unhooked, plus brown leather loafers. I got this idea from a magazine I saw once.

Riley walks up to me and leans that sexy body against mine.

My gaze flicks to Cyneric, who stands a dozen feet away watching us. He's not wearing the clothes I picked for him. Okay, maybe I chose baggy cargo pants and a Mickey Mouse T-shirt. So what? The jerk needs to learn humility. But naturally, he conjured his own stuff—leather pants, leather jacket, leather boots, and a shirt with half the buttons unhooked. His entire ensemble is black, of course.

Showoff. He just had to outdo me by unbuttoning more of his shirt. How does he look tanned? The vamp needs to stay out of the sunlight. I don't have time to worry about that, though. We need to sneak into that club and gather intel. Yeah, I'm suddenly James Bond.

Now I need to transport us to that club. When I try it, though, nothing happens.

"Everything okay?" Riley asks. "You look tense."

I do not want to admit I can't teleport while Cyneric is watching and listening. So I try again, focusing all my mental and magical energy on accomplishing the task. This should be easy. I've been doing it all my life. But my head starts to pound, and my heart starts to thud, while sweat beads on my forehead. I keep pushing, pushing, pushing until I finally whisk us away.

We land in a river.

Shit. I try again but can't make it happen. We're both treading water, trying to keep from going under, though our clothes don't help matters.

I focus all my energy on moving us out of the water. My head pounds like somebody is trying to crack my skull with a hammer, but I get us to an alley near the club. We're both soaked and dripping, so I wave a hand to dry us off. Since air isn't my element, it takes a ton of energy to accomplish that. We now look like nothing happened, but my head still hurts like the devil, and I'm having trouble catching my breath. Riley seems fine, though she gazes up at me with a cute little wrinkle of concern between her eyes, right above her nose.

"What happened?" she asks.

"My targeting went off the rails for a minute."

That wrinkle deepens.

"I'm okay," I tell her. "Just tired, that's all."

She doesn't look like she believes that. Hell, I don't believe what I said either. It must be the curse, but I don't feel like discussing that while Cyneric is within earshot. He didn't get dumped in the river, and he looks way too smug about that fact. I want to tell him to go back to the Unseen and stay there, but I know he won't listen to me. I bet he wouldn't listen even if Riley asked him nicely to go home.

The vampire is obsessed with my girlfriend, and I don't like it one bit.

I clasp Riley's hand. "The club should be about a block away. Let's get moving." I glance down at her shoes. "Should I, uh, conjure you something more comfortable for walking?"

"No, I can manage. We are masquerading as club whores, after all."

We exit the alley, and nobody pays attention to us, probably because everyone on this street is dressed for a night of clubbing. As we amble down the sidewalk, Riley and I smile and laugh like a real couple on a real date. But Cyneric hangs a few paces behind us, and every time I glance behind me, he's staring at the back of Riley's head. Well, at least he's not staring at her ass.

Up ahead, I see the club. A sign declares it to be The Dragon's Den, so I know we've found the right place. Every time someone opens the double doors, music filters out to us. A line of people waits to gain entry, but a velvet rope holds them back. I conjure some of the money I had legally obtained in this world and sidle up to the bouncer, slipping several hundred-dollar bills into his palm.

He glances at the money and hikes up one brow. When he turns his attention to Riley, he rakes his gaze over her entire body. Then he pulls back the rope and lets us into the club.

I glance back, expecting to see Cyneric, but he's gone.

Perfect. The unstable, obsessive bloodsucker has gone rogue—again. I can't worry about him right now. Besides, I'm pretty sure he won't go far from Riley.

We wander into the building, heading down a darkened entryway lit only by soft, golden bulbs recessed into the walls. As we step out into the club proper, the music gets louder, but not so loud that we can't speak to each other. That's weird. I thought clubs all operated at high volume with bass beats that create mini earthquakes. The Dragon's Den features lots of furniture with a relatively small dance floor. Patrons gather on curved velvet couches or huddle around tables. A few strobe lights flare occasionally. But otherwise, the club offers subdued lighting.

Not quite what I expected.

I lead Riley around the perimeter of the main area, where most of the patrons are hanging out, and watch for some sign of the elemental who cursed me. Yeah, it would help if I knew what that person looked like. I can sense there are elementals in this club, though I can't spot them. They would be glamouring to appear human, I'm sure.

A deep voice chuckles behind us. "I knew you would find your way to me eventually."

The male voice sounds American. But I'd bet my life that he's an elemental. I can feel subtle magics licking at me.

Riley and I turn around.

A big man with black hair and a beard smiles at us with wolfish delight. "I thought it would take you longer to find me, but I'm glad you're here, Triskaideka."

"Who are you?" I ask.

"Drakon, of course." He grins, his big white teeth gleaming, though it doesn't seem like a friendly expression. "I am the one who cursed you."

"Am I supposed to be shocked? I got a tip the curse-maker owned this club, so I knew I'd find a dick like you waiting for me here." I scan the club and sigh with sarcastic disappointment. "I expected more from a place called The Dragon's Den. I mean, this looks like a slightly fancier version of a nursing home."

"This is the lounge." He starts walking past us, gesturing for us to follow him. "Let me show you the real club."

I want to send Riley home, right now, but I can't leave her alone while Cyneric is out in the world unsupervised. So I clasp her hand a little tighter and follow Drakon. He guides us around the periphery of the lounge to a set of gilded double doors that have images of dragons carved into them. Our host waves a hand. The doors swing open, and we follow him into a large room full of...gambling tables.

Oh, it's *that* kind of club.

Riley surveys the big room, taking in the various games and the people huddled around the tables praying they'll get lucky. I see roulette, blackjack, poker, baccarat, and craps. Slot machines line the rear wall, and I notice a couple of pool tables too, tucked into a little alcove in the far corner. When someone walks out of a door on the left side of the room, I even glimpse a bingo game underway before the door shuts again.

I don't care about the games, though. I want answers from our host. "So, Drakon, you're an elemental."

He throws me an annoyed look. "You are a master at stating the obvious, aren't you?" He offers his hand to Riley. "I am Drakon, Crown Prince of the Western Kingdom of Dragon Shifters. And you are Riley Jordan, a mere mortal."

She doesn't accept his hand. "How do you know my name?"

"Anthea told me, naturally. She is my lover, and ensorcelled too, so she can't stop herself from sharing every bit of information with me." He claims her hand, turns it over, and kisses the palm. "You are delectable, Riley. I could give you far more pleasure than any other male in any world."

"I'm with Tris."

He scans his gaze over me. "I wouldn't be averse to a ménage à trois."

Oh, like hell I'm letting this dirtbag screw my girlfriend. Maybe I should conjure that endued sword right now.

"I appreciate the offer," Riley says as she wriggles her hand free of Drakon's. "But like I told you, I'm with Tris. And I believe in monogamy."

Drakon kisses her palm again, then releases her hand. "We'll see about that."

I insert myself between Riley and the dragon shifter, which means I'm standing inches away from the dirtbag. "Stop flirting with my girlfriend and tell me why you put a curse on me."

"Because you stole from me."

"What? I never did any such thing. I hadn't heard of you, much less met you, before tonight."

"Perhaps you hadn't known of me, but you managed to steal from me consistently for five months."

"You're insane." I lean in until our noses almost touch and glare into his iridescent purple eyes. "I never stole from anybody."

"Of course you did." He spreads an arm. "Let's go into my office to discuss this."

Riley and I follow him across the gaming room and through a door labeled "PRIVATE." Once we're inside the room with the door closed, Drakon waves for us to sit down on two chairs in front of his desk, then he takes a seat behind it.

"You have been frequenting my clubs," Drakon tells me. "And you always win. That means you have cheated."

"I don't cheat. And I never heard of The Dragon's Den until tonight."

"But you visited my properties. I own fifty-eight establishments around the world, mostly gaming facilities but also other sorts of clubs." He opens a drawer in his desk and pulls out a manila envelope, then dumps the contents onto the desktop. "Here is the proof."

A stack of eight-by-ten photographs lies fanned out across the desktop. He picks them up one by one to show them to me. I see pictures of myself. They show me standing at tables in various casinos, playing games like poker and blackjack.

I lodge one ankle on the other knee and force myself to relax into my chair like I don't care that Riley and I are basically hostages in Drakon's club. Yeah, I doubt he'll let us walk out of here, and I can sense the club has wards around it. That means I can't zip us away either. "So you've got pictures of me gambling legally inside legal casinos. I didn't commit any crime, and I didn't steal anything. I won small amounts of money. Unless you're admitting your own casinos aren't on the level…"

"Do you think I'm an idiot? You never lost. Never." He crosses his arms on the desktop and slants over it, sharpening his gaze on me like he thinks that will intimidate me. "You have abused your leprechaun luck to fleece my businesses."

"Luck?" I say with a chuckle. "Did you get all your info about the copper fae from a cereal box? We don't dole out luck, and we don't have any special good fortune we can tap into either. Every dollar I won in your casinos was legit."

"That is not possible. I live by the odds, and I know the chances of you repeatedly winning and never losing are astronomically low."

"Not my fault I had good luck. Besides, I mostly won at poker, which is a game of skill with a bit of luck thrown in too."

Drakon slams his fist down on the desk. "I want compensation for what you stole from me. The curse is your punishment, but I will make sure you live long enough that I get the payback you owe me."

"I won maybe three hundred bucks total. What kind of petty asshat are you? Cursing me for a few hundred dollars."

Drakon rises from his chair. He glowers at me while he fists his hands and hunches his shoulders. Then his body shimmers and swells, growing bigger and bigger while his skin darkens and wings emerge from his back. He snaps his fingers straight, and those wings unfurl. Drakon has grown taller and stockier, towering over us like a giant gargoyle.

"Still want to annoy me?" he says. His voice has become rougher and deeper. "Now you understand what I am, but perhaps I should demonstrate what I can do."

He leaps over the desk and grabs Riley, folding his black wings around her.

I jump up and kick my chair away, determined to face the dragon. I try to conjure the endued sword, but I can't, of course. The wards around this place won't allow it.

Chapter Twenty

Riley

D RAKON RUBS HIS ROUGH, GREENISH-BLACK CHEEK AGAINST MY face. "I could take her right now. Defile her body viciously for hours and hours. Do things to her that would make the worst serial killer in the mortal world seem tame by comparison. Is that what you want, little leprechaun?"

The fact that I can feel his dick swelling does not make me any less terrified. Tris has an endued sword, but I'm guessing he can't conjure it from inside this building. It must be warded. I still don't quite understand what that involves, but I know it means all magics are squelched, at least for me and Tris. Not that I have magical powers. I wish I did. Then I could ice this dragon jerk and get us the heck out of here.

I really wish I weren't dressed like a nightclub slut right now.

Tris stands an arm's length from Drakon and me, and he looks furious. It's kind of hot, but now is not the time to think about that. Tris fists his hands and clenches his jaw, making a muscle tick there. His eyes whorl with shades of bright green and fiery red while golden sparks ignite within them. "Let her go."

He spoke those three words with more menace than I've ever heard from anyone—except for Drakon.

The dragon shifter flutters his wings just enough to graze Tris. "I am five seconds away from ravaging your girl and forcing you to watch. Agree to any punishment I wish to mete out on you, or I will fuck Riley to death."

A chill rushes through me, so frigid and sharp that my throat goes thick. He means what he said. I can feel the truth of it. But I will not let anyone rape me. I'd rather die. Since I can feel Drakon's dick rubbing against my lower back, maybe I have some leverage after all. If I can wriggle just enough… I manage to slide my hand behind my back, right over the dragon's private parts.

Drakon retracts his wings and grabs my wrists, holding them over my belly with one of his big, scaly hands. I'm effectively leashed now. He must've realized what I intended to do—grab his balls and twist as hard as I could—and he made sure I can't do that.

"Your decision," Drakon growls. He clamps his free hand around my breast and squeezes hard enough to make me gasp. "Your answer. Right now."

Tris glances at me and grimaces.

"Don't do it," I say. "Tris, you can't let—"

The dragon slaps his hand over my mouth, covering my nose too. I can't breathe.

"Fine, anything you want," Tris tells the dragon. "Just let her go."

Drakon releases me with a shove, and I stumble into the desk. "Let's go out into the gaming room. The roulette wheel will decide your fate."

Roulette? That's a game of chance, but I have a sick feeling in my gut that tells me Drakon won't leave the result to random luck. He wants to punish Tris.

Drakon shifts back into human form and ushers us out into the gaming room where desperate people are praying for miracles. When we reach the roulette table, Drakon commands the miserable people crouched on stools there to leave immediately. Nobody argues. Even a guy who's clearly drunk scurries away the instant Drakon issues his order.

Tris and I climb onto stools.

Drakon stands beside me, leaning against the table. "I assume you are familiar with roulette, little fae. Roll and lose, that's how it works." He leans across me to bare his teeth at Tris. "The house always wins, even if it takes months."

"Am I supposed to make a bet?" Tris asks.

"No need. Just roll the wheel. If you hit black, you win. Red, you lose. Normally, the croupier starts the wheel spinning, but I want you to do it."

He snatches up the little white ball that will roll around the rim of the wheel and gives it to Tris.

My boyfriend sets the wheel rolling and drops the little white ball onto the outer rim so that it spins around and around in the opposite direction from the wheel itself. We all stare at the roulette wheel until the ball bounces into a slot.

"Black thirty-five," the croupier announces. "The player wins."

Drakon growls through his gritted teeth like a wild animal. "That is impossible. Roll again, leprechaun."

Tris repeats the process.

"Black twenty-four," the croupier declares. "The player wins again."

Drakon slams his fist down on the table, making the white ball bounce out of its slot and roll across the table toward Tris. He grabs the ball. Drakon seethes, his nostrils flaring and a hint of flames flickering in them.

Tris offers him the little ball.

Drakon snarls so loudly and with such menace that the other gamblers in the room scurry out. The double doors clap shut after the last person has fled. Only the croupier, Drakon, Tris, and I remain here.

"You cheated," Drakon snarls. "And you lied to me. You clearly have leprechaun luck, or you would never have beaten the house twice tonight and a dozen times over the past five months."

"I didn't cheat," Tris says. "And everybody in the Unseen knows that leprechauns don't have any special good fortune. I told you that earlier. It's the truth, whether you like it or not."

"Why don't we all calm down," I say. "I'm sure we can come up with an explanation for all of this if we just sit down and behave like adults."

"Adults? You are mere infants compared to me." Drakon steps back and shifts into dragon form, his wings spread wide. "I was born a dragon prince millennia before humans mastered the power of fire. You two are mere fetuses. My kind has walked the multiverse since the beginning of time."

Not sure if I believe that, but I don't doubt dragon shifters could have existed long before humans. I don't really care about placating Drakon. I want to save Tris. But how can I do that? We're trapped inside a warded casino with an actual dragon.

An unholy pounding erupts outside the gaming room. People scream and shout, and feet scuffle as everyone tries to escape—from what, I have no idea. But the building quakes with every concussion.

Drakon stalks over to the double doors and pushes his head through them. "What in the worlds is going on out here?"

Someone responds, but I can't make out their words.

"A vampire is doing what?" Drakon says. He listens a bit more, then growls and spins around to stalk back to me and Tris. But he only glances at Tris, then stomps up to me so close that I can feel the heat from his faintly flaming nostrils. "Why is a vampire attempting to breach my club while shouting your name?"

Oh, crap. Cyneric is back.

Well, maybe that's not entirely a bad thing. If he can break us out of here…

Drakon clamps a hand around my throat, squeezing only enough to make his point—that he will murder me or worse if I don't say what he wants to hear. "Who is the vampire?"

I shrug. Yeah, I'm reverting to my dumb-blonde persona. Will Drakon buy it? I think I only need to fool him for long enough to let Cyneric do whatever he plans to do. I'm assuming the unstable vamp has a plan. Jeez, we're screwed.

An explosion racks the entire building.

I stumble just as Drakon loses his grip on my throat and scramble over to Tris, who wraps his arms around me.

"The wards are down," he whispers to me. "Hold on."

Everything around us blurs and disappears, then we rocket down a tunnel full of writhing darkness that nips at my skin. We pop out in a field beneath a starlit sky.

"Where are we?" I ask.

"Uh, not sure. I was aiming for..." He stumbles backward, and his arms are torn away from me. "This is bad. I can't—What just happened?"

He seems so disoriented that I know something has gone horribly wrong. With his teleportation skills? Or with his curse?

Tris staggers sideways, then collapses.

I race to him and kneel at his side. His eyes are open, though bleary. I brush my fingers over his cheek. "Are you sick?"

"Elementals don't get sick, not unless..." He slaps a hand on his forehead and groans. "Not unless dark magics are involved. Not sure if this is a natural degradation because of the curse, or if Drakon did something to make me even weaker. Maybe he accelerated the curse."

"Can you get us back to the rock shop? Maybe your friends can help."

He shakes his head slowly. "Can't teleport. That last jump sucked me dry."

"Do you have any idea where we are?"

"No. This is my fault, Riley. You're in trouble because of—"

I seal his lips with my fingers. "Hush. I don't want to hear any self-recriminations. Drakon did this to you, and Drakon took us hostage. It is not your fault."

A figure appears on the other side of Tris.

"You cannot remain here," Cyneric says. "The dragon might find you."

"Did you meet Drakon?"

"No. But I saw him from a distance. Dragon shifters are powerful."

I hate to ask, but we do need help. "Can you whisk us back to where you found us earlier? To the portal?"

He nods.

But Cyneric doesn't just transport us to the cavern behind the waterfall. He takes us through the portal without even pausing and sets us down on the far side of the small pool in front of the rock that marks the entrance to the mortal world. I don't have time to worry about what it means that the vampire could teleport us directly into the Unseen. I'm concerned only with Tris, who seems to be fading away with every breath he takes.

Did Drakon do something to him? He might've enhanced the curse when he realized we had escaped. The bastard wants to punish Tris for winning at stupid casino games. Drakon clearly has plenty of money, so I'm sure this is macho dragon-shifter nonsense, the elemental equivalent of a pissing match. Except Tris is not playing his game. He can't. Tris can barely move now.

Cyneric hoists Tris onto his shoulders, then grabs my hand and spirits us away again. This time, we land inside the courtyard of the copper fae village.

The fae milling around freeze and stare at us. Well, I think they're actually staring at Cyneric. One woman raises an arm to jab her finger toward him. She screams, "Vampire!"

Well, at least they aren't screaming because we're dressed like rejects from a sex club. That woman noticed Cyneric's fangs, though he quickly retracted them.

More people scream or shout, and everyone starts running around like a bunch of scared mice. I don't give a damn about frightening these people, though later I will probably need to apologize—without technically apologizing. Right now, my only concern is the leprechaun lying half-dead in a vampire's clutches.

I remember where the house Tris's parents live in is located, so I tell Cyneric to follow me as I jog down the streets. He doesn't complain. I swear I can feel the vamp's gaze boring into the back of my skull, but I don't have time to worry about his obsession with me either. We round one corner, then another, and I at last see the house where Nyara and Frimis live. I'm gasping for breath as I bang on the door.

Frimis opens it, and his brows cinch up. Probably because of the way I'm dressed. Then his attention swerves to the vampire and Tris. "What's happened?"

"Explain later. We need help right away. Tris's curse has kicked into high gear, and he's going downhill fast."

Frimis steps aside, gesturing for us to enter. He lifts his brows a teeny bit when the vampire crosses the threshold, then he leads us to Tris's bedroom. Cyneric drops my boyfriend on the bed like he's a sack of potatoes. Oh, who cares. His jealousy is not my problem.

Tris's dad leaves us.

I glance down at my leather dress. "Jeez, I wish I had my old clothes."

My dress vanishes, replaced by what I'd worn before we went to Drakon's club—shorts, tank top, gauzy cover-up shirt, and hiking boots. I look at Cyneric. "Did you do this?"

He nods.

The vamp is still wearing his leather outfit, but when I glance at Tris, I notice the vamp gave him back his usual jeans and T-shirt.

I sit down beside Tris on the bed and caress his cheek.

His lids flutter open, though only halfway. "If this is heaven, I volunteer to stay forever." He winces a touch. "That was a dumb thing to say. I don't want you to die with me."

"Do copper fae believe in heaven?"

"Yeah, we do." He starts coughing, and it swiftly mutates into hacking that racks his whole body. Once the fit ends, he grasps my hand. "You shouldn't be here. Go home where you'll be safe. I'll drag you down with me."

"No, you won't. And what makes you think I'll be safe in the mortal world? Drakon lives there. And he knows my name, so I'm sure he can find out where my apartment is." I lean in to touch my lips to his. "The way we get through this is to stay together."

CHAPTER TWENTY-ONE

Tris

"S HE'S RIGHT, DEAR," MY MOTHER SAYS AS SHE BUSTLES INTO THE ROOM carrying a tray that's loaded with first aid supplies, food, and water. She sets the tray over my hips. "Try to sit up and eat something."

Ma will not give up until I do what she wants, but she's stubborn only because she cares about all fifteen of her crazy kids. I don't know how she puts up with us. It's no mystery why we do what she tells us, though. Our mother is one smart cookie.

I shimmy backward while pushing up into sitting position so I can rest against the wall, then I nibble at the food. Riley watches me with a faint smile on her lips, though she doesn't move any closer to me. I don't feel all that hungry, but Ma will worry if I don't at least try to eat. My gaze wanders to the first aid supplies, and I pluck up a roll of gauze. "How is this going to help me? Bandages won't stop a curse."

Ma hugs herself, and her eyes shimmer with burgeoning tears. "It was all I could think to do."

I reach out to lay a hand on her arm. "It's okay, Ma. I'm not dead yet, and I don't plan on giving up."

She kisses my cheek. "I love you, dear. You are my sweet ginger boy."

"Ginger?" Riley says.

"Ma means that I have red hair," I explain. "She loves to watch TV shows from the mortal world, and especially the British ones. Those people call redheads 'ginger,' which sounds pretty dumb to me. But Ma gets a pass on goofy nicknames."

"All moms do." Riley glances up at my mother and smiles. "Your son is tough. He'll get through this."

Ma turns her attention to something behind Riley, which I can't see from my position on the bed. I lean over to look. Duh, Ma is staring at

Cyneric. I almost forgot the bloodsucker was there. He loves to blend into the background and stay so quiet and motionless that everybody overlooks him. Then he can turn around and become scarily intense. I doubt I will ever trust him, but he did kind of help save my life by spiriting Riley and me away to my parents' house.

Should I introduce my parents to Riley's semi-stalker? Not sure there's an etiquette protocol for a situation like this.

"Who is your friend, Riley?" Ma asks, while inching backward toward the doorway.

"His name is Cyneric," Riley says. "He's not exactly a friend, but he has helped us."

"Don't get too close to him," I warn Ma. "He drank the blood of a living being yesterday, and I think he enjoyed it."

Cyneric tips his head to the side the slightest bit, but I can't decide what that means.

Ma's eyes have gone wide.

I stretch a hand out to pat my mother's arm. "Relax. He won't hurt you." I aim a hard look at the vamp. "Will you, Cyneric."

That was not a question. Why should I ask politely? The vamp does whatever he wants without worrying about the consequences. Cyneric does not respond to my statement in any way, not even with a facial tic.

"No, he won't hurt anyone," Riley says when the vampire refuses to speak.

Ennea appears beside our mother. She gives Ma a peck on the cheek. "Go see what Pa's doing, okay? I need to talk to Tris and Riley and their…friend."

She glances at Cyneric but only shakes her head once. Then my sister perches on the bed's edge right beside me. "I'm going to help you, but it won't cure the curse."

"You found something that might give me more time?"

Ennea squeezes my hand. "It'll be like a big shot of adrenaline. You'll have more energy for a while, but there will be a crash later."

"How long will it last?" Riley asks.

"Not sure. Several hours, at least. Maybe even a full day."

I grasp my sister's hand. "I'll take it. We need time to stop Drakon and make him undo the curse."

"Drakon?" Ennea's jaw goes slack. "I've heard rumors about him. That shifter is seriously bad news."

"No kidding? Glad you told me that. I thought Drakes and me were becoming besties." I turn my attention to the vampire. "You can go home, Cyneric, wherever that might be. We can handle this on our own."

I would prefer it if he returned to the training camp, but I doubt he will ever agree to that.

Cyneric fists his hands but otherwise remains calm and stoic as he gazes at me. "I will not leave Riley. You cannot protect her."

"Yes, I can. Besides, she knows how to handle herself." I touch Riley's cheek. "You are amazing, and you don't need a bloodsucker to look out for you."

She bites her lip and lowers her gaze as if I've embarrassed her. I told the truth, that's all. She is amazing.

Ennea flicks her gaze between me and Riley. "Are we doing this, then? The magical adrenaline shot?"

"Yeah," I reply. "We're doing it."

My sister stands up. "Better stay off the bed while I do this, Riley. He might flail or something. I've never tried anything like this before, so I can't be sure how it will go down."

"Gee, sis, what an inspiring pep talk."

Riley gives me a quick kiss and a smile, then hops off the bed to stand near the opposite wall beside Ennea. Cyneric stands in the corner, his gaze zeroed in on me while I set the tray Ma gave me on the floor and shimmy back down the bed to lie stretched out on the mattress.

Ennea whispers to Riley, apparently assuming I can't hear it—but I do. She murmurs, "Time to pray."

I close my eyes and fold my hands over my belly, feeling oddly relaxed, which I wouldn't have expected. Maybe I'm just too weak to get anxious, thanks to the sucker punch to my soul that Drakon gave me right before Cyneric whisked us away. I peek out the corner of my eye and see Ennea raising her arms in front of her, palms out, as she begins to chant in the ancient fae tongue, a language so old that only witches and sorcerers still speak it, and then only during rituals.

Golden energy flows from Ennea's palms, slithering through the air toward me. Though I shut my eyes again, I can feel the magics licking at my skin, brushing over my face, exploring me while they assess the situation. Yeah, magics often seem to be sentient, though I don't know if that's true or just an illusion. The energies coil around my fingers and toes, then spread across my whole body. They burrow through flesh, clawing their way deep inside, making me wince and jerk. Yeah, the magics hurt briefly.

"Tris!" Riley calls out. "Is he okay? He looked like he was in pain."

As much as I want to reassure her, I can't speak or move a single muscle.

"He's all right," Ennea says. "Take it easy, sweetie. Your panic might knock the spell out of whack."

Now the magics slither into the deepest parts of my body and soul, their warmth tingling through me. The sensation grows stronger every second, until the pressure of the spell steals my breath and makes my heart thrash in my chest. I can handle the pain. If this is what it takes to destroy Drakon and get rid of my curse, I'll swallow the pain for as long as I need to do it.

The energies abruptly vanish.

I lie here stone-still, feeling dazed by the power of those magics. Then something incredible happens. An indescribable sensation rushes through me, invigorating my body from head to toe, plunging deep inside to strengthen every part of me. I open my eyes and spring into a sitting position, flexing my arms and reveling in this newfound strength.

"Oh, yeah," I say. "I could get used to this."

"But you won't," Ennea says. "This is a temporary thing, not permanent superpowers. Don't abuse the gift I just gave you."

"Wouldn't dream of it." I jump off the bed. "Feel like I could lift a mountain. But I'll settle for pounding Drakon into dust, then pummeling anybody else who annoys me."

Ennea and Riley both give me pained looks.

"Relax, I'm kidding," I tell them. "But I will destroy that dragon bastard with this."

I conjure the endued sword Travis had lent me.

"Put that away for now," Riley says. "We need Drakon to think we're unarmed."

"But I can't conjure inside his club. It's warded against that kind of intrusion, which means I need to have the sword with me when we go back to the club."

"The wards are gone," Cyneric says. "I destroyed them."

We all stare at him. The vamp did what? Not sure if I believe that, but then, he is no ordinary bloodsucker. Is it safe to have a ward-busting, portal-hopping vamp on the loose on earth or in the Unseen? Seems like we don't have much choice in the matter. I'll worry about Cyneric later. We've got bigger problems.

Like one big, nasty nutjob of a dragon shifter.

But Cyneric wins the award for Number One Nutjob.

"That spell was awesome," I tell Ennea. "You did great. But now it's time for me and Riley to confront Drakon. Somebody will be destroyed today, and I plan on making sure it's Drakon instead of me."

"If that's all I can do for you," Ennea says, "I should get back to my lab. Got a client coming in for a cloaking spell."

"Go on. We've got it from here."

My sister vanishes.

Cyneric is staring at Riley—at her throat—with a hunger that triggers every hair on my body to stiffen. While Riley and Ennea were focused on the adrenaline spell, the vamp had inched closer to my girlfriend. Too close.

"Step away from Riley," I tell him. "Do it now, Cyneric."

He acts like I didn't even speak and moves even closer to Riley, who just stands there without blinking, moving only her eyes to glance at the vamp. She must be worried about how he might react if she tries to sidle away from him. I've never tried to conjure a living thing, so I don't know if I can do that safely. I need physical contact to teleport, which means I can't whisk her to me.

I try taking one small step toward her.

Cyneric throws an arm around her waist so fast that I didn't even see the movement. He hugs Riley to his side and sniffs her neck. His nostrils flare, and a low growl resonates in his throat.

Screw this. I conjure the sword. "Move away from her now, Cyneric. Last chance."

His gaze veers to my sword. His nostrils flare again.

"Put the sword away," Riley says in a surprisingly calm tone. "He will let me go. Won't you, Cyneric? You don't want to hurt me. You've been trying to protect me, right?"

The vamp nuzzles her throat, flicking his tongue out to taste her skin. He groans with so much hunger that I know I can't just stand here. I need to stop the bastard now.

I take half a step.

Cyneric bares his fangs, tugging Riley into his body as he prepares to sink his teeth into her throat.

I zoom across the distance and slam my fist into the wall, effectively barring the vamp from biting Riley. His fangs sink into my forearm—and he guzzles my blood.

"No, Cyneric!" Riley shouts. "Stop! Let go of him!"

I yank my arm away from Cyneric, ripping flesh and sinews, but I don't care about that. The fucking vampire just drank my blood. He wanted to feast on Riley, but I got in the way. Anger erupts inside me, scorching and too powerful to resist. I seize the vamp by the throat and hoist him off his feet, holding his body several feet above the floor with his back against the wall.

"Never touch her again," I snarl while tightening my grip on his throat. "Riley is my girlfriend, not yours. If you ever look at her the wrong way again, much less come within fifty feet of her, I will conjure that sword and turn you into a pile of cosmic dust."

The bedroom door bursts open, and Ma rushes inside with her eyes wide and her hand on her chest. "What happened? I heard screaming."

Her attention shifts to Riley huddled against the wall, then to me holding the vampire up by his throat. She might've also noticed the massive dent in the wall.

Ma's hand flies to her throat. "Tris, you're bleeding."

I glance at my forearm. Yeah, blood is pouring from the wound where the scumbag bloodsucker ripped into me. Well, better me than Riley.

Ma grabs the first aid supplies off the floor. "Lie down on the bed."

I wrench my hand away from Cyneric's throat, and the vampire vanishes. I do what my mother wants and sit down on the bed's edge. While she tries to use gauze to stop the blood pouring from my arm, I shoo her away. "That won't help. I need a vortex."

"Can you heal yourself?" Riley asks.

"No, but I can get Pendi to do it. She took care of the healing vortex while I was going through the transmutation." I grasp Ma's hand to stop her frantic attempts to bandage my arm. "It'll be okay."

I rise and grab Riley's hand, then whisk us away.

We land in the center of the healing vortex, surrounded by the natural stone benches. I holler for Pendi, and she arrives within seconds. My parents blip in a second after my sister.

"Your ma insisted we had to come here," Pa says. "She needs to know you're okay."

Pendi waves for Riley to exit the vortex. She halts just past the stone benches, standing beside my parents.

I sit down on a bench.

My sister cradles my wounded arm in both her hands. She doesn't technically need to touch me or do anything other than eat copper to power up the vortex. She doesn't even need to be here. But I think she's trying to placate our mother with a little show. Ma probably cried and begged Pendi to save me. It's overkill. I'm not in danger of being destroyed.

"Have you eaten enough copper?" I ask my sister.

"Yes, little brother. I was manning a vortex before you were even born. I know how much I need to eat to make the healing energies strong enough."

I lower my voice to barely a whisper. "You don't need to stand here."

"Ma will freak if I don't."

Sighing, I slouch on the bench and resign myself to watching my sister perform for our mother. She waves a hand over my arm as the healing energies flow into me, starting with my fingers, traveling up through my wrist and settling in my forearm. The tingling warmth infiltrates my flesh and dives deep to knit the veins and sinews back together. Once that's done, the magics get to work on repairing the damaged flesh, returning my arm to its normal condition.

Golden energies had surrounded my arm during the healing process, which means nobody except for me and Pendi could see what was happening.

I flex my arm and my fingers. "Feels good."

Pendi pats the top of my head. "Try not to get ravaged by a vampire again. I get gassy from eating that much copper."

"Don't worry. Next time I meet that bloodsucker, I'm running him through with Travis's endued sword."

My sister looks at our parents. "He's fine. Show's over."

Our mother rushes over to hug me from behind. "Oh, my poor boy."

"Jeez, Ma, you're going overboard."

Pa pulls her away from me. "Let's go home, Nyara. Tris is a mature fae now, and we should trust him to handle his own business."

Ma kisses the top of my head. "All right. We'll go. But never scare us that way again."

"I'll try, Ma."

Once everyone has left, and Riley and I are alone again, I rise and pull her into my arms. "It's time to confront Drakon. You sure you want to come with me?"

"Positive."

I zip us away.

Chapter Twenty-Two

Riley

THE SECOND WE LAND AT THE CLUB, TOUCHING DOWN JUST OUTSIDE THE main doors, I notice something odd. The parking lot is empty. The lighted sign is no longer lighted. Sure, it's daytime here. But a gambling establishment seems like the type of place that would be open in the daytime too, possibly even twenty-four hours a day. When Tris tries to open the doors, they swing out, which means they weren't locked.

Something about this whole situation makes my skin crawl.

Tris holds my hand firmly as we enter the building and traverse the darkened hallway. The lights that had provided partial illumination aren't on right now. I trust Tris to guide me through the darkness until we step out into the main club area. Lights do burn here, though I see only a smattering of people. They've all gathered around sofas to the left of the entrance or at tables nearby.

"Come in," a familiar voice calls out to us. "You are welcome to join us for a drink."

Drakon raises a glass of amber liquid as if to encourage us to accept his offer of a drink.

We don't want booze, though. Tris and I make our way to Drakon and his friends, or maybe "minions" is a better word. Scantily clad women hover around Drakon, either sprawling on the sofa beside him or leaning over the sofa's back to drape their arms around him. A few men relax on another sofa, while several more sit at the nearest table.

They all stare at me and Tris.

Drakon shoves the women away from him, and they scatter to the other sofa or the tables. The dragon prince waves for us to take a seat beside him.

I glance at Tris.

He shrugs.

We sit on the sofa, but not close to the crown prince of whatever-it-was he told us last night. Drakon spreads an arm across the sofa's back, angling toward us. Tris made sure he's between me and the dragon shifter, which I doubt Drakon appreciates.

He eyes me up and down, then swerves his attention to Tris. "How are you still upright? I enhanced the curse. You should be a useless lump who needs help to use the bathroom."

"Yeah, I feel horrible about disappointing you."

"Tell me how you managed to grow stronger instead of weaker."

"How should I know? I'm just a leprechaun. We're all morons, you know."

"Stop toying with me. I don't appreciate it." Drakon's eyes narrow to slits, and his nostrils flare, emitting the faintest hint of fire. "Someone helped you."

My boyfriend shrugs. "Don't ask me."

"Enough of this. Tell me how—"

Tris conjures the sword Travis gave him, springs off the sofa, and lands right in front of Drakon. The shifter's eyes flare wide.

And Tris rams the sword straight through Drakon's chest.

He must've skewered the shifter's heart, but Drakon doesn't move or cry out or act like he even noticed. Blood pours from his chest wound, streaming down in crimson rivulets that soak his fancy shirt. Yet Drakon still just sits there calmly.

And he chuckles.

Tris gapes at the dragon shifter, and that's all I can do too.

Drakon grasps the sword's hilt, all that protrudes from his chest, and slowly pulls it free while Tris keeps hold of the handle. I should move. Do something. Anything. If an endued sword can't get rid of Drakon, do we have any hope of defeating the curse and the shifter himself? But I seem to have become frozen in place, able to do nothing except watch as Drakon rips the sword from Tris's grasp and flips it around so the tip of the blade brushes his chest.

"I'm tired of this game," he says in a soft yet menacing tone. "I think I'll kill you now."

Tris grabs me and whisks us away.

But we wind up right back where we started—in the club, with Drakon and his minions. Now we find ourselves in the gaming room, though, instead of on that sofa. Drakon stands beside the roulette table with one hand on the outer rim. He taps one finger on it.

"I've changed my mind," Drakon says. He swings his gaze to me. "Rather than destroying Tris, I will force him to watch while I corrupt you. That will be far more entertaining than turning your lover into a puff of molecular dust."

"How did you survive being gored with an endued sword?" Tris asks. "Nobody can live through something like that."

Drakon's lips curve into a smug smile. "You should have listened when I told you I've been alive since before humans mastered fire. That makes me a primordial being. Not quite a primordial god, but certainly a far more powerful elemental than you or any of your friends."

"You're immune to endued weapons."

"I believe you're finally catching on." Drakon picks up the little white ball that's part of the roulette game and rolls it in his palm. "A cheater like you deserves to be punished, and in a way that will both humiliate and demoralize you before you finally fade away, thanks to my curse."

He starts the roulette wheel spinning, then tosses the white ball onto the rim, where it begins to whirl in the opposite direction.

I'm not liking this situation at all. An unkillable dragon shifter? Suddenly, I wish I had never gone searching for cryptids. But no, I don't really wish for that. I would never have met Tris if I hadn't gone into the woods in search of mysterious creatures. If Drakon kills Tris, I will find a way to swallow all the dark magics in the universe and destroy the winged freak.

"I stopped you from escaping this time," Drakon said. "Your vampire friend seems to have abandoned you. So when the wheel stops spinning, your fate will be sealed. Black, you die. White, I take your girl and defile her. It's a fair deal, eh? Yes, I agree it is."

He didn't let us respond to his question. Yeah, I'm really shocked by the fact he's gaming his own system to cheat his way into winning.

The white ball settles in a slot, and the wheel gradually stops spinning. Drakon taps the ball with his finger and grins with feral delight. "White. Your girl is mine."

"Like hell she is," Tris snarls.

Drakon chuckles again. "You have no say in the matter. But I think a change of venue is in order."

The world shifts around us, and we wind up in another club that resembles the outer section of the casino, where patrons lounged on sofas and at tables. Here, though, the club offers a gloomy atmosphere lit by the strobe lights on the dance floor. People do dance there, and music plays, but not super loud. Couples, and larger groups too, leave the dance floor to head for curtained areas along the periphery of the club. Still more sneak away to private rooms with closed doors.

What kind of club is this?

Drakon hooks a thumb under my chin. "You're wondering where I've brought you. Let me enlighten both you and Tris. This is a sex club."

My throat goes thick. Sex club? Considering that he vowed to "defile" me, I don't want to know what sorts of things people are engaging in behind those curtains and doors. But I doubt I'll have a choice. Drakon is crazy powerful and, well, just plain crazy.

The shifter freezes, his attention focused on something behind us.

I glance back—and see Cyneric hovering a few feet behind me.

"Well, well," Drakon says with a nasty smile. "Isn't this an interesting turn of events. But I can rearrange my plans to accommodate our new arrival. After all, I've corrupted more humans and elementals than anyone in the multiverse. Never tried to corrupt a vampire, but then, Eros kept them to himself until recently. How selfish of him."

Tris curls a protective arm around me. "You won't touch her. Cyneric won't let you."

The dragon prince chuckles yet again, but this time with a disturbing amount of sensual menace. "You clearly didn't grasp the meaning of my words. I intend to corrupt your vampire friend. Right now."

Drakon snaps his fingers, and I suddenly find myself in his arms, hugged to his rock-hard body. I'm facing Tris with Drakon's chin nudging the crown of my head. One of his arms holds me in place, and kicking him does no good. It only makes him laugh again.

The scene shifts around us, and we now stand inside a room with black walls and instruments of torture hanging on the walls. At least, that's what they look like to me. A black bed in the middle of the room has black silk sheets too. Various types of furniture occupy the space too, though I've never seen chairs like the ones in this room.

When I look around for Tris, I see he's being restrained by two large men who might well be dragons too. They share the same weird glint in their eyes that Drakon has.

I swallow hard as my throat goes dry.

"Sex club, remember?" Drakon whispers into my ear. "An innocent like you probably knows nothing about BDSM."

"I've heard of it." But no, I don't want to find out what Drakon's idea of BDSM involves. The version I've heard about sounds tame compared to what I sense this evil winged creep wants to do to me. "If you're going to tie me up and defile me or whatever, just get it over with."

"No, I have a much better idea." He snaps his fingers. "Come here, vampire. I want to give you a delicious gift."

Cyneric doesn't move, and his gaze remains locked on me.

"Leave her alone," Tris snarls. "You want to hurt me, not Riley. So do your sicko shit to me and leave her alone."

"Where would the fun be in that?" Drakon drags me to the nearest wall, and I realize it consists of padded black leather. He spins me around and backs me up to the wall, holding me in place with one hand around my throat and his body pinning me to the wall. Then he rotates his head to glance over his shoulder at Cyneric. "Come, vampire. Slake your lust for this woman. I can sense your desire for her. Why fight it? Haven't you been subjugated for long enough? First by Eros, then by the Four Winds and the ones they tasked with keeping you down. Set your hunger free, my friend."

Cyneric gazes at me with an expression I've never seen before, and I know Drakon's tactic is working. The volatile vampire can't fight his desires for much longer, not with a dragon prince luring him to give in.

Drakon slides his hand up to my cheek and forces me to turn my head to the side. With his free hand, he waves for the vampire to approach. "Don't be shy. Come closer and take what you want."

Cyneric slowly walks toward us like a panther stalking his prey. His focus remains on my neck as he comes closer and halts right next to Drakon. The shifter peels his body away from mine just enough that he can move his palm onto my chest, between my breasts, to hold me to the wall. I can't move a muscle. He must be using magic to constrain me, since I should be able to at least move my arms and legs. But I can't.

Drakon smirks at Cyneric.

The vampire comes up beside me and lowers his head to sniff my exposed throat.

"Yes, that's right," Drakon virtually purrs. "Listen to her heartbeat pulsing inside her body. Imagine what she will taste like, how good it will feel to feast on her blood. Here in this room you can do anything you want, so go for it. Sink your fangs into her flesh."

Cyneric growls softly. His lips brush my throat. While I stand here immobilized, he touches his fangs to my neck and drags them over my flesh so slowly that it feels like a sensual act.

My heart is pounding, which probably isn't a good thing right now, but I can't control the fear rising inside me. What if Cyneric loses control and drains me? I'm not indestructible. A mere mortal like me has no chance of surviving a vampire's assault.

"Yes," Drakon purrs. "Take her. Have her. Devour her."

Cyneric sucks in a breath and exhales it in a ragged rush.

Then he sinks his fangs into my throat.

CHAPTER TWENTY-THREE

Tris

"STOP, CYNERIC," I SHOUT WHILE I STRUGGLE TO BREAK FREE OF MY guards. But they're too damn strong. "Stop, you're killing Riley. She's human, you bloodsucking moron. I know you don't want to hurt Riley, so stop *right now.*"

Cyneric had closed his eyes, but now he cracks one lid open to look at me. Even while he studies me, he keeps guzzling Riley's blood like she's a bottle of tequila and he wants to get drunk.

"Look at her," I snarl. "She's pale. Her lips are blue. Can you feel her pulse? Because I bet it's way too fast. If you don't stop now, *she will die.*"

And if that happens, I'll rip the heart out of his chest with my bare hands and shove it down his throat.

Cyneric stops drinking. I can tell because his throat has stopped working. Though he still has his fangs sunk into her neck, he just watches me with no discernible expression. Have I gotten through to him? Or is he too far gone to care about anything except his lust for blood?

The vampire gently removes his fangs from Riley's throat. Then he gazes at her face, seeming confused, and his eyes gradually widen. Cyneric stumbles backward several steps.

Riley slumps down the wall, struggling to take shallow, fast breaths.

But Drakon catches her before she hits the floor and forces her to stand. He glowers at Cyneric. "What are you doing, vampire? Keep drinking. You know you want to consume her completely, so just do it."

Cyneric shakes his head. "No. I will not."

He vanishes, crashing through the wards around this club with an audible explosion that rocks the building.

Riley looks deathly pale. Her eyes are glossy and unfocused. Her lips have fallen open too, and she seems incapable of moving.

I clench my teeth and my fists as I spear Drakon with a searing glare. "I am going to destroy you."

"No, you are not. I'm too powerful, and you are nothing but a puny leprechaun."

As I watch Riley drifting away from me second by second, her consciousness fading, I experience a sudden revelation. I'm not helpless. I'm not weaker than Drakon either. Ennea gave me the magical version of an adrenaline shot, and it has done something more than keep me on my feet. I feel like all the neurons in my brain have activated at the same instant, coursing power through me the way the adrenaline shot had reinvigorated my body.

All I need to do is set that power free.

I take two slow, deep breaths, and a kind of supernatural energy I've never experienced before rushes through me. I look at Riley one more time, then I do it. I roar as I shake off the bastards who constrained me, and I barrel across the small room, heading straight for Drakon.

He freezes, not even blinking.

I slam my fist into his chest and hear bones crack. Drakon's eyes almost bulge out of their sockets. I punch my fist into his chest again, hearing more bones crack, while at the same time I thrust my knee up into his groin.

Drakon howls and doubles over, cradling his privates.

I ram my knee up into his chin. More shattering bones. More howls from the dragon prince. Blood streams from his mouth, dripping onto the floor. Drakon's men rush at me, but I grab Riley and whisk us away. We land inside the healing vortex behind the rock shop in Michigan.

Laying her down on the grass, I press my ear to her chest. Still breathing. Barely. I touch my forehead to hers and whisper, "You'll be okay, you'll be okay."

Then I wait for the vortex to kick in.

Nothing happens. Riley still lies there pale and drained in the most literal sense, hanging on by the barest thread of life. Why isn't the vortex healing her?

More copper. I need more copper.

I zip straight into the shop, not caring if customers might see me, and scramble for the bins of copper ore, knocking down bins of other stuff and racks of postcards in the process.

"What are ye doing now?" Nevan demands. "You'll scare away our customers."

I spin around to glare at him. "Shut up, Nevan. Where's the rest of the copper? I need more *now*."

"That's all we have in stock at the moment." Nevan's expression goes blank, then his gaze narrows. "What's happened?"

"Drakon made Cyneric drink Riley's blood, and he went too far. She's dying of blood loss." I frantically hunt through more bins, and rocks tumble to the floor. "I need more fucking copper right now."

Nevan comes up beside me and lays a hand on my shoulder. "Take it easy, Tris. We will help you in whatever way we can, but we don't have any more copper here."

I'm breathing so hard my ears have started to ring and I see black spots in my vision. When I try to take another step, I trip and fall on my ass on the floor. "She's dying, Nevan. Don't you understand? Healing is my thing, but I can't do it without fuel."

Nevan kneels beside me, laying a hand on my shoulder again. "There is another way to obtain more copper. It won't be quite legal, but—"

"Don't care. Tell me how."

"Steal it from another rock shop. There's one ten miles away that keeps a much larger stock of copper than we do. The shop is called Land of Ore."

I don't even wait for Nevan to say anything else. With that other shop's name in my mind, I teleport straight into the building. A woman shrieks. Children point at me. I barrel past them and find the display of copper, which includes polished bookends and raw ore. Grabbing as much as I can carry, I hurry back to the vortex.

Riley lies on the ground, deathly pale and barely breathing. Nevan crouches beside her.

"She won't live much longer," he says. "I called for an ambulance, but I doubt it will arrive in time."

I wolf down copper like a maniac, and when I've consumed my entire stockpile, I drop to my hands and knees to scoop up the dust created by my chomping. I shove dirt into my mouth along with the copper dust, but I don't care. Now I'm so stuffed that I feel nauseous, but I don't care about that either. My chest heaves, though I feel like I can't pull in enough oxygen. Energy roils off me in glittering copper tentacles that slither toward Riley and wrap around her body. Soon, I can't see her at all. The magics have surrounded her.

That only happens in the most critical circumstances, like the time I'd healed Nevan after Skeiron gutted him with a big black sword.

I gaze down at Riley, and my throat constricts. *Come on, baby, wake up.* The coppery magics fade away. Riley just lies there as still as death. But she can't be dead. She can't.

Nevan had moved outside the vortex, but now he kneels beside Riley and takes hold of her wrist. "She has a pulse. Riley is alive. Her cheeks have more color too."

Dropping to my knees beside Riley, I brush hair away from her face. She does look less pale. The fang marks on her neck have disappeared too. But I won't feel any better until she wakes up and smiles at me.

Cyneric appears on the other side of the stone benches, directly across from me. He gazes down at Riley, and his faces pinches up a touch.

"What the hell are you doing here?" I snarl. "Get away from Riley. You did this to her. *You.* She nearly died because you couldn't stop yourself from guzzling her blood."

The vampire staggers backward a couple of steps. "I did not mean to—"

I spring to my feet, leaping over Riley and the benches to land inches away from Cyneric. Then I clamp my hand around his throat. "I should rip your head off right now."

He glances at Riley, and I swear his lips quiver the faintest bit.

"Do you even care that you almost killed her?" I demand. "Or are you so drunk on the blood of living beings that all you think about is where to get your next fix? How many people have you drained?"

His expression reverts to stoic mode. "None."

"Well, hurray for you. Do you expect to get a medal for that?"

A moan originates from behind me. A moan I recognize. I leap over the benches to touch down beside Riley.

She has her eyes open. For a moment, she just lies there seeming dazed, but then her gaze clears and she aims those beautiful eyes at me. "Hey. What did I miss?"

I drag her into my arms and hold her tight.

Cyneric watches us with no discernible expression.

Nevan touches my shoulder. "I believe my assistance is no longer needed."

"Yeah, we're okay now. I appreciate your help."

Nevan wanders off down the trail to the rock shop.

And Cyneric stares at Riley.

"You're smothering me," she says with a laugh, while her face is mashed to my chest.

I loosen my hold on her so we can look at each other. "Didn't mean to smother you. But you almost died, and I—" My throat has constricted again, and I need a moment before I can finish that thought. "I thought I'd lost you, and I didn't like that at all. I've never felt so helpless and hopeless."

She kisses me sweetly. "You don't need to feel that way anymore. I'm here, and I'm not going anywhere. Not without you."

"Good. Because I never want to be away from you."

Her gaze wanders to Cyneric, and she sighs. "I need to talk to him."

"Like hell you do. That creep nearly drained you dry."

She swerves her attention back to me. "Are you serious? Or is that an exaggeration?"

"It's the truth. Your lips were blue."

"Oh." Her eyes grow large, but then she blinks rapidly and recovers from her shock. "I had no idea it was that bad."

"Well, it was." I stab a finger in the air toward Cyneric. "And if that bloodsucker ever comes within fifty feet of you again, I will rip him into so many tiny pieces that even a vortex can't put him back together."

Riley brackets my face with her hands. "Relax, Tris. I think Cyneric learned his lesson."

"But he's still dangerous. All it took was for Drakon to tell him how good it would feel to drink you, and Cyneric did it."

"Yeah, I know." She scrambles to her knees. "But I need to talk to him one more time. Okay?"

"Only if I'm right next to you."

"Absolutely."

I help her up, and we walk around the benches to reach Cyneric. The vampire still shows nothing in his expression, which doesn't make me feel any better about his need to check on the woman he nearly killed.

Cyneric focuses on Riley. "I regret hurting you."

Okay, he has managed to shock me. But an apology hardly makes everything peachy. I resist the impulse to slug him only because I know Riley wants to say something to the vamp, and a broken jaw would make it harder for him to respond.

"I'm glad you realize you did something wrong," Riley tells the vamp. "But you need to give up this obsession with me. Only Tris's healing skills kept me from dying. That wouldn't have been necessary if you hadn't listened to Drakon when he told you to bite me."

Cyneric bows his head. "I know."

"The fact that you feel bad about what you did suggests you can change—if you want to. But only you can decide to do that."

He nods with his head still down.

"I really think you should go back to the training camp," she says. "Let Max and Travis and the others help you."

Cyneric's head pops up. "I cannot do that."

"You mean you don't want to," I say. "You're addicted to human blood now, aren't you? Elemental blood probably doesn't do it for you anymore. Am I right?"

A muscle in his jaw ticks.

"That means yes," I say. "Eros made it so you couldn't enjoy drinking blood from living beings. But now that he's gone, you found out you enjoy it plenty, but only when you devour human blood."

"Something has changed," Cyneric admits.

"That's even more reason for you to go back to the camp."

Cyneric shakes his head. "Alone is the only way. Since I tasted mortal blood, nothing else can satisfy me."

He vanishes.

"The vampire tells the truth," a familiar voice says as a familiar figure materializes beside us. Bob hooks his thumbs inside the waistband of his slacks. "The first taste of blood from a mortal altered his needs. He can never go back to donated blood from elementals. Now, he must deal with the consequences of the change."

Fantastic.

CHAPTER TWENTY-FOUR

Riley

I COMPLETELY UNDERSTAND WHY TRIS DOESN'T LIKE THE IDEA OF A rogue vampire on the loose who must consume the blood of mortals to survive. Is it my fault this happened to Cyneric? I shouldn't have let him tag along with me like a lost puppy. But he decided to follow me, and he decided to drink my blood simply because Drakon seduced him into doing that. So no, it's not my fault.

"What are we supposed to do now?" I ask. "Cyneric shouldn't be left alone with all that temptation. He nearly killed me. Since he can cross the veil whenever he wants, we can't keep him contained to the Unseen, which means he might drain a mortal to death without meaning to do it."

"I realize the dangers inherent in letting him live," Bob says. "But the Four Winds are the only beings allowed to weigh life-or-death decisions concerning elementals."

"Can Cyneric reform himself?"

"My foresight doesn't show me the end result. I know only that he cannot consume elemental blood, but he will need nourishment to survive. Are you familiar with the salamanders and what happens when they starve?"

"Tris has told me about them."

"If Cyneric starves, the result will prove far more catastrophic than what happens when a salamander is malnourished."

Fabulous. A starving vampire sounds like a recipe for disaster, but nobody can destroy Cyneric except for those Four Winds, whoever they are. When I'd asked Tris about them, he told me it was a long story. "Who is going to explain to me what the Four Winds are?"

"They're the balancing power in the Unseen," Tris tells me. "It's their job to keep in check all the beings who live in that world and to make sure those beings don't abuse their power to take advantage of mortals. The Four Winds were the driving force behind the Great Bargain."

"Um, the great what?"

"The Great Bargain." Tris clasps my hands, aiming his supernaturally blue eyes straight into mine. "A long, long time ago, the elementals started running wild. They would enslave mortals for their own pleasure, cast black spells, and basically do all kinds of naughty stuff. And they could go anywhere in the mortal world. Based on your limited experience with bad elementals, I'm sure you can imagine how awful things had gotten back then."

Oh yeah, I can imagine. And the thought ripples a shiver through me.

Bob clears his throat. "Perhaps I should finish the story. To halt the abuse of mortals, the Four Winds convened the elders of all the elemental races and the gods too. They hashed out a bargain that would create limits on what elementals can do. Gods cannot be limited, which is a problem. But less so than when the elementals had free rein. The Great Bargain created the basic rules—that elementals cannot travel beyond a one-mile radius from any natural water feature in the mortal world, and that bargains and debts only have power in the Unseen."

"Why would elementals agree to that?" I ask.

"Because the only alternative was destruction. The Four Winds were prepared to annihilate every being in the Unseen—except for the gods, whom they could not destroy—and start over with new species."

I guess it takes an apocalyptic threat to keep supernatural beings in check. And that brings up a question. "What about Drakon? I doubt he gave up and went to Tahiti."

Bob rubs his forehead, wincing. "Yes, that dragon shifter is already giving me a migraine. He wants revenge."

Tris rolls his eyes. "I didn't steal from him. I won those games fair and square, thanks to dumb luck."

"Is it dumb luck?" Bob raises a hand when Tris starts to respond. "That was a rhetorical question. Find the answer on your own. But remember this. Even a primordial shifter can be destroyed with the right motivation."

Bob disappears.

"Oracles are so annoying," Tris says. "Might as well have stuck his tongue out at me, because that's about how useful his so-called information was."

"Actually, I think it was a lot more informative than that."

He gives me an oh-please look.

I tap his chest. "Don't scoff until you hear what I think."

"All right. Go on and tell me."

"Drakon is ticked because you had such amazingly good luck in his casinos."

Tris shoves his hands into his pants pockets. "I know that already."

"Shush. I'm not finished yet." I settle both my palms on his chest, strictly because I love to feel his muscles under his T-shirt. What? I might as well cop a feel whenever I can, in case we die in five minutes. "Drakon couldn't understand how you got so lucky. He believes you have a special kind of luck, and he thinks you cheated with magic to achieve that good fortune. What if he's right?"

"I don't cheat."

"Of course not. But maybe you have acquired a special type of magic that gives you amazingly good luck."

He huffs. "That would be cheating."

"Not necessarily. You said your transmutation was supposed to turn you into your true self, but you didn't think you had achieved that yet. I told you I was sure you had, but you didn't believe me."

"How could you know? Even I'm not sure if or when that might happen."

I slide my hands up to his shoulders. "I've gotten to know you, Tris. You are a strong, capable, mature man. I can't explain how I know this for sure, but I do. I'm positive you have become your true self, and that's how I know your good luck must be more than chance. You are a leprechaun, after all."

"We don't dole out luck, and we don't have any special good fortune for ourselves."

I lean against his body, tipping my head back to study his face. "Does every fae of a particular tribe come out of the transmutation with the same changes? I mean, does every copper fae change their accent, grow big muscles, and become incredible in bed?"

He smirks. "How do you know I wasn't incredible in bed before the transmutation?"

"Were you?"

Tris scratches his cheek and screws up his face. "No, I wasn't. The only girls who wanted to sleep with me were undines, but they're like the elemental equivalent of a cheerleader. You know, they'll do it with any guy."

"Not all cheerleaders are sluts, but I understand what you're saying."

"The cheerleaders in mortal TV shows always screw their way onto the squad."

I shake my head, though I can't help smiling. "You need to stop watching teen soap operas."

"Pendi loves them. Since I don't have a TV, I need to beg my brothers and sisters to let me watch theirs."

I pat his chest and sigh. "Getting back to the issue of your good luck, did you ever hit the jackpot that many times before you went through leprechaun puberty? Or did you not gamble before then?"

"Only once in a while. I never won anything, so I eventually gave up. I played poker with my friends, but we didn't wager on our games." He puckers his lips as if he's deep in thought. "Come to think of it, I only started gambling again after the transmutation. Didn't think about it at the time, but it does seem weird that I immediately had awesome luck. That's why I kept gambling after I won my first game of poker in one of Drakon's casinos. I didn't know he owned it, though, not at the time."

"So, will you admit that it's at least possible you developed a new power after your elemental puberty? You might have acquired the power of good fortune."

He says nothing for a moment while he stares at me, then he bows his head and groans. "If that's true, I've become a stereotype. Might as well slap my face on a cereal box."

"Instead of thinking it's embarrassing, maybe you could try to view it as a gift."

"Never heard of the Unseen giving an elemental the gift of beating the house in every casino."

I boost myself up on my tiptoes to clasp his face in my hands. "Maybe you're meant to do more with your gift than just gambling. What if you can grant that luck to other people too?"

"Maybe…" His gaze goes distant for a moment. Then he grins and pulls me close to kiss me. "You are a genius, Riley. But I need to test my luck to make sure it wasn't a fluke all those times I won at Drakon's casinos."

"How do we test that?"

Tris grins again. "Oh, I've got a great idea. Let's go to Las Vegas."

"Casinos got you into trouble. Maybe we shouldn't—"

"Just a quick test, not a prolonged attempt to beat the house. Okay?"

I consider his plan, but quickly realize he's right. This is the fastest way to test his luck. "Okay, let's do it."

He spirits us away to the Vegas strip, in an alley, then he leads me out onto the sidewalk. It's daytime, so the lights of the casinos and hotels aren't as spectacular now. Everything looks kind of dingy in the light of day, but we aren't here to admire the scenery. We keep walking until we reach the first casino, then we go inside to try his luck.

First, he tries a slot machine—and he wins. Next, he heads for the roulette wheel—and wins again. Tris suggests we go to a different casino now so nobody will get suspicious. We wind up testing his luck at five establishments, and he wins every time. After that, we return to the rock shop in Michigan because Tris wants to "prove to the air fairy" that he does have a new power that allows him to beat the odds at every game. By "air fairy" he means his friend Nevan, who he tells me used to be a sylph aka an air elemental.

Nevan suggests we gather "the gang" for a poker match, so he shouts for Max and Travis. They show up seconds later. Though the men invite me to play too, I tell them I have no interest in card games. Instead, I sit on Tris's lap, which was his idea. He claims it will increase his luck twenty-fold. He does win three rounds of poker, but I doubt my rump on his lap made any difference.

Nevan tosses Tris a quarter and tells him to test his luck with that. Tris correctly guesses every toss.

"I must admit," Nevan says, "that you've had extraordinarily good luck today. Maybe you have developed a new power."

"You believe that?" Tris says. "I expected you to make fun of me and act all high-and-mighty about it."

"Nevan is right," Max announces. "This is unusually good fortune that would seem to indicate a new power."

If his friends believe that, maybe he will too.

"Do any of you guys know Drakon?" I ask, while I'm still perched on Tris's lap.

"The dragon shifter?" Max says. "I've heard of him, but he lives in the mortal world. I prefer the Unseen."

"So you have no idea if Drakon can be killed. Bob sort of implied that he can, but we don't know how to do that."

"Even the toughest elemental infused with the darkest magics will have a weak spot." Max leans back in his chair and lifts one shoulder. "Afraid I can't tell you what Drakon's weakness is, though."

It's up to us. At least now we have solid evidence that Tris has developed a new power, though I'm not sure how that will help us. He doesn't even know how to activate that power on purpose, much less how to direct it to his advantage. But we will figure it out. I know it.

We say goodbye to Nevan and Max, then return to the little trailer where we'd spent most of yesterday. Lying on the bed, we discuss our options. But we don't have many of those. When I suggest Tris should try to use his new power on purpose, he gives me an exasperated look.

"I have no idea how to activate it," he says. "Or what to do with the power once I get it to work. I already have improved luck."

"You could try to grant me luck. Give me the quarter."

"What quarter?"

I nudge him with my elbow. "The one Nevan gave you, which you did not return to him."

"Oh, that. I didn't steal it. Just forgot I had it." He digs the quarter out of his pocket. "Here it is."

I take the coin from him. "Try to grant me good luck."

CHAPTER TWENTY-FIVE

Tris

GRANT HER LUCK? THIS FEELS LIKE A BAD IDEA, ESPECIALLY SINCE MY CURSE is still in effect. Testing my luck is one thing, but trying to use my apparent new power on her feels like tempting fate. But I need to know if I can do this, and I've learned enough about Riley to realize she's too stubborn to just give up if I refuse to do it. So I scrunch up my whole face, concentrating hard, then blow out a breath. "Did it work?"

"Time to check. I say it'll be heads." Riley tosses the coin, and it lands heads up. "Let's try it a few more times."

She gets the first ten tosses right, but then her luck gets spottier until, eventually, it becomes no better than chance.

"So much for that theory," I grumble.

"Maybe you can only grant someone good luck for a little while. Or maybe you just need to get more comfortable with your new power."

"Great. How do I do that? Can't remember ever receiving a new power. I was born with the ability to activate the healing vortex, though I didn't come into that power until I was old enough to handle it."

She sits up, braced with one arm, and looks at me. "You were born with that power? Wow. All I got was a little moon-shaped birthmark."

I slide a hand onto her hip, right at the spot where her thigh meets it. "I know all about that birthmark. You gasp every time I lick it."

She lays a hand over mine on her hip. "Yeah, I do. And I love it every time you touch me."

"Maybe we should have sex, strictly to test my luck."

"You don't need special powers to get lucky with me." She twists around to set the coin on the bedside table, balanced on its edge. Then she starts it spinning. "I say this will not fall down. It will stop on its edge, and the tails face will be toward us."

"Okay. We'll see if that works."

She lays her body on top of mine. "Kiss me."

Like she needed to tell me to do that. The second she smiled at me, I wanted to kiss her. We make out, with lots of groping and some soft moans from her, until we finally realize the coin has stopped spinning. We both look at the table at the same instant.

The quarter stands on its edge, and the tails face is aimed at us.

"Now that seems like more than chance," I say. "Maybe I need to kiss you to confer my good luck power on you. That suggests we should get it on, strictly to find out if the luck I gave you is still working or if it's worn off."

"Oh, sure, that's why you want to get naked with me. For science."

"No, for magic." I push a hand inside her shorts to palm her ass. "Let's accumulate more data."

She laughs.

The trailer door explodes inward.

I throw my arms around Riley to shield her from the debris the explosion scattered inside the trailer and keep my eyes shut until the noise of it fades away. Then I crack one eye open. The door hangs half off its hinges.

And a dragon shifter hovers in the doorway with his wings tucked behind him.

That's not Drakon. He must've sent one of his lackeys to retrieve us. I zip us away to the falls and jump through the cascade into the cavern. All I can think to do is to go into the Unseen and hide until we can figure out how to stop Drakon. But as I raise my hand to open the portal, the dragon minion appears in front of us, blocking the way.

"You are not leaving this world," he says, and he spreads his wings just to show off. "Drakon wants you."

"Really? It's always nice to be wanted, but my social schedule is all booked up."

I wave my hand. The second the portal opens, I raise my foot to slam it into the dragon's gut, kicking him toward the portal. Then I whisk us away to another portal.

The dragon appears right in front of us, once again blocking the way. "Nice try, leprechaun. But we came prepared."

He flicks his wrist, and shimmering handcuffs appear, encircling my wrists and Riley's. Two more dragon shifters materialize too. Our guards have arrived. I try to move, to fight, but I can't even get my pinky finger to bend.

The dragon who had destroyed the trailer door saunters up to us. "Your powers of good fortune will not help you now."

"How did you even find us?" I ask.

The dragon's lips form a smug smile. "Drakon will explain that to you. I'm sure he will enjoy telling you all about it."

"Well, I live to make Drakon happy."

Our guards set their hands on our shoulders and take us away. We materialize inside Drakon's BDSM club. *Oh, perfect.* There's nothing like black vinyl walls and racks of torture devices to make a person feel at home. I've never visited any other BDSM club, but I doubt Drakon's version looks at all like the way mortals play around with it.

I don't see the dragon prince, but I'm sure he'll pop in to swagger and threaten us anytime. I still can't move, thanks to these damn cuffs. Could I use my luck power to get out of them? I have no idea how to do that, but necessity is the mother of invention. Isn't that what mortals like to say? Okay, but I don't know how to harness that power. I can't invent a way. Or can I?

Drakon saunters into the room and faces us. "Welcome back. You won't live long, but I will feel much better once I've rid myself of you, leprechaun. Then I can claim Riley as my mate."

I'm sure he said that mainly to tick me off. It's working. But I won't let him see how much I want to beat the crap out of him. "Riley doesn't date oversize chickens."

"Chicken?" Drakon chuckles. "Your insults need work."

"You're right. 'Chicken' is the wrong word. You're more of a whooping crane."

Drakon stalks up to me. "Stop talking. Every word you say irritates me."

"And I feel awful about that. Your feelings are my top priority." I need to keep him talking as a distraction, but I can't focus on using my new power while drumming up more sarcastic jibes. I move only my eyes to glance at Riley, hoping she'll understand my intent when she realizes what I'm about to do. "You know what? I think we should play a new game and wager on who will win."

Drakon crosses his arms over his chest. "You assume your luck will hold out, and you'll win the wager."

"You're hoping my luck has run out. That's part of the bet and the game."

"I have cursed you." He lays his hand on my chest. "I agree to your wager. But first, I will enhance the curse a bit more."

Aw, shit. Then again, maybe this isn't a bad thing. I'll have a chance to test my newfound power in a real-world situation. But I need a test like none I've conducted so far, something too outrageous for Drakon to resist.

"What are the stakes?" Drakon asks.

"Anything you want. If I win, I get anything I want." Will his arrogance rule his decisions? Or will he get wise to my game? "Do we have a deal?"

Drakon studies me for a moment, then slaps my arm. "We have a deal. What is the game?"

I resist the urge to glance at Riley and pull in a deep breath. "Russian roulette."

The dragon prince tilts his head to the side and scrutinizes me like he can't quite believe what I suggested. "You do realize the ultimate penalty for that game is death."

"I know."

"Your luck might protect you, or the curse might override it—and you will die. Even if you win, I will destroy you. That is the 'anything' that I want."

"I figured."

He eyes me with a strange expression. "You don't care what happens to Riley after I destroy you."

"She can take care of herself. Riley is the smartest, strongest person I've ever met."

"Yes, she is unusual." He slants toward me. "That's why I look forward to defiling her after your demise."

Will this guy ever shut up about "defiling" people? He needs a new schtick.

Drakon nods to one of his minions, and the dragon dude guides me away from Riley and the other shifter minion. We halt on the opposite side of the room, right in front of the black vinyl wall. The shifter minion strides back to his master, leaving me alone over here. I still can't move. These handcuffs prevent it—for now.

The dragon prince ambles up to me, halting about ten feet away. He conjures a revolver and flips the cylinder out to show that it holds only one bullet. Then he spins the cylinder and flips it shut.

My eyes want to look at Riley, but I force myself to keep my focus on Drakon. I won't even glance at the gun once he aims it at me.

Drakon raises the revolver, targeting it on my forehead. "You will have at most five chances to test your luck. Then the final bullet will pierce your skull. The rounds are endued, naturally. I always keep endued weapons and ammunition on hand."

Of course he does. "Just get on with it."

"As you wish."

I stare into his eyes and wait for the click—or the boom. If I hear that, it might be the last thing I ever hear.

Click.

At least I didn't flinch when I heard that sound. Now I brace for the second attempt.

Click.

Though I keep my gaze on Drakon, my psyche retreats into the depths of my mind as I gather all the good luck I've been granted and channel it into a ball of energy. I visualize it that way to help me focus my magics.

Click.

The third chamber has revealed nothing inside it. I keep channeling my luck power, and though I have no idea how it works, I focus on believing it does work and will protect me. As I continue condensing the magics inside me, I swear I can feel Riley urging me on, almost like she's inside me. But I don't dare glance at her.

Boom.

The explosive sound of a round being fired detonates inside the small room. I wait for the bullet to slam into my forehead, but nothing happens. Smoke wafts up from the gun's muzzle, and still I feel nothing. I raise my hand to palpate my forehead, then lower my hand to look at it. No blood. I didn't feel anything on my forehead either, certainly nothing like a gunshot wound. It should've punched a hole through my skull. But there's nothing.

Drakon's attention shifts to the floor. His nostrils flare, emitting a wisp of fire.

I look down at my feet, and a feeling of euphoria rushes through me. Because there on the floor lies a spent round, squashed like it slammed into an impenetrable barrier and dropped at my feet. My luck did that.

I can't help grinning at Drakon. "I won."

His face contorts into the nastiest expression I have ever seen. Not even a harpy could look as enraged and disgusted as Drakon does right now. "You cheated again."

I shrug. "It's just my luck, I guess. That's a new power I've acquired, by the way. Even your curse couldn't get past my good fortune."

He seethes as flames shoot out of his nostrils.

"You know what?" I say. "I don't even feel cursed anymore."

Drakon shifts into dragon form, now standing as tall as the ceiling of this room, and snaps his wings out to encompass half of the space. "You will suffer for this insult. You and everyone you love in both worlds."

Oh, no. I hadn't meant to tick him off quite this much. But what can he really do? Snarl and breathe fire, that's all I've seen from him.

Drakon drops into a crouch, sucks in a big breath, and gusts flames out of his mouth and nostrils as he flies up, shattering the ceiling, to blast straight out the top of the building. The sunlight makes his dragon scales shimmer, and he lets out a deafening shriek full of a fiery rage that matches his fiery snorts.

He flaps his wings slowly, hovering just above where the roof had been, and fixes his glare on me. "This is war."

Chapter Twenty-Six

I'VE NEVER BEEN INVOLVED IN A REGULAR WAR BEFORE, SO AN INTERDImensional one sounds extremely scary. Dragons fighting with leprechauns? That doesn't sound like a fair fight. I mean, the shifters have wings and fire breath. Tris has luck and muscles and healing power. But Drakon did say he wants to destroy Tris and everyone he loves in both worlds. His friends will step up to help, won't they? Maybe they've fought wars in the past. That would give us two salamanders, Tris's brothers and sisters, and a few humans.

Yeah, that doesn't sound too promising.

While I'm still thinking about interdimensional warfare, Tris grabs me and transports us to a nearby portal, which lies on the banks of a river. I can see the city of London all around us, but I don't get a chance to take in the scenery. Tris tells me to hold my breath, then leaps into the river with me hugged to his body. We sink down, down, down through the murky water. A light shimmers below us. Tris dives straight toward it, kicking his feet to speed up our downward trajectory. We fly through the portal and splat onto the earth in a place I don't recognize. It must be the Unseen, since that's where the portals lead, but I've never seen this particular spot. We've wound up lying facedown on the grass.

Tris jumps up while still holding me and peels my wet hair away from my eyes. "I don't have enough energy to summon a puff of air to dry you off. Took a hell of a lot of power to do that before."

"It's okay. I can handle being drenched. Where are we?"

"Not sure. I've never used this portal before." He takes a step back and fists his hands in his shirt to wring the water out of it. "I didn't want to aim for the portal behind the rock shop. The dragons found us there, so that location is burned for us. At least until we beat Drakon."

"Do you think that's possible?"

"Yes, I do." He smiles with a confidence I haven't seen from him until now. "I beat Russian roulette, after all. I should've taken a slug to the brain, but my luck power saved me."

"Will that be enough to stop a war?"

"No, I kinda doubt it. But this gives us a start. Time to rally the troops."

I can't help smiling. "You're cute when you get gung-ho. Have you ever fought a war?"

"Sure. I helped Lindsey and Nevan in three battles—when they took out Skeiron, when they eighty-sixed that evil sorcerer, and when the harpy Aello tried to rewrite time and then started a war because Lindsey saved the timeline. We won all three battles."

"You really do have experience. Let's rally the troops."

He slings an arm around me, molding my body to his.

"Is this really necessary?" I ask. "Or do you just like feeling me up?"

"Holding your hand would work just as well. But where's the fun in that?"

"This way is much better."

He takes us to the vampire training camp. I don't expect to see Cyneric here since he ran away to who knows where, but I still feel a touch of anxiety about revisiting the camp. Two dozen or so vamps remain on the premises. What if they can smell that another vampire fed on me? What if that makes them crazed with hunger for human blood? But I know Tris wouldn't bring me here if he believed there was even the slightest danger to me.

He sets us down just inside the doorway to the makeshift arena. Now we walk across the space to reach Max and Travis, who seem to be observing while two sylphs instruct the vamps. What are they learning? How not to drain a living being? That would be my number one priority if I ever took bloodsuckers under my wing. Actually, I did do that with one vampire. Yeah, and look how it turned out. Think I'll leave the vamp training to the guys who can't die except at the of tip an endued sword.

Travis and Max meet us halfway and greet us with smiles.

"You're not destroyed," Max announces when he sees Tris. Then he gives my boyfriend a playful slug in the shoulder. "That's a positive result. Travis and I were making bets about how long it would take Drakon to kill you. Did your luck help you dust him?"

Tris winces. "Not exactly."

Max narrows his gaze. "What does that mean? I'm getting one of those 'imminent death' feelings. What have you done?"

"I beat Drakon at Russian roulette. He was, uh, slightly annoyed about that. And he might have, well, vowed to destroy me and everyone I know."

"Everyone you know? That's bloody perfect. You had to get me involved in a vendetta, and I don't even like you."

"Yes, you do," I say. "Men don't like to admit to things like that, but you and Tris are bosom buddies."

"Bosom?" Max says as he curls his lip. "I don't have breasts, love. If Tris's little problem involves giving me tits, I won't be a happy salamander."

"I wouldn't worry about that," Tris tells him. "What you should really be concerned with is the impending war."

"War with who?" Travis asks.

"Drakon."

"Oh, bloody hell. I had enough of war after all those incidents with Lindsey and then the thing with three gods trying to reclaim Larissa."

"Of course you're only thinking about yourself." Tris scowls at his friend. "You could try caring about somebody else for a change."

I know these guys are arguing only because they're scared. Men get that way over piddly things like one guy stealing another guy's girl. But these three have slightly more reason for turning on each other right now. A looming apocalypse feels like a good excuse, but I can't let them keep sniping at each other.

"Shut up!" I holler.

The three men stop arguing and swivel their gazes to me, each wearing an expectant expression, like they think I can solve all our problems just because I shouted at them to shut up.

"Arguing doesn't help," I say. "Let's try working together to solve the problem. Tris told me you guys have fought battles before, so taking down Drakon shouldn't be a big deal."

"Not a big deal?" Max says. "The dragon shifters are primordial elementals with immense power."

"And Tris has his new luck power. You and Travis have powers too, right?"

Max rolls his eyes. "Oh, yes, I'm sure our pheromones and powers of seduction will help us annihilate a powerful dragon prince."

Maybe their seductive powers could help. I need to think about that, though.

"We need lots of help," I say. "Don't you guys know lots of people? Well, get moving on that. Rally the troops. Right, Tris? Max and Travis will help. Won't you?"

All three men nod and exchange glances as if they might actually be considering what I said. Then they start talking about how to do what I suggested. Wow. I ordered men to do something, and they did it. Maybe I've developed a special power too.

The guys pull me into their discussion, and soon we've come up with a plan for rallying all our allies and potentially defeating the dragon shifters. Though we need to flesh out the plan a bit more, I feel better knowing we've gotten a start on that. Now it's time to gather all the allies we can.

"How do we make sure the dragons don't surprise us?" Tris asks. "You know, while we're taking a whiz in the woods or something."

"That is a concern," Travis agrees. "How can we defend against a surprise attack? We need more information about the dragons."

Max claps a hand on Travis's shoulder. "Brilliant. You go ahead and sneak into the palace of the western dragon shifters. We'll sweep up the dust after they've destroyed you."

"You're not helping, Max," Tris says. "Ditch the sarcasm and use your brain."

"Maybe Bob could help," I say. "If we tell him how serious the situation is, he might be able to give us insight or something."

"Okay, that's not a half-bad idea. Bob likes you, Riley, so you and I should go see him. Max and Travis, you guys can handle the other stuff we talked about."

The salamanders nod their agreement.

While they jog over to the sylphs to let them know what's going on, Tris and I teleport to the periphery of the oracle's precinct. The atmosphere feels eerily still and quiet, but that might be my anxiety affecting how I perceive things. I can't help being on edge with a war coming. As we approach the path that leads through the woods, a shiver of awareness tingles down my spine.

I grab Tris's arm to stop him. "Do you feel that?"

"Yeah. Reminds me of when Anthea was stalking me."

"Do you think Drakon sent one of his minions to follow us? Maybe they couldn't track us until now."

"I don't know. This feels different." He lays a hand on my back, urging me to start walking again. "Let's keep going, but have our eyes and ears on high alert."

"Good idea."

As we continue through the dark and creepy forest, I hear strange birdlike noises originating above our heads. I suppose it could be actual birds. But I remember what Tris told me about the kerkopes, the flying monkey-like beasts who live inside the oracle's precinct. The more I hear that noise, the more I need to ask Tris about it.

"Will the kerkopes hurt us?" I ask. "They sound agitated based on the noises they're making."

"They work for Bob. The ones who attacked Lindsey way back when had gone rogue."

"If they went rogue once, they could do it again. Don't you think?"

Tris stops walking. "Yeah, you're right. We need to get to Bob fast."

He sweeps me up in his arms and starts running—faster than any human could go. We fly across the sulfuric river, and he keeps running at an insane speed until we pop out into the clearing that surrounds the mound-like entrance to the oracle's lair. Tris puts me down and knocks on the little hill.

Nothing happens.

Tris knocks again and shouts, "Hey, Bob! Let us in."

Still nothing.

"Maybe he's not home," I say. "Even an oracle must need to get outside for some fresh air."

"I can't picture Bob lying on a lawn chaise tanning himself."

"You will never see that," a familiar voice declares, "because I do not sunbathe."

We both turn toward Bob, who now hovers several yards away, behind where we had been standing. And when I say he "hovers," I mean that literally. His feet float just above the ground.

"I knocked," Tris tells Bob. "Why didn't you answer?"

"You can't go inside my lair. It isn't safe to open the door for anyone." He floats a little closer. "And it isn't safe for the two of you to enter this precinct."

"Not safe? You should've warned us. What's going on, Bob?"

"Some of the kerkopes have been seduced into joining the dragon prince Drakon in his war against you."

"Oh, perfect. We should get out of here, but we did come to ask for your help. Are you able to do that? Or are you trapped inside your lair?" Tris waves toward Bob's feet. "You're actually inside, aren't you? That's why you're floating."

"Yes, I've had to resort to hiding like a frightened mouse. But I will find a way to leave and get past the kerkopes. You can count on me for assistance when the time comes."

"We appreciate that, Bob."

"Better hurry. Exit the woods as fast as you can. I can sense the kerkopes plotting against you."

Wonderful. I'd hoped the oracle might have a smidgen of good news for us, but I guess not. *Armageddon, here we come.*

Bob disappears, and Tris picks me up again to race through the dark and eerie woods. We've just crossed the river when the shrieking of wild creatures erupts overhead. Tris keeps hold of me while we both peer up into the abyssal darkness created by the canopy of trees. I can't see a thing up there. But I hear wings flapping and branches cracking.

Tris's features tighten. "This is not good."

He takes off running down the trail even faster than before, springing up to leap over big rocks and veering sideways to avoid downed trees. I swear those obstacles hadn't been there before. Did the kerkopes purposely try to block our escape route? Those creatures must be way smarter than I assumed they were. Calling them flying monkeys must've skewed my perception.

But these creatures are clearly smart. They set up obstacles, after all.

Up ahead, I can see the sunlight streaming down inside the clearing at the edge of the oracle's precinct. Oh, thank goodness. We're almost clear. The kerkopes won't follow us out into the wider world of the Unseen. Will they? I guess I've assumed those creatures can't leave the oracle's domain, but if they've gone rogue, who knows. I have so little knowledge about magic and this world.

Inches from the edge of the woods, Tris trips over something. We both go tumbling, rolling across the ground until we smack into a tree, tangled up together. I scramble to my knees and stare up at the canopy above us.

A dark shape swoops down. Long, curving talons clamp around me under my arms. Then I'm swept up into the canopy in the grip of a monkey-beast.

CHAPTER TWENTY-SEVEN

Tris

ONE OF THE KERKOPES JUST KIDNAPPED RILEY. I CAN BARELY SEE them as they rise through the canopy into the pitch darkness. I can't fly. Can't jump that high either. I hesitate for exactly three seconds, then I leap up and latch onto the nearest tree, climbing up the slimy, oozing bark. My feet slip, but I cling to the tree with my fingers and dig my nails in to solidify my hold. Though every muscle in my body screams for me to stop, I will never do that. Not until I get Riley back.

"Tris!" she shouts. "Tris, I'm up here!"

Her cries came from the left, so I crawl across a thick branch to reach an adjacent tree and start climbing up its trunk. Those flying freaks took my girlfriend. Once I catch them, they will all pray for destruction because what I plan to do to them will make dying seem like fun.

I'm breathing hard, almost wheezing, but I will not stop. *Get to Riley*, that's all I can focus on right now. I know she's strong and capable and can handle herself, but these are supernatural creatures. She has no powers, and her body is so fragile compared to all the elementals living in this world.

By the time I get halfway up the tree, I can barely catch my breath. Sweat pours down my temples and has soaked my shirt. I throw my head back and holler, "Riley! Where are you?"

"Here!" she shouts.

At least she sounds closer now, which means I'm not that far away from her. What will I do once I get to Riley? I have no weapons, and I can't conjure the endued sword since the oracle's wards prevent that. I'll use my bare hands, my teeth, whatever it takes to save her.

Bob materializes beside me. He looks a little pale, but I've never seen him like that before. "You can conjure anything you need. I've cast an arduous spell to create a loophole in the wards just for you."

"That's great, Bob. But are you okay?"

"I'll recover faster than Riley will if those beasts harm her. Hurry, Triskaideka."

The oracle is gone.

Well, he gave me what he could, and I'm grateful for that. I can't ever tell Bob so, but I'm sure he knows. He's a seer, after all, so he probably knows what I'm thinking before I do.

I shout for Riley again, and she calls out to me in response. Then I hear the screeching of kerkopes—more than one of them, I'm sure—and I realize they won't let her keep alerting me to her position for much longer. So I scramble across a branch that's not as sturdy as I'd like, heading for a neighboring tree. The branch creaks like it might break, but I keep going, moving even faster. The gunk oozing out of the bark sticks to my clothes and skin. A crack resounds behind me, and the limb I'm on tips downward. I'm relying on my new power to get me where I need to be.

Don't crap out on me now, luck.

I throw an arm out to grab onto a thicker branch on the neighboring tree just as the sagging limb beneath me gives out. I hang from the other tree, clinging to the branch while I struggle to swing my legs up and wrap them around the limb's girth. Finally, I've gotten a bit of luck. This tree has much thicker branches and rougher bark, which gives me more leverage.

The kerkopes have gone eerily silent. That's never good.

Up through the canopy I climb, but now I can move faster and more easily thanks to the composition of this tree. I gradually start to hear faint noises, like wings gently flapping and soft birdlike noises. But I don't hear Riley anymore. That doesn't mean they've hurt her. Maybe they gagged her so she can't call out to me, and that's why I can't hear her. Every muscle in my body begs me to stop, but I keep pushing beyond my limits, ignoring the signs that I might be injuring myself in the process. A healing vortex will fix that.

I pause about twenty feet from the top of the tree and climb onto a limb for a better view. My eyes have adjusted to the darkness reasonably well, so I can make out shapes at least. As I scan my surroundings, I spot movement three trees over, at the same level as where I crouch. Bob said I can conjure anything I need, so I wish for a pair of binoculars. They materialize in my hand. I could've gotten myself a pair of night vision binoculars, but that would ruin my natural vision, which is innately better than anything a mortal could hope to have. Raising the binoculars, I adjust the focus and survey the area.

There. I see it. The kerkopes have a nest three trees over, and inside it lies a shape that's distinctly not a flying monkey-man. I adjust the focus more until I can make out the shape of a head covered with long hair.

Riley. It must be.

I hook the strap of the binoculars around my neck and crawl over to the next tree, then sidle around its trunk until I can see the nest again. Another peek through the binoculars confirms my suspicion. That is Riley over there. Now I just need to climb over to her without rousing the suspicions of the kerkopes. Two of them seem to be guarding her. I send the binoculars back to wherever they'd come from, but now I need a distraction.

Oh, I've got a great idea.

I conjure a handful of firecrackers and a matchbook, then light up the tiny explosives as I drop them one by one. The bright flashes as they ignite, combined with the sizzling sound they make, draws the attention of the kerkopes. Their heads pop up from where they crouch on the adjacent tree, but some also pop up on nearby trees too. When the first firecracker bursts, they all screech and fly up out of their hiding places. Then they swoop down to check out what's going on below.

And I have my opening.

I leap across to the adjacent tree, landing on the branch beside Riley. The nest she sits in lies cradled between two other branches. I carefully scoot over there and hold out my arms to her. "Come on, we need to hurry."

She waddles toward me, hindered by the fabric binding her wrists and ankles. I was right about her being gagged. The second I have her in my arms, I yank the gag out of her mouth. But I don't have time to free the rest of her. Bob had said I could conjure things, but he didn't mention if I could teleport. Worth a shot. I picture us landing just outside the oracle's precinct.

And we're there. Poof. Free of the kerkopes.

I set Riley on her feet and tear off her bindings.

She yanks the gag off and tosses it away, then grins at me. "That was the most amazing rescue ever. You're my hero, Tris."

"Uh, maybe you shouldn't give me that label yet since I haven't even released you from your debts to me."

"Have you tried since you developed a new power?"

"No. I'm still cursed, though." I consider her for a moment, then decide to give it a try. And I groan. "Tried again. Don't think it worked."

"Order me to do something."

"Stand on your toes and cluck like a chicken twice."

Riley does that. Then she sets her hands on her hips and shakes her head. "You liked making me do that, didn't you?"

"Well, you are adorable when you cluck like a chicken."

"It's a good thing you just rescued me, or I'd have to kick your butt for that trick."

"But you told me to do it."

Her lips twitch at the corners, which I know means she's teasing me.

"Okay, fun's over," I say. "Time to head back to Coppertown so we can rally the troops there."

"How many of them do you think will join our army?"

"Everybody who's able to fight."

Riley's eyes widen. "Everybody? That village seemed like it had lots of people in it."

"And they've all fought in wars before this. The Unseen isn't all sunshine and daises, you know. I've told you about the battles we all fought with Lindsey."

"You're right. I shouldn't be surprised, but I can't help that I am."

I sling an arm around her, about to take us away.

But something slams into my back, and I feel my flesh ripping. The heat of blood streams down my skin, and I stumble sideways, losing my hold on Riley.

Two kerkopes stand there, and one of them holds up his blood-soaked talon. He licks it and makes an appreciative sound. "Leprechauns taste better than they look."

I grab Riley and whisk us away, but the monkey-man who thinks I taste good latches onto my ankle at the last second. My hitchhiker tries to gnaw on me while we rocket through the abyssal tunnel and emerge at the periphery of the copper fae village. The beast drags me to the ground and bares his razor-sharp teeth, lowering his mouth toward my nose. I conjure the endued sword, but I can't get leverage with this creep on top of me. His wings create even more of a barrier. So I push the sword across the ground, out of the range of the beast's wings.

Riley snatches it up and grasps the hilt in both hands, raising it tip down.

The monkey-man has pinned my hands with his knees, and the weight of him on top of me means I can't kick him either. Damn, this monster is strong. I bash my head into his, but that only slows him down for a few seconds. It's enough.

Riley rams the sword's blade into the beast's back. The tip pierces my belly, but I'll survive that. It takes a far more grievous wound to trigger destruction, even with an endued weapon. Riley yanks the blade free and plunges it into the monkey-man's skull.

Blood pours over me, but most of it is not mine. I shove the creature off me and scramble to my knees, then scuttle backward away from the beast. Since Riley used Travis's endued sword, that means the bastard will not live to tell his friends where we went.

I throw my head back and holler, "Get the wards up now!"

My cry echoes through the courtyard, and people begin to run in various directions. Some are trying to hide, for sure. But most are rushing off to tell the mayor to activate the wards and to warn everyone in town that one of the kerkopes invaded our home.

Since I know they will defend the village at any cost, I grab Riley's hand. "Go to my parents' house. I need to find the nearest vortex and get Pendi to heal me."

"I'm not leaving you."

"Please, Riley. I need to know you're safe."

Those words cause a magical tether to snap taut between us, but my debt to her vanishes instantly. She owes me her life, twice over, and my piddly gratitude can't nix that.

She reluctantly turns and runs in the direction of my parents' house.

They'll take care of her. Now I need to take care of myself. So I use the last ounce of energy I have to teleport to the nearest vortex, which happens to be the one where my sister Pendi serves as guardian. She appears a few seconds after I arrive. I'm already lying on the ground in the center of the vortex, though not because I'm trying to make her job easier. I landed in this spot, and I can't move. The injuries that monkey-man inflicted have taken a toll, and even a fae can't stay upright after losing this much blood.

"Triskaideka," Pendi says as she kneels beside me. "What kind of trouble have you gotten into this time?"

"Kerkopes. Long story. Just heal me, okay?"

She closes her eyes.

"Have you eaten enough copper today?"

Pendi opens one eye to look at me. "Shut up, Tris. I'm trying to do my job."

"But how much—"

"I'm all fueled up. Don't worry."

She shuts her eyes again, and I can feel the healing energies cocooning my body, sinking under my skin to suffuse every cell. The pain dissipates gradually while I float on an imaginary cloud of magics. My eyes remain open throughout the healing process.

Pendi's lids flutter open. She gives me a serene smile. "It's done."

I push up into a sitting position, stretch, and yawn. "That feels better."

She punches my arm. "Now stop getting into life-or-death trouble, would you?"

"I'd love to, but I can't. Haven't you heard about the impending war with the dragon shifters?"

"No. Which dragons did you tick off?"

"Drakon's clan."

She throws her head back and groans. "Tris, you're the most trouble-some little brother I have. Even Quin isn't half as much bother."

"I don't mean to be such a pain."

Pendi sighs. "Yeah, I know."

I kiss her cheek. "Love you, sis."

"Uh-huh. I'll tell you how I feel about you after the war." She gives me a quick hug. "Try not to get destroyed."

I rush back to Coppertown, straight to the front door of my parents' house, and walk into the kitchen just in time to see them all laughing. "What's so funny?"

Pa turns to smirk at me. "Riley told us how you rescued her from the kerkopes, but then she had to save you from them too."

"I was bleeding, and you guys think it's funny."

"No. We think it's funny that a woman saved you."

"Why? I'm not a sexist. If women want to save me, I'm cool with that." I sit down at the table beside Riley and clasp her hand. "Especially if this girl's the one saving me."

Pa leans back in his chair. "So, tell us about the war you started."

CHAPTER TWENTY-EIGHT

Riley

HE DIDN'T START THE WAR," I TELL TRIS'S PARENTS. "DRAKON DID THAT. The dragon prince is insane and jealous of Tris's luck power. Tris also saved me when Cyneric nearly drained me to death."

"Cyneric?" Nyara says. "The vampire? Oh, I don't like that you two have become friends with him. I met him once, and already I know that creature is dangerous."

"We aren't friends with him. Cyneric just kind of shows up whenever he feels like it."

"You need wards, dear. He couldn't reach you then."

Tris makes a somewhat rude noise. "Yes, he can, Ma. Somehow, that vamp has the power to penetrate wards and cross the veil without Janus's permission. He was supposed to keep the vampires contained in the Unseen."

"Have you asked Janus about that?" Frimis asks.

"Not yet. I've been kind of distracted."

"It's not Tris's fault," I say. "He's doing the best he can while he's still cursed and we have the threat of war."

Tris's parents stare at me. Then they both break into big grins.

"What?" I ask. "Did I say something dumb?"

Nyara reaches across the table to pat my hand. "No, dear. We're happy you two have fallen in love, that's all."

Love? It's way too early to declare that. I like Tris a lot, and we had amazing sex. But love… No, I can't even think about that yet. Maybe after the war, we'll have time to discuss our feelings and our future, if we want to have one together.

Frimis lays a hand on his wife's arm. "Take it easy, Nyara. You're scaring poor Riley."

"I'm not scared," I say. "Well, not because of what you said. I'm terrified about this war."

"Every able-bodied adult in Coppertown will pitch in," Frimis declares. "We've done it before. When we add in Tris's friends in both worlds, and the oracle Bob, that's a darn good start on an army."

"Not sure how long we have to amass a big enough army," Tris tells his father. "Drakon is royally ticked, and he's crazy enough to try anything."

"You and your friends have a plan, though, right?"

"We do. But I'm worried my curse will screw up our plans."

"You have a new power, though. Believe in your luck and share it with your allies."

I bump my shoulder into Tris. "And you've got me. I have a special power too, you know."

"What's that?"

"You've seen it before. Remember? That's how I fooled you when we first met."

Tris just stares at me for a moment, his expression blank. Then his mouth slides into a sly grin. "Oh yeah, right. *That* power."

"What are you two talking about?" Nyara asks. "When did Riley develop elemental powers?"

"Oh, it's not elemental. Trust me, Ma, my girl can handle herself."

I love that he called me his girl. He's my guy, for sure.

"Do we have time for dinner before the battle begins?" Nyara asks. "I have leftovers if you need a quick meal."

"That would be great," I say. "A meal before we fight is a good idea."

Nyara seems more relaxed about the upcoming battle now that we've agreed to eat first. I guess every mom feels the need to take care of her children even once they're adults, and even under dire circumstances. How will this battle end? We will be victorious. I have to believe that, or I'll never get through the trials ahead of us.

Frimis and Nyara need to stay here in Coppertown. They're the elemental equivalent of an elderly couple, and Tris doesn't need to work hard to convince them to stay put. Besides, they can prepare for any wounded fae who come home in need of treatment. Both of Tris's parents have been trained in magical triage, which will make sure the wounded won't suffer too much while they wait for a spot at a healing vortex.

Wow, I just realized none of this weird stuff bothers me anymore. Talking about vortexes? No big deal. Discussing battle tactics? We handle whatever comes. Fending off dragon shifters? They'd better watch out, because we are ready to rumble.

After dinner, Tris and I head for the courtyard that serves as the town square. Everyone already knows what's going on, since Nyara informed the mayor who sent out supernatural signals to alert everyone else. Now Tris climbs onto a wooden platform and speaks to the crowd.

"We have a tough road ahead," he says. "But I know every single person in this town, and I know we can all handle it. The dragons will not destroy us or our resolve to stop them. Conjure your weapons and be ready when the call comes. Riley and I need to meet with our allies for final preparations. Be safe, be strong, and know how much we appreciate and admire all of you."

He hops off the platform.

And the crowd cheers.

Fae rush up to shake Tris's hand or hug him, and no one questions what needs to be done. The copper fae might be the most loyal and hearty individuals I've ever met. Their determination gives me a morale boost too.

The fae even hug me, and several of them kiss my cheek.

Now it's time for us to leave. The wards protecting the village allow me and Tris to exit the town, but if we come back, we'll need to wait at the village boundary for someone to let us in. Just as we're about to zip away, Frimis jogs up and shouts for us to wait. He carries a silver sword that glistens with a sheen of copper.

"Take this," Frimis tells his son. "This endued sword has seen me through more battles than I can count. It will serve you well."

"Pa, this is—" Tris gets a little choked up, then clears his throat and slaps his dad's arm. "This is amazing. I'm honored to bear your sword in the coming battle."

Frimis nods curtly, and tears shimmer in his eyes. "Take care of each other. We'll see you on the other side."

Of the battle, I hope he means. Not the other side of death. But I refuse to think that way. We will prevail.

Now that everything is set, we have nothing to do except wait for the dragons to attack. Fortunately, Bob stops by as we're leaving the fae village, and he tells us he has foreseen the time and place for the war. Though Bob remains trapped in his lair because of the rogue kerkopes, his ability to astral project means he can still participate in the big battle to come. Another bit of good luck for us. Did my boyfriend subconsciously engage his new power to help Bob give us the information we need? I don't know, and it doesn't matter, not now. Maybe later we'll all discuss luck and curses and fate.

Our friends meet us in a place called Fae Valley, where Bob told us the war would begin—in exactly fifty-two minutes from when we last saw him. These fae really need to get more creative with their place names. But Tris told me this valley is a gathering place for all fae tribes, not just the leprechauns, so I guess it makes sense to give it a generic name.

Tris and I gather with his fourteen siblings to discuss our strategy. The sylphs turn up next, followed quickly by the salamanders, both male and female, all of whom wear coppery metal armor. I guess they forgo nudity when a war is on. Max and Travis seem to have taken the lead with the salamander battalion, who all carry swords. The sylphs also have swords. Whether they're endued, I can't say. But I sure hope those blades are invested with enough magics to destroy the dragons.

The fae battalion consists of several platoons—copper fae, silver fae, gold fae, and more. Yeah, the elementals actually use military terms from the mortal world. The fae have weapons, mostly bows and arrows, but also blades that resemble machetes. The undines join us too, though I'm still fuzzy on what kind of elemental they are. Those guys wield small, curved swords that have jagged edges.

We have our army.

Tris and I move to one end of the clearing, where the ground rises a bit like a natural stage. He sucks in a big breath and hollers, "Listen up, everybody!"

All the battalions turn to face us and listen.

But Tris looks tired. Is it the curse? Or just stress? Maybe his magical adrenaline boost is wearing off.

"Bob has told us the battle will begin any minute," Tris announces. "With Bob's help, Ennea and her fellow witches have super-endued all the weapons they could, but not all of you received that gift. They couldn't do that for everyone without stripping all their own magics. Now, keep your eyes peeled, stay calm but alert, and remember the plan. Riley will be up first. Now, take your positions."

The elementals all scatter into the woods that surround the large field where the battle will begin. Some of the warriors will glamour to become invisible and hide their positions that way, while others prefer to apply mundane camouflage face paint to blend into the background. Glamouring is more like holographic camouflage, or that's how my brain interpreted the explanation Tris gave me.

Tris and I remain in the clearing alone.

"What does super-endued mean?" I ask.

"It's a way stronger version of enduing a weapon that will hopefully allow us to destroy the dragons. Takes a huge amount of magics to make that happen, so the witches need to relax and recharge now."

He means they've done their part, and now it's up to the rest of us to save the world.

Tris takes my hands in his hands and gazes at me with a depth of emotion I've never seen before. "Whatever happens, I need you to do your thing and then get the hell out of the line of fire. You're way more vulnerable than the rest of us."

Because I can die. They can't—unless an endued weapon or magically enhanced poison gets them. I'm not offended by his statement that I'm vulnerable and should hide once the real fight begins. I nearly died when Cyneric sank his fangs into my throat. So yeah, I'll stick to the plan.

A figure appears on the far side of the field.

Oh, no. It can't be him.

Tris's lip curls, and he snarls, "Cyneric. That bastard has some nerve showing up here."

He zips us down to where the vampire waits. He seems as unreadable and stoic as usual, though he avoids looking at me. His stunningly pale blue eyes almost glow in the fading light of the sun, though he stays just beyond the reach of daylight, in the shadows of the trees. Soon, he won't need shade anymore. The sun will have set by the time the battle begins.

"What do you want?" Tris asks the vamp.

"To help. I can fight."

"And how many people will you eat in the process? How many allies, I mean. You can chow down on the dragons all you want."

"I have no wish to drink from any of you, and in fact, I cannot tolerate your blood anymore." Cyneric flicks his gaze to me, then focuses on my boyfriend again. "But I cannot guarantee that I will be capable of controlling the hunger in the heat of battle. I might consume anyone's blood if I become too weak."

"Then leave. We don't need you."

"I must stay."

My guy is about to get nasty with the vamp, I can tell. He's fuming. But we don't have time to argue with Cyneric, and we can't stop him from doing whatever he wants. All we can do is pray he doesn't harm our allies.

"Let him stay," I tell Tris. "He'll do what he wants, anyway. Might as well see if he can be useful. All hands on deck, right?"

"This is an army, not the navy." Tris sighs. "Okay, Captain Fang, you can fight with us."

Cyneric nods once, then retreats into the deeper shadows inside the woods.

Here in the Unseen, the sun sets quickly, and the two moons rise just as fast. Their milky glow provides all the illumination we need. They are much brighter than Earth's moon.

Bob pops in to tell us the dragons will arrive at any moment.

Tris cups my face in his hands and kisses me. I feel magic tingling over my skin and sinking deeper to suffuse my entire being. I can't breathe because the intensity of those magics combined with his intoxicating kiss steals my breath. When he peels his lips away from mine, he pecks a kiss on my nose. "That should give you enough luck to last through the battle."

But he seems more tired than earlier, though he manages a spry gait when he hurries back to the elevated far end of the field.

Earlier, he had thrown out a net of magics, as he called it, that would spread good luck to our entire army. I retreat to the edge of the woods and wait. I'll be up first once the dragons arrive. I might not have actual armor, but Tris believes his new power will protect me. I trust him with my life, so I know what he says must be true.

Drakon materializes in the center of the field. He spreads his wings and his arms. "Come out, little leprechaun. It's time for me to destroy you. Or are you too cowardly to face me?"

This is my moment.

I traipse out onto the field, wearing the outfit Tris loved when we first met—shorts, a tank top, a gauzy cover-up shirt, and hiking boots. I twirl around and around, humming and singing "la-dee-da" while I make my way toward the dragon shifter. He stares at me while wearing a baffled expression, and his gaze tracks my every movement. I fling my arms wide and dance in a circle around Drakon.

"La, la, la," I sing. "The dragon is here. La, la, la."

Drakon grabs my wrist to stop me. "You seemed reasonably intelligent back in my club. But I suppose having nearly all of your blood drained from your body caused brain damage."

"Brain what?" I say with a giggle. "Can you conjure liquor? I'd love some bourbon or rum. Mm, rummmm. That word feels yummy on my tongue."

Drakon releases my wrist and studies me with squinted eyes. "Are you drunk?"

"I don't think so. What does drunk feel like?" I spin in a circle around him, and out of the corner of my eye, I glimpse the army sneaking into position. "Would you like to dance with me? I bet dragons are great dancers."

The crown prince of the western dragon shifters scrunches up his entire face.

"La-dee-da," I sing as I raise my arms above my head and link my fingers. "The moons are so pretty. Do you think they smile? Maybe I'm having double vision. Or are there really two moons up there? I bet one has blue cheese, and the other has yellow cheese."

Drakon draws his head back. "Cheese? You are insane, child, but I'll still fuck you."

"Really? Oh, that's nice."

Peripherally, I notice that the army is in position. So I give up my ditz act and pat Drakon's chest. "You're not too bright, are you?"

He tries to grab my wrist again, but I vanish before he can do it. Oh, yes. He isn't too bright at all.

Because our army now surrounds him.

Chapter Twenty-Nine

Tris

RILEY IS INCREDIBLE. WHEN SHE TALKED ME INTO HER PLAN TO GO FULL-on ditz to distract Drakon, I'd agreed with reservations. I trust her, and I know she's a strong woman. But Drakon is a powerful shifter. He wouldn't fall for her dumb-blonde routine, would he? Of course he did. Riley is just that good.

Though we now surround Drakon, only a portion of our army has revealed itself. And we know the rest of the dragon shifters will show up any minute. I brandish the sword my father had given me and that Ennea had super-endued. She spent hours today enhancing the weapons of everyone in our army. We're as ready as we'll ever be.

The flapping of wings draws our attention to the sky as more dragon shifters land to flank their leader, the crown prince of western dragondom. But they haven't come alone. The dragons brought their skankiest buddies—the harpies and the kerkopes.

"Surrender now," Drakon growls at me. "And perhaps I will spare your pitiful army."

"No dice. We're ready to fight."

"As you wish, then."

Drakon conjures a sword and roars as he rushes at me. I sidestep him and swipe my blade toward him, but he flies up away from me to swoop down behind me. I spin around and jab him in the side. He snarls, thrusting his sword at my belly, but I zip behind him. His blade meets air. I grasp my sword in both hands, about to jam it into Drakon's back, when he flies into the sky again.

Everywhere around me, our army clashes with dragons, harpies, and kerkopes. I see the bad guys fall, screaming in agony as destruction devours their bodies. No, it's not a pretty sight. But Drakon and his gang left us no choice.

The dragon prince whumps down behind me. I hear him, though I can't see him, yet I know it's Drakon. I whirl around and jab at him, but he parries and laughs.

"You are pitiful," he says. "A leprechaun is no match for a primordial elemental like me."

I slice my blade across his midsection, but that kind of wound isn't enough to trigger destruction. I need to inflict a much more grievous injury. The cacophony of swords clashing and arrows whacking into bodies fills the air. I smell blood too, which makes me worry about Cyneric. But I don't have time to focus on him.

Drakon flies up to hover above my head and slash his sword down at me. I jump around to avoid his strikes, but he slices me a few times. Not enough to kill me, though. I glance sideways to check on everybody else, and I see Riley hiding behind a tree. My night vision is excellent, and the full moons provide even more light. I wish Riley wouldn't make herself so visible. Drakon slashes at my legs, causing me to stumble and fall onto my back. Then he grasps the hilt of his sword and drops down to straddle me, about to ram that blade straight into my chest.

A shape soars through the air, sailing down toward me and the dragon. Cyneric snares Drakon's wing and yanks him off me, then hurls the dragon halfway across the clearing.

Did the bloodsucker just save my life? No way in hell will I thank him for that. Indebting myself to a vamp is not on my to-do list. And I wonder why Cyneric helped me. He's obsessed with my girlfriend, after all.

Cyneric stands near my feet, breathing hard, his fists clenched. "Where is Riley?"

"Safe. Stay away from her, Captain Fang."

He races into the fray, and I can't see where he went or what he's doing. Not guzzling anybody's blood, I hope.

A scream reverberates through the battleground, so piercing that it breaks through the melee.

Riley.

But she doesn't sound terrified. No, that seems like an angry scream.

I zip myself straight to the edge of the trees, where Riley is struggling with Drakon, who has her pinned to his body with one arm under her breasts and his free hand clamped around her throat. She kicks and thrashes and tries to bite him, but she can't hurt him enough to even make him wince. He's too big, too strong, and too determined.

Riley finally manages to twist her head around and sink her teeth into his forearm.

Drakon growls. "You stupid little—"

"Shut up, monkey brains," I snarl. "Let her go."

"I think I'll kill her instead."

Lunging toward him, I pierce his shoulder with my endued sword, but that wound isn't enough to trigger destruction. I can't hit him anywhere else, not with Riley trapped in his arms. As strong and brave as she is, she can't fight a powerful elemental warrior.

Drakon laughs. "A pinprick won't kill me, you brainless little fae." He tightens his grip on her throat, which makes her choke. "Watch your lover die."

I know he's about to snap her neck. I can see the intent in his eyes and in the way his fingers twitch in anticipation of the kill. The only way I can destroy him is if I thrust my sword straight through his chest, preferably his heart. But doing that would kill Riley too. I try teleporting her to me, but Drakon must have magics that prevent me from doing that. He came prepared, and he wants to force me to watch Riley die.

I can think of only one thing to do. I conjure a dagger that technically belongs to my brother Quin, and it appears in Riley's hand. Her eyes widen for a split second as she tightens her fingers around the dagger.

She flips it around and rams the blade into Drakon's privates.

He howls and staggers backward.

Riley races to me, and I place my body in front of hers, wielding my sword. I'm starting to feel weak, probably from the curse, but I can't stop fighting now. My adrenaline boost must be fading too. Though I want to teleport Riley to someplace far away from the battle, I doubt I can do that. I'm getting weaker every minute. I should never have let her join the fray. I had foolishly assumed I could stay strong through the battle.

But I can't. I'm dying, and I can feel it.

Drakon straightens and conjures his sword. "Your girl will pay for that little stunt later, after I've dispatched you."

"Like hell. You're the one who's going down."

He chuckles. "I've given the curse more vigor. You'll be dead in ten minutes at most."

I hate that fire-breathing asshole so much.

Drakon laughs again, louder this time, and he sounds way too gleeful.

I push Riley further behind me, grip my sword in both hands, and lunge for Drakon. He vanishes, and I fall face-first onto the ground, getting a mouthful of grass and dirt, while the sword pops out of my hand. It flies backward, out of my sight.

Riley screams—in anger again. Then she hollers, "Tris! Watch out!"

I roll onto my back.

And Drakon bends forward to plunge his sword down toward my chest. I watch as the blade lowers in slow motion, but I know that's an illusion. My brain has slowed everything down, and I can't seem to move a muscle.

Riley tackles Drakon from behind, screaming like an enraged banshee, and slices her dagger across his throat. The dragon shifter shakes her off with one violent twist of his torso. She tries to jump on his back again, but he glances back and sees her coming. When he spreads his wings, she gets knocked backward. Drakon turns sideways to me and Riley, glancing back and forth between us like he can't decide who to kill first.

I struggle to my knees, and though I want to stand, I wobble so much that I can't go any higher than a kneeling position. "Forget about her, Drakon. You want me."

"Might as well get rid of you first, then defile your sweet girl."

I can feel all the luck I'd acquired with my new power sifting away from me, along with my energy and magics. The way Drakon is looking at Riley makes me want to clobber him, but I can barely stay on my knees. I cannot let him have her, but I know of only one way to get her out of here, to a safe place. I haul in the biggest breath I can and shout, "Cyneric! Riley needs you."

Riley stares at me, her eyes wide.

The vamp appears beside her.

Drakon roars and punches his sword through my torso. He doesn't hit my heart. Whether the blow is enough to destroy me, I have no idea.

"Get Riley away from here," I tell Cyneric. Blood streams from my mouth. "Now, you bastard. Save her."

"No!" Riley screams. She tries to rush for me, but Cyneric seizes her around the waist and hoists her off the ground. She claws at his hands, to no avail. "No, Cyneric, let me go!"

They both vanish.

Drakon brandishes his blood-drenched sword, twirling it like he's giving an exhibition for spectators. But no one else is paying attention. They're too busy fighting for their lives, and I'm too busy dying to care. Am I dying? Drakon has an endued sword, but he missed my heart. The rules of destruction can get murky in a situation like this. The fact that I'm still breathing seems like a good sign.

I might hate Cyneric, but I know he will protect Riley, no matter what.

Travis appears beside me. "Tris, what…"

Drakon flourishes his big, black sword. "I have destroyed him. That's what happened."

"If he were destroyed, he wouldn't be lying there bleeding." Travis brandishes his own sword. "You missed the mark, you tosser. Are all dragons too stupid to know where an elemental's heart is?"

Drakon growls. "I can finish the job right now—after I behead you."

The world grows darker every minute, but I can still see Travis and Drakon battling like shadows on a wall, their swords clashing. Since I've never been destroyed before, I don't what it's supposed to feel like. I want to close my eyes and just let go of everything. But I've seen elementals die. They don't fade away. They scream and thrash while the scalding magics rip them apart down to the tiniest molecule, then the remnants float away on the breeze.

I don't feel like that.

Cyneric took Riley. Sure, I told him to do it. But I don't trust that guy, which means I need to get up and go find them. If I'm not dying, then I can do this. Ennea mentioned I would experience a crash once the adrenaline shot wore off. The curse has made the crash worse, I'm sure, but I can fight it.

A manlike shape flies past me, whumping down a few feet away from my head. Is that Travis? Or Drakon?

Get up and do something, moron, right now.

I suck in the deepest breath I can muster and exhale it slowly, repeating the process again and again until I feel a seed of energy, both physical and magical, growing inside me. The warmth of it enlivens my body, and I keep chanting in my head. *You can do it, you're not dying, you can do it, you're not dying.* The pulse beats faster and stronger. My vision gradually clears and sharpens. The noises around me grow louder, and I can make out words too.

"You are about to die, salamander," Drakon growls. "Say goodbye to everyone you love."

I push up onto my elbows and blink swiftly until the last of the blurriness clears up. Then I see it. Drakon has Travis pinned to the ground, and my friend seems dazed. Why doesn't he whisk himself away? Maybe Drakon injured Travis, and he doesn't have the energy to teleport. I sit up and glance around, searching for my sword.

There. I see it lying on the ground about six feet away—right next to Drakon's big, booted foot.

I feel a lot better now. But do I have the strength to conjure my sword? One way to find out. I focus on the sword and will it to come to me, squeezing my entire face into what must look like an agonized expression. But I don't feel agony. I'm concentrating harder than I've ever needed to before, that's all.

The sword appears in my hand. *Eureka.*

Drakon finally notices me and turns his head to glance my way. His lips peel back from his teeth. He growls and gnashes his teeth like an enraged bull.

I lunge at Drakon just as Travis does the same. My sword punches into the dragon's lower back while Travis plunges his blade into Drakon's belly. I doubt either blow will destroy the bastard, but I have bigger problems.

Drakon roars, but the sound quickly transforms into an anguished howl. He vanishes.

I offer Travis my hand to help him get up off the ground. "You okay?"

"Yes. What about you? I thought I was about to watch your body turn to molecular dust."

"That's what I thought too. But I'm okay, for now."

"Good." Travis eyes me with a strange expression. "I, ah, saw Cyneric take Riley away."

"I know. I told him to do that, but now I need to find them both. Can't trust the vamp."

"Go on. We'll keep fighting until someone finally takes Drakon down."

"I think it's time for Riley's plan B. Think you can handle that?"

His mouth slides into a devilish grin. "Oh yes, we can handle it. Your girlfriend is a genius, by the way."

"Yeah, I know. Be careful, Travis."

"Don't worry about us. Go get Riley."

Since I have no idea where Cyneric took Riley, I focus on her and pray my vague targeting will get me where I need to go. And I pray everyone I love will survive this battle.

Chapter Thirty

Riley

CYNERIC SETS US DOWN NEAR THE HEALING VORTEX BEHIND THE ROCK shop. When Tris takes me into and out of the Unseen, we need to stop inside the cavern behind the falls to open or close the portal. Then if we're heading into the mortal world, we have to jump through the waterfall and jump off the rock ledge onto the ground.

But the vampire didn't do any of that.

Tris told him to take me away, and poof, we appeared right in this spot, mere feet from the healing vortex. How is that possible? Cyneric is far more powerful than anyone realized, which makes him far more dangerous too.

But right now, I care only about what happened to Tris.

"Take me back to the battle," I tell the vamp. "Right now."

"I will not."

"Yes, you will. Right now, Cyneric."

He shakes his head.

I plant my hands on my hips. "Since when do you follow orders from Tris? You don't even like him."

"The leprechaun was correct when he commanded me to spirit you away to a safe place."

"No, he was not. He acted based on fear."

"You should remain here. Safe."

I step closer to the vampire, angling my head back to nail him with my best steely glare. Not that I've ever tried to intimidate anyone. I'm desperate and pissed off, and though I understand why Tris wanted Cyneric to take me somewhere else, I will not just wait here to find out if Drakon murdered him and all our friends and allies.

"Listen to me, Cyneric," I say in the toughest voice I can muster. "I need to go back to the battlefield. Do I seem like a wuss who wants to hide while everyone I care about might be dying? The answer is no, I am not that kind of person."

"You must remain here."

"Screw that. Take me back to the battlefield now, or I'll find a way to get there myself."

Cyneric stares at me without expression. The intensity of his gaze makes every fine hair on my body stiffen, and a shiver rushes through me. But I will not let him see how much he unsettles me. So I lift my chin and square my shoulders.

The vampire's gaze drifts down to my mouth. He licks his lips, and his nostrils flare.

No, I don't like that at all. I try to take a step backward.

Cyneric seizes my upper arms and hauls me into his body, then lifts me up to crush his mouth to mine.

I hold perfectly still, my heart racing and my eyes wide open, while the vampire presses his lips to mine even harder. His eyes are open too, and they swirl with shades of blood red and shimmering silver, like a hurricane of lust and hunger. He wants me. For more than a snack. I can feel his dick hardening. Cyneric wants to have sex with me, and I'm not entirely sure he cares how I feel about that.

So I ram my knee into his groin.

He grunts and jerks his head back, but maintains his hold on me. His voice becomes a rough growl. "Want me."

"No, I don't want you. I love Tris."

"I have tasted your blood, and it was the sweetest nourishment I have ever had. You must be my fated mate."

"Afraid not. I belong with Tris. He is my fated mate, not you."

I can't believe I said that, but I meant it. In this moment, when an off-balance vampire wants to fuck me and drink my blood, I suddenly realize the truth. Being with Tris is my destiny. Nothing that happened since I came to Michigan happened by accident. A force beyond our control brought me to Tris, and though we chose to be together, fate gave us the nudges we needed. We both had issues that made us doubt ourselves and each other, but we have overcome all of that.

Cyneric mashes me to his body more tightly. His hot breaths gust over my face, and I swear I can smell the faint metallic scent of blood on his breath. "You are mine."

"No. If you force me to have sex with you, there will be no turning back. You will be destroyed, and my boyfriend will make sure of that."

"No one can stop me."

"Is this really what you want to become? A rapist? The kind of creep who abuses women for his own pleasure? Maybe you'll ensorcell me so I'll have no choice but to enjoy it. But underneath the fake pleasure, I will hate you until the day I die."

Cyneric stares at me, but something in his eyes makes me wonder. Have I gotten through to him? Does he understand the consequences? Most important of all, does he want to stop himself?

"Don't do this," I say. "Think about what you'll become if you assault me. If you really care about me, you will stop."

The vampire's grip on me loosens just enough that I slide down his body until my feet touch the ground. Whorls of white and ice blue clash in his eyes. Are those the colors of fear? His lips fall open. His gaze searches mine.

Cyneric is yanked backward. His body flies through the air until it smacks into a tree. He slumps to the ground.

Tris stands a few feet from where the vampire had been a moment ago. Though blood soaks one side of his shirt, and he seems rather pale, he still clenches his fists tightly. His shoulders bunch up. A muscle jumps in his jaw. He speaks through gritted teeth as he says, "What the hell was that bloodsucker doing to you?"

I won't lie, especially not after what Cyneric just did. I believe he realized he had gone too far, but I will not cover up for him. "He kissed me. Then he seemed to think I'd want to have sex with him."

"He did what?" Tris's eyes flare with the hottest red I've ever seen. "I am going to beat him down so hard."

"We have bigger problems right now. Let's get back to the battle and worry about Cyneric later."

I focus on Tris and the dark circles under his eyes, not to mention his bloody shirt. "Are you okay?"

"Not yet. But I will be." He marches into the healing vortex. "Give me a minute."

Cyneric watches me while I watch Tris. My boyfriend settles onto a stone bench and shuts his eyes. Then he just sits there. After a few minutes, he rises and sighs while stretching his entire body.

"All better," he says as he strides up to me.

He does look better. The color has returned to his face.

Tris doesn't try to talk me out of going with him this time. He throws a molten glare at the vamp, then slings an arm around me and whisks us away.

We materialize in the center of the field.

Everywhere around us, our friends and allies wage war against the dragons and their allies. But the harpies don't seem to be participating anymore. The salamanders have surrounded them, and the harpies appear dazed.

Tris teleports us directly to the salamander battalion. Max and Travis grin when they see us.

"Welcome back," Max announces. "Did you sneak away for a quick shag?"

Tris rolls his eyes. "No. It's a long story that we'll tell you later."

Max spreads an arm to indicate the dazed harpies. "How do you like what we've done? Riley's idea worked like a charm."

"You actually did it?" I say.

"That's right. Every last salamander on the field, incubus and succubus alike, sent out a massive blast of pheromones that stunned the harpies." He smirks. "Now they all want to shag us."

A harpy sidles up to Max and drags the tips of her talons down his cheek. "Remove your armor and show me what a salamander can do."

"I'm married, pet. Try one of the other salamanders."

The harpy pouts, but saunters away to hook up with someone else.

My plan worked. Wow.

Tris hooks an arm around me. "This was all your idea, Riley. You pulled your ditz routine on Drakon, then you spearheaded the campaign to defeat the harpies with pheromones. You rock."

I can't help grinning.

But a battle still rages at the other end of the field. We need to do something to end the war. Could my idea be expanded?

I clear my throat, which draws the attention of Max, Travis, and Tris. "Could you guys hit the kerkopes with a big dose of pheromones? Like you did with the harpies?"

Travis lifts his brows, then shrugs. "Why not? Let's give it a go."

Max and Travis gather several other salamanders and pop over to the section of the battlefield where the kerkopes keep dive-bombing our allies. Tris and I watch for a moment as the salamanders unleash their pheromones on the monkey-men. Are they all male? I have no idea. When they abducted me, I couldn't tell what kind of genitalia they have, if any. Now, the kerkopes land near the salamanders. They approach the incubi and succubi at a slow pace, and they begin to sway slightly as if they're drunk.

On pheromones, I'm sure.

A huge, winged figure dives out of the sky, barreling toward us with such speed that we barely have time to recognize what that shape is—a dragon shifter aiming straight for us.

Tris pushes me out of the way. "Go! Hide in the woods."

He conjures his father's endued sword, the one Ennea enhanced to increase its killing power.

"Tris, no, I—"

"*Go*, Riley. He's wicked strong, and I can't worry about you while I fight him. Don't make me invoke your debts to me."

"Okay. But one thing first." I fling my arms around him and mash my mouth to his. A strange feeling of electricity zings through me, and the strength of it steals my breath for a moment. When I pull my mouth away, I feel a touch lightheaded. "Be careful."

"Don't worry. I'm not dying today."

I sprint into the woods but stay close enough that I can run out there if something goes wrong, then I hide behind a massive tree. From here, I can peek around the trunk while still hiding. I wish I had a weapon.

Tris has luck on his side. His new power assures that.

Drakon hits the ground hard, making the earth shudder. He unbends his knees and raises his sword. "Time to end you, little fae."

Tris wields his sword, twirling it in elegant half-circles. "Bring it on, birdbrain."

Drakon flaps his wings, flying up just enough to hover above Tris's head. Then he dives at Tris while gripping his sword in both hands, held at belly level. Tris bends his knees while gazing up at the dragon as if he's waiting for the right moment to strike. Just as Drakon thrusts his blade out for the kill, Tris leaps out of the way, and the dragon shifter winds up plunging his sword deep into the ground.

Tris whacks the flat face of his blade into the dragon's back.

Drakon shouts and struggles to free his weapon, but ends up smacking facedown onto the ground.

Tris grasps his sword with both hands, raises it, and thrusts the blade straight through Drakon's back, pinning him to the ground. Tris wrestles his weapon free of the shifter's body.

Has he wounded Drakon enough to destroy him?

Drakon abandons his sword and leaps to his feet. The wound Tris inflicted went through the shifter's chest, but must have missed his heart. Drakon unfurls his wings and swipes them back and forth in front of him, forcing Tris to keep hopping out of the way. When the dragon opens his mouth and spews a roaring gust of fire breath, it brushes Tris's shirt and sets it on fire.

He slaps his palms on his shirt until he's doused the fire. "You jackass. I loved this T-shirt."

Since he had to drop his sword to snuff out the fire, he now snags his weapon again.

Drakon leans to the side and sweeps one wing to hurl Tris up into the air, then spin him several times fast. When Drakon releases him, Tris hits the ground so hard that the sword flies out of his hand, and he seems momentarily dazed.

The sword lands no more than six feet from me.

Drakon heaves his blade out of the earth and rushes at Tris, who still hasn't recovered his wits. The shifter plunges his blade down toward Tris's chest.

I bolt out of the woods and snare Tris's weapon along the way, heading for the battling duo, not thinking about the consequences of what I intend to do. Not thinking much at all. It's pure instinct. I reach Drakon and Tris just as the sword is about to plunge into Tris's chest. I raise my sword and scream with rage as I slash the blade toward Drakon's neck.

The sword lodges partway into his throat. Blood pours from the wound, and Drakon freezes while gurgling.

I try to yank the blade free, but it's jammed in his neck.

Tris rolls out from under Drakon an instant before the shifter falls to the ground. He's still alive, though, and still bleeding profusely. Tris jumps up and smacks his feet down on Drakon's neck. The sword's blade slices all the way through the shifter's throat, severing his head.

I'm breathing hard, unable to move or speak. I can't even tear my gaze away from the headless dragon shifter.

"Step away from him," Tris tells me. "He's about to be destroyed."

We both back away to the edge of the woods.

Drakon wails in agony and clutches at his head while rocking side to side. His eyes bulge, his jaw gapes, and every muscle in his body convulses as the searing energies of destruction eat away at his body. They slither into his nostrils and mouth, making him gag and convulse. A curtain of pure white energy arcs over him like electricity as Drakon screams.

This is destruction. Tris had mentioned it to me several times, but he never explained it in detail. Now, as we watch Drakon disintegrate, Tris cradles me to his body while the shifter blurs and dissolves, the particles of his atomizing flesh swirling in the air and spiraling up toward the sky as a fine mist that eventually dissipates.

Drakon, Crown Prince of the Western Kingdom of Dragon Shifters, is dead. For good. Forever.

We are free.

CHAPTER THIRTY-ONE

RILEY AND I RETURN TO THE BATTLEFIELD TO CHECK ON EVERYONE who had fought with us. We lost three allies—two sylphs and a silver fae. Though we mourn every loss, we're grateful that more hadn't died because of Drakon's arrogance and his determination to destroy me. The rest of the dragon shifters gave up swiftly once they realized Drakon was dead, and that we had incapacitated the kerkopes and the harpies, the only allies the dragons had.

The woman I love saved my life. We destroyed Drakon together. At least it's over now, and we can move on with our lives.

But how will we move on? Together? Apart? I'm an elemental, she's a mortal, and those facts make merging our lives very complicated. We don't know each other as well as we'd like. All the insanity that happened since the day I met Riley complicated the heck out of everything. Now we have time to figure things out. And that's unsettling. Not sure why. Well, maybe it's because of Cyneric and the fact that I have no idea where he went or when he might show up again to do…whatever he wants to do. To Riley. To me. To whoever he wants. We can't stop him, not even with endued weapons.

Will he ever get over his obsession with Riley? Cyneric needs to move on too. Even an unbalanced vampire must realize that.

I spirit Riley away to my parents' house to let them know the battle is over and we won. They seem anxious when we walk into the house to surprise them, but then they realize we've brought good news, and they start grinning. We believe my curse ended when Drakon died, but we haven't gotten confirmation of that from Bob. He was summoned by the Four Winds for an ethereal confab in the clouds. We'll have to wait a while to find out for sure.

One thing I do know without any doubts. Riley's determination and love helped me survive until Drakon bit the dust, but her kiss gave me the power to keep going despite my curse. I can't prove that, but I know it's true. She kissed me right before Drakon made his final attack.

After spending the night in my childhood bedroom, we enjoy a big breakfast with Ma and Pa, as well as all fourteen of my siblings. Riley smiles while she watches me helping Pa set the table for our morning feast, which requires opening up a wall in the dining room to accommodate the very long table we need for gatherings of the entire brood. Riley loves chatting with every member of my family, but especially Quin and Ennea. They share stories about me that make Riley laugh so hard tears roll down her cheeks.

I had absolved Riley of her debts to me the instant the battle ended. I'd forgotten about that until then. She's with me now because she wants to be, not because of a magical tether that binds her to me.

After the feast, we say goodbye to my family. Riley announces it's time to introduce me to her parents. I assure her I don't mind if she wants to wait until we know each other better, but she insists she doesn't want to delay any longer. I can understand that. Sometimes it's better to just get things over with, because a person's expectations can be worse than the reality.

I need to tell Riley something first, though. We've just crossed the veil, and I manage to dry us off with a gust of air once we touch down by the wooden railing. My energy level has skyrocketed since we destroyed Drakon. Yeah, my curse must be gone. But I don't understand why I feel even better now than I did before a dragon jackass hexed me.

No more worrying. I need to tell Riley that thing I've been thinking about a lot this morning. She starts to walk down the trail, but I halt her with a hand on her arm.

"What is it?" she asks.

"I need to tell you something."

"Okay." She watches me and waits. But when I just stand here like an oak tree, she clasps my hand. "Whatever it is, you can say it. Don't you trust me?"

"All the way."

She slides her arms around my waist. "Then tell me."

"Okay." I suck in a breath and do it. "I love you, Riley."

"I love you too, Tris. Was that the thing you needed to say?"

"Yeah, it was."

She raises onto her tiptoes to kiss me. "See? It was nothing to worry about."

Riley loves me too. But I still don't know how we can merge our lives. For now, I won't worry about that. First, I need to support Riley while she deals with the bombshell she's about to drop on her parents. She grows more anxious as we head for the rock shop, and I think she's worrying about how to introduce me to her parents. I'm currently glamouring to appear more human, which will give her mom and dad time to adjust to all our revelations before we reveal my true nature. In the rock garden, we stop so Riley can pull out her cell phone and call her parents to let them know she's coming home—with her new boyfriend. After the call, Riley tells me her parents are happy she met someone, but they "show their enthusiasm in the subdued way they adopted after the humiliation of being ridiculed by their fellow scientists and losing their jobs."

I get that. There's nothing like ridicule to make someone wary of getting to know other people. Maybe what we're going to tell her parents today will reinvigorate their love for cryptids. And I think I've finally got the hang of pronouncing that word.

Riley and I wander down to the rock shop so we can share the good news with Nevan and Lindsey. They cheer and hug us when we explain how we took down Drakon. Then it's time to head for Galena, Illinois, where Riley's parents have lived ever since they lost their zoo jobs. Now they've become science teachers, working for an online school. They enjoy their jobs, Riley tells me, but she feels like they'd rather be working at a zoo again. Right before she called her parents earlier, we had both agreed she ought to fib a little. Since we didn't want to drop that bomb yet, she couldn't explain that we would arrive via teleportation. So Riley told them we would "fly" there. Which is sort of true. I mean, I do often refer to teleporting as "whisking" and "zipping," words that could indicate flight. Okay, yeah, Riley had to lie. But for a good reason.

Now, I whisk us to her parents' house, and she knocks on the door.

When it swings open, a woman who looks like an older version of Riley smiles at us with more joy than I'd expected. Subdued? Yeah, right. The woman drags Riley into a suffocating hug while babbling about how beautiful her daughter looks and how gorgeous her boyfriend is. I can't understand the rest of what she says. It's genuine babbling.

Riley gives me a confused look.

A man walks up behind her mom and encourages her to stop suffocating their daughter. Then he gives Riley a hug and shakes my hand.

"It's great to meet you," he says. Then Mr. Jordan looks at his daughter. "Are you going to introduce us? Or do I need to do that myself?"

"Oh, sorry, Dad. I forgot."

"Come inside first."

We all head into the living room, where Riley's parents sit in matching armchairs, side by side. Riley and I take the sofa that also matches the chairs. Photos of animals, taken at zoos and in the wild, cover every wall. Her parents might have lost their faith in the colleagues they'd thought of as friends, the ones who turned on them, but they've held on to their love of wildlife and nature. Just like their daughter.

"Mom, Dad," Riley says. "This is my boyfriend, Tris. He's a wonderful man, and I know you'll love him. Tris, meet my dad, Glenn Jordan, and my mom, Valerie."

Mrs. Jordan smiles so hard that her cheeks dimple, then she clasps her hands on her lap. "We're just tickled pink to meet you, Tris. Where are you from?"

Riley and I exchange glances. Should we tell them the whole truth now? Or wait a little longer? It's her decision, not mine.

"Guess you don't want to talk about yourself," Glenn says to me. "Are you an escaped fugitive or something?"

"No, Dad, he's not." Riley glances at me again and smiles. I think she's waiting for me to confirm it's time to tell the truth, so I nod. She sits up straighter, faces her parents, and dives in. "This is going to sound insane, but I swear it's all true. We'll prove it to you. When I told you I was going to Michigan on vacation, that was, um, not the whole truth. I went there because I'd found a lead in a discussion forum that led me to believe I might find cryptids in the woods behind a certain rock shop."

"Oh, Riley," Valerie says as she exhales a long sigh. "You shouldn't have done that. You have a good job. If anyone finds out you're studying things that don't exist, you might get fired or at least become a laughingstock. We don't want that to happen to you."

"I don't care. Being a flight attendant was awesome, but I've found something far more rewarding and exciting. Besides, I got fired a while back. Somebody found out I'm interested in cryptids, and my bosses thought that was unprofessional."

"Riley, we had no idea. Why didn't you tell us?"

She hunches her shoulders. "I was embarrassed."

"We made you feel that way, didn't we? I'm so sorry, sweetie."

"It's not your fault." Riley grasps my hand, like she needs an anchor before she can go on. "I haven't told you the good part yet."

They seem skeptical, and I'm sure we'll need to give them proof of what Riley is about to say. I'm cool with that. We both knew we'd need to expose my true nature to convince her parents. Once they see, though, I bet they'll accept the truth quickly. After all, they spent years researching mysterious creatures. Now their daughter has brought one home.

Riley grips my hand more tightly and keeps her focus on her parents. "I found cryptids. Lots of them. They're real, but they aren't exactly how we expected them to be. When I got to Michigan, I bumped into Tris—and that's when I learned the truth. There's another world parallel to this one, and the creatures that live in it are more fantastic than you guys ever could've imagined."

We glance at each other, and I know it's time. So I stand up. "My full name is Triskaideka, and I was born in the Unseen realm. I'm a copper fae, or if you prefer, a leprechaun."

Glenn rolls his eyes. "This is not a funny practical joke."

"Not a joke, sir." I release my glamour, revealing my true appearance as a mostly human-looking man with glowing, swirling eyes. "I am a leprechaun. Mortals have silly ideas about what we're like."

Riley's parents just stare at me.

I raise a hand, palm up, and conjure a flower unlike anything anyone in the mortal world has ever seen. It's gorgeous and alien, beyond exotic by mortal standards, exactly the sort of thing Riley's parents ought to love. I offer the flower to Valerie. "For you, Mrs. Jordan. A gift from my world."

She gapes at me for a few seconds, then accepts the flower and takes a delicate sniff. Her eyes widen. "That scent, it's unbelievable."

"You're holding a moon flower that was cultivated by nymphs. You won't find anything like it on earth."

Glenn's eyes have gone wide too. "Nymphs are real?"

"Yeah, sure," I say. "Lots of beings that humans think are myths live in the Unseen, though we don't look the way you might expect. The legends are exaggerated."

Valerie sniffs the flower again and smiles. "What other creatures live in your world?"

"I'd be happy to tell you about them, Mrs. Jordan."

"Please, call me Valerie. Riley has never brought a man home to meet us, which means she must care for you a great deal. So you should call us by our first names."

"Absolutely," Glenn agrees.

Riley's parents have accepted the truth even faster than I expected. A couple who studied cryptids must've always been open-minded, and they trust their daughter would never trick them. This is the ultimate vindication for them, though they can never share it with the world. Who cares? Knowing the truth matters way more than getting the approval of all those jerks who humiliated them. It's vindication for Riley too, but neither she nor her parents care about that anymore. They stopped worrying about what other mortals think the moment I revealed myself to them.

"Lots of creatures live in the Unseen," I tell Riley's parents. "Want to meet one of my friends?"

"Oh, yes, please," Valerie says as she breaks into a joyful grin.

I holler, "Max! Get your butt in here now."

Max appears beside me—buck naked, of course.

"Oh!" Valerie exclaims as her eyes widen almost to the point of bulging. Then she blinks rapidly and skims her gaze over the salamander from head to toe and back up to his groin. Her attention stalls there. Yeah, that's how most mortal women react to their first look at an incubus.

I shake my head. "Put on some pants, Max. You're meeting Riley's parents."

Leather pants materialize on Max's body. He spreads his arms. "Happy now? Leprechauns are such prudes."

Max's wife, Harper, joins us a few minutes later with their new baby, and Riley's parents get even more animated. They joke and laugh with our elemental friends. Valerie keeps glancing at Max's muscles, but she also ogles me. *So there, salamander, women like leprechauns too.* Once, Valerie winks at Riley while nodding toward me, but I have no idea what that means.

Never again will I need to slum it with a succubus to get laid. I found the only woman in any world who makes me feel like I can do anything as long as I'm with her. Maybe Riley is my fated mate. The way she came into my life sure felt like destiny, and I've learned never to doubt what the Unseen wants. Especially when I want it too.

Life is perfect today.

CHAPTER THIRTY-TWO

Riley

TWO DAYS LATER, AFTER MY PARENTS HAVE MET ALL THE NICEST ELEMEN-tals as well as Lindsey and Nevan, Tris and I decide it's time to show Mom and Dad the Unseen. They've done fine with coppery skinned salamanders and unearthly flowers. Now we want to show them what else the elemental world has to offer. Tris teleports my parents to the rock garden behind the shop. They love the concrete statues of fantastic animals like unicorns, but I can tell they're anxious to visit the Unseen.

We lead them down the trail to the healing vortex, where we pause so Tris can explain to them that this is real, not a hokey New Age thing, despite the cheesy sign beside the vortex. It really can heal people. Tris and I agreed, last night while we were in bed together at my parents' house, that we wouldn't tell them about the battle with the dragons and how a vampire nearly killed me but I came back to life. Not yet. What we're about to show them will test their open-mindedness to its limits. When we're sure they can deal with it, and not have simultaneous heart attacks, we will share the bad stuff too.

Now it's time to take them through the veil.

Tris can't carry all of us through the waterfall at once, which means he needs to make two trips. Once we've all entered the cave, he opens the portal. Mom and Dad gape at it for a moment, then they both smile like they've just found the entrance to nirvana.

And we step into the Unseen.

Mom and Dad are like kids who just walked into the biggest toy store in the universe. They can't resist touching the trees and the moss-like stuff that serves as foliage. Mom pets the grass and picks little wildflowers, smiling with intense satisfaction when she sniffs them. I have never seen my parents this happy before.

Tris encourages Mom to stand up, then he takes the flowers from her. "These can be kind of…intense. You might want to take it easy with them."

"Why? What's wrong with these flowers? They smell divine."

"Yeah. They're imbued with magics. Elementals aren't affected by it, but mortals can go a little…woo-woo."

"Woo-woo?" I say with a laugh. "Nice technical terminology, Tris."

"I'm a leprechaun, not a scientist."

We take them on a walk through the woods, but after that, we switch to zipping around so my parents can see as much of this world as they want. Well, we avoid the areas where nasty elementals live—like the harpies and the kerkopes.

At midday, in the Unseen, we drop my parents off at the home of Tris's parents. They are thrilled to meet my family, and the four of them become instant besties. We feel comfortable leaving Mom and Dad there. Tris's brothers and sisters will probably show up too since, according to Tris, they are "some of the biggest busybodies in this world."

Bob had sent us a message—an actual piece of paper inside an envelope—a little while ago. The message appeared in Tris's pocket. Bob's note explains that he has important stuff to tell us, and we need to meet him at his lair as soon as possible. Well, the rogue kerkopes aren't there anymore, so it ought to be safe. The sylphs took care of those monsters. Bob was glad to clear out the ranks and get rid of the creatures who had betrayed him. Tris had asked him, right after the dragon battle, why he didn't foresee that the kerkopes would turn on him. He replied that his foresight doesn't apply to himself as well as it does to others. That's weird. But I guess it's one of those features built into the Unseen to stop elementals from abusing their powers.

Yeah, Tris has told me more about this world. I think I could spend the rest of my life learning about the Unseen and still not know everything.

Tris and I have no trouble crossing through the oozing woods this time. We reach Bob's lair quickly, but we don't need to knock on the little hill. The door is already open. Tris takes my hand as we head down the pitch-dark passageway toward the oracle's lair and the door shuts behind us. We reach the main chamber in a few minutes and step up to the giant bronze bowl with its eerily flickering amber flames.

Bob stands behind the bowl. He spreads his arms wide. "Welcome. And congratulations on your great victory against Drakon."

"That's nice of you to say, Bob," Tris replies. "But you said there was an important reason you summoned us."

"Yes. Several reasons, in fact." Bob places his hands on the rim of the bronze bowl. "First, you should know that your curse was lifted the moment Drakon died."

"What a relief. That's a huge weight off my back. You're sure? Like, really sure?"

Bob rolls his eyes. "Yes, I am one hundred percent sure. Do you want to hear the rest? Or would rather make inane comments?"

"I didn't mean to annoy you. Go on, tell us the rest."

The oracle shakes his head, flicking his gaze up to the ceiling briefly. Then he continues. "Your new power is here to stay, but you must use it wisely. Do not abuse your supernatural good fortune by employing it for gambling."

"No, I will never do that again. Getting cursed taught me a big lesson about appreciating what I have."

"I'm glad to hear that. While I have another issue to discuss with you two, right now I'd like to hear your questions. I know you have some."

"How do you know?"

Bob taps his temple. "Foresight. Duh."

Tris laughs, apparently because Bob the oracle, a mystical being with incredible power, just used the word "duh." I think he was teasing us too, which is even more shocking. But I'm not sure if Bob will appreciate Tris's reaction.

I lift onto my tiptoes to whisper in Tris's ear, "Should you be laughing at the oracle?"

"It's all right, dear," Bob says. "I am not offended. But you have questions, and it's time to ask them."

He seems to think we know what questions to ask. I don't, but maybe Tris does.

My boyfriend clears his throat. "Why did you invite us into your lair so we could have sex in your spare bedroom?"

"What makes you think it's my *spare* bedroom?"

"Because, well, we sort of heard you and Miriella, uh…" Tris winces. "Well, you know."

"We were making love." Bob gives Tris another exasperated look. "Honestly, it shouldn't be that hard to figure out. As for why I invited you two into my home…" He smirks. "You needed to establish a strong bond so you would be ready for what was to come, and nothing accomplishes that faster than a good roll in the hay."

"Establish a bond? I don't understand."

"I foresaw the battle ahead. You and Riley needed to be prepared to do anything for each other, or else the war would be lost." He leans forward, his hands still curled over the bowl's rim. "When you made love, it accomplished more than giving you physical pleasure. You experienced something unexpected, didn't you? Something that changed your relationship irrevocably."

"Uh…yeah. I guess so." When Tris glances at me, I smile. And I hope that expression conveys everything I feel for him. He smiles in return, and I know he gets it. "Yeah, Bob, it changed everything."

Bob raises his hands above his head. "The oracle is never wrong. You may bow down to me now."

We stare at him. Is he teasing us again? Or does he seriously want us to bow down?

The oracle winks. "That was a joke."

"Oh, of course," Tris says. And he sounds a touch uncomfortable. A playful oracle is a new and bizarre experience for both of us. "Did you have anything else to tell us?"

Bob sighs heavily, bowing his head. Then he looks up at us. "What did I say? You have questions, plural. That means you aren't done yet."

"Right." My boyfriend scrunches up his face as he's thinking hard. "What about Anthea? We haven't been able to find her to make sure she's okay."

"The succubus is fine. The moment Drakon perished, she was freed. I believe she's now… What do mortals call it? Bed-hopping, I believe."

Well, at least she's all right. Drakon forced her to do his bidding, so we can't blame her for what happened.

Tris glances at me. "Do you have another question? I'm drawing a blank."

"I think I know what he expects us to ask." I face Bob. "Can Tris and I have a future together? He's immortal. I'm not. That seems like a problem."

"Not necessarily. But there is one question you must ask yourselves before you can decide." He folds his arms over his chest. "What are you willing to sacrifice to be together?"

"Riley is human," Tris says. "That means we can't have children together. A hybrid pregnancy could kill her."

"What?" I veer my attention to Tris. "You never mentioned that before."

"I know. I should have, but there was so much going on. I did tell you I can't get you pregnant unless I consciously decide to do that. The pregnancy issue is why elementals have that ability."

Bob flicks his gaze between Tris and me several times, then he sighs. "I can't make this decision for you. Just know that whatever you decide, it will be the right choice. I've foreseen that. And remember, you have options. But I'll leave that for Tris to explain."

Tris gazes at me with a look that I can't decipher, but I can't help wondering if he's afraid I'll run away once he shares those options with me.

"Not all the choices involve Riley making a sacrifice," Bob says. "Remember that."

I would sacrifice anything for Tris, and I know he would do the same for me. But that doesn't help me figure out what Bob meant.

"Now for the last item on my agenda," Bob says. "The problem of Cyneric."

I sidle closer to Tris and slip my hand into his. I don't see how anyone could blame me for feeling uneasy. The problem of Cyneric? No, that's not an ominous statement at all.

"The Four Winds have taken him," Bob says. "Now they must deliberate over what to do with him. Something unprecedented has occurred. An elemental being has undergone spontaneous changes without the intervention of the Unseen itself or the Oversoul. Evolution is a natural part of any ecosystem, but this sort has never been witnessed before."

"What are you trying to say?" Tris asks. "Spit it out, Bob. Um, I respectfully ask that you spit it out. That's what I meant."

The oracle smirks. "Relax, Tris. I am not about to smite you."

"Oh, good."

Bob rubs his forehead. "Cyneric has developed certain traits that even the Four Winds are having trouble reconciling with the way Eros created the vampires. The god made Cyneric first, then the others came later. Perhaps that explains Cyneric's new powers. You see, he has become literally invincible. Even endued weapons can't destroy him, and he may cross the veil with impunity. He also has the ability to breach the boundaries in the mortal world."

"That bloodsucker can go anywhere he wants? What if he kills somebody? He's obsessed with Riley and almost killed her because Drakon told him to do it."

"I am aware of that, as are the Four Winds. They will weigh the options and, I'm certain, devise a plan to deal with the vampire. Cyneric is a singular elemental. His fate must be considered at length before a decision is reached." Bob walks around the bronze bowl to stand right in front of us. "Rest assured, no one will allow Cyneric to harm either you or Riley."

"What about the rest of the Unseen and the mortal world?" Tris asks. "Are all the living beings in both worlds now an all-you-can-eat buffet for a starving vamp?"

"You should know better by now. The Four Winds will never allow that to happen. Trust the balancing powers. Trust the Oversoul." He stretches an arm out to indicate the doorway. "Be on your way now. I've shared all that I can."

Tris and I leave the oracle's lair and go back to his parents' house in Coppertown. His family and my family are in the backyard starting up a barbecue grill. I can't help feeling surprised by the fact that leprechauns enjoy slapping some burgers on a grill, but I'm sure I'll get used to the way elementals like to adopt mortal habits.

We wait until after dinner to discuss the subject Bob had mentioned. Then Tris leads me into his old bedroom, and we sit on the bed side by side with our backs to the wall.

"We need to talk about some stuff," he says. "What Bob mentioned. We need to discuss our future together."

"Okay. Bob said there are options."

"Yeah." He sandwiches my hand between both of his. "Option one, we decide never to have kids. Option two, we adopt kids. And option three... Well, that's not a viable solution."

"Why not? Tell me what it is, and we can decide together if option three might work."

He shifts uncomfortably on the bed and releases my hand. Tris can't look at me when he says, "The only other option is the forging."

"You mentioned that before, but you didn't explain."

"The forging is a process that turns a mortal into an elemental."

I sit up straighter, and my pulse beats faster. "That's possible? Why didn't you want to tell me that?"

"You don't understand what the forging involves. A mortal needs to be on the verge of death, near enough to a natural water feature that their blood spreads into it. Water is the portal, but blood is the key."

I turn halfway toward him as my excitement wanes. Something in the tone of his voice has brought a darker edge to this conversation. "I don't understand."

"All the portals in both worlds can be activated in one of two ways—by summoning magics to open them, or through blood that spills into the water and triggers the portal. The Unseen senses when a mortal lies dying near a portal, and a kind of dog whistle call goes out to let elementals know a potential new recruit is waiting."

I bite my upper lip as I study him. "I can tell you think forging is a bad idea. But why? Wasn't your friend Travis forged? You mentioned that before."

"Yeah, he was forged. But only because Max felt compelled to do it. He was Lindsey's familiar at the time, and her grief over losing her friend pushed Max to forge Travis." He shuts his eyes for a moment, and when he looks at me again, his expression has taken on a graveness that chills me. "Listen to me, Riley. Really listen. The forging is a violent and extraordinarily painful process. It rips a mortal's body apart at the molecular level, then reassembles it in a new, elemental form. I don't want you to go through that."

"But if that would mean we can be together—"

"Don't you get it? You would have to die and then suffer more agony than any human could possibly imagine. It will change you. Afterward, you might not even want to be with me anymore."

I know he means every word of what he said.

Tris covers his face with his hands. Then he blows out a breath and meets my gaze. "I can't lose you, Riley. If the forging is the only viable option, I might as well destroy myself right now. Because I know I can't spend the rest of eternity without you."

And I couldn't live forever without him. Where does that leave us now?

CHAPTER THIRTY-THREE

Tris

I LOVE YOU, TRIS," RILEY SAYS. "IF THE FORGING WOULD MEAN WE CAN spend eternity together, I'll do it. And of course I'll still want you afterward. Travis went through the forging, and he's okay. Why are you convinced I'll wind up hating you afterward?"

"Travis had a long road to travel before he was okay enough to go out in public. The forging is brutal."

Riley gazes at me in a way I've figured out means she's going to be stubborn about whatever I'm telling her. I love that side of her—but not right now.

"It's not just that you'd be different," I say. "You wouldn't be like me, and I wouldn't know how to guide you through the transition. You'd need to spend years, maybe even centuries, adjusting to your new existence. And you'd need an elemental of your own kind to guide you through it."

"You can do that for me."

I shake my head slowly. "No, Riley, I can't do that. The fae don't procreate through the forging. We are one of the few races in the Unseen that believes tricking a mortal into dying and being reborn as an elemental is immoral. We reproduce by having children the old-fashioned way. Other races, like the salamanders and the sylphs, expand their numbers by forging mortals."

"Why would they do that?"

"Because they think childbirth is dirty and unseemly." I scrub a hand over my cheek. "But I think they also like being able to handpick their so-called children. The sylph who forged Nevan chose him because he was one of the strongest warriors in his tribe. The sylph glossed over the bad parts of the forging, but honestly, Nevan was already mostly dead and in no condition to give legitimate consent. Elementals often abuse their power to create new beings."

"You wouldn't do that."

"No, but I don't have the power to forge you even if I wanted to do it." I rest my head against the wall and close my eyes while I consider how to convince her this is a bad idea. "The fae elders cast a spell to prevent any of us from ever trying to create new members of our race. They realized the power was too easily corrupted. That spell was cast eons ago, and nobody would know how to break it even if they tried."

Does she really understand what I'm saying? She can't imagine what the forging would be like. Honestly, I don't fully understand it either, but I've seen it happen, and it's beyond brutal. I could never watch her go through that just to be with me. But I've never met anyone like Riley, and I've never cared about anyone as much as I care about her. I'm in love with a mortal, but I can't see a viable way past this issue.

I would gladly spend the next fifty years with her, knowing I won't age but she will. Can Riley handle that? I'll stay young while she grows old. What if she resents me? Then I'll watch her die, but I will go on living—without her. I know she's the only one I ever want, which means I'll go through eternity grieving for her. Maybe that's a selfish thought, but I can't help feeling this way. Mostly, though, I worry about how our relationship might hurt her. She should find a mortal man, get married, have kids.

Riley snuggles up to me, and I curl an arm around her. We sit here for a long time just enjoying the intimacy of holding each other. The sun has set, and the two moons of the Unseen begin to rise, but still we sit here. Eventually, we undress and crawl under the covers together to sleep while her body is molded to mine. I think mortals call it spooning. I inhale the scent of her and relish the warmth of her, knowing I might not have Riley for much longer.

But I rouse in the middle of night, and an epiphany strikes. Somehow, I manage to get back to sleep. My idea needs to wait until we've both had a decent night's rest.

In the morning, Riley wakes up to find me already awake. I've still got her body cradled against mine when she rolls over so she can look me in the eye.

The woman I love kisses me softly. "Good morning, Tris."

I kiss her forehead. "Good morning, Riley."

"You look like you want to talk."

"I do." I trail my fingers along her bare arm. "Did you sleep okay?"

"Well enough. But I couldn't help worrying about what's going to happen with us. You're convinced we can't be together."

"Actually, I have an idea." I keep trailing my fingers up and down her silky skin, focusing on that task instead of meeting her gaze. She might not approve of my solution. "I was, uh, thinking about our dilemma. And I have another option."

"What is it?"

"I could give up my immortality."

"That's possible? You didn't mention it yesterday."

"That's because I'm not sure it is an option." I sit up and bend one knee, resting my arm on it. But I can't look at her while I explain. "I'd need to convince the Four Winds to do it. They removed Travis's immortality, but he's still an elemental."

"I'm guessing it's not easy to talk the Four Winds into doing that."

"They could also make me a mortal, a regular human being. But I don't know if they'd be willing to do either thing. They stripped Travis's immortality because he couldn't be made human again so soon after his forging. And we still wouldn't be able to have kids."

She lays a hand on my cheek. "I don't care if you stay an immortal leprechaun. I'll still be with you. We can always adopt children, like you said yesterday. Travis and Larissa did that."

"This is all irrelevant unless the Four Winds grant me an audience to discuss my idea."

"We should at least try that, right? Today."

"You should stay here. I have no idea how the Four Winds will react to me or you. They only allow those they deem worthy to enter their temple."

Riley sits up and wraps her arms around my neck. "I am going with you, whether you like it or not. Couples do things together."

"But this is—"

"Stop it. I'm going with you, period. No arguments."

I can't help smiling. "You're so hot when you get bossy."

Though I'd rather spend the morning making love to Riley, I realize that delaying will only increase my anxiety. So I conjure fresh clothes for us, and we tell my parents where we're going. They worry about what might happen, of course, but Ma and Pa trust me and know I can take care of myself. Ma hugs us both, but Pa just slaps my arm and kisses Riley's cheek.

Now we are on our way.

I zip us to the side of the mountain that houses the Temple of the Four Winds at its summit, but I can't take us all the way there. The wards around the temple prevent it. We touch down on the slope of the rocky mountain, just below the level of the fog that conceals the temple, where a gale whips around us and lashes Riley's hair to her face. Somehow, the fog remains in place despite the blustering wind. We didn't bring any weapons with us since we can't take them into the temple, but I doubt we would need them, anyway. From here, we must climb up the steep slope until we reach the summit.

But not yet. First, I need to request permission to enter the temple precinct. I don't shout to the sky, though. No, the Four Winds prefer a quieter approach. So I shut my eyes and formulate the request in my mind, though it's more of a feeling than a thought. When I open my eyes, the fog bank above us is churning fiercely.

Then the fog lifts, revealing the giant white-stone temple high above us. Sunlight shining on the building's facade seems to make it glow.

"Is that it?" Riley asks. "Have we been deemed worthy?"

"Guess we have."

Maybe I grip her hand more tightly than I should, but I'm not ashamed to admit I'm afraid of what the Four Winds might tell me. I haven't been a perfect elemental, and I haven't always been grateful for what I have. I've changed, but I have no idea if the most powerful beings in the Unseen will care about that.

We mount the steep steps to the portico, where massive wooden doors block our way.

A horrendous grinding noise erupts, making my ears hurt as the giant doors inch open.

I lead Riley into the temple—a vacant building that seems to stretch on forever to our right and our left. High above our heads, carvings on the wall depict winged beings dressed in flowing robes. We are about to meet the beings shown in that artwork.

Four figures materialize in front of us, hovering above the floor.

Their white robes graze the floor, but their arms and heads remain exposed. I used to think of the Four Winds as ethereal beings who never set foot on the physical world, but after hearing Bob and Miriella going at it in his lair, I can no longer view the Four Winds that way. I'm having trouble looking Miriella in the eye. She gets down and dirty with Bob. How am I supposed to see her as one of the most powerful beings in the Unseen? And knowing she has carnal urges makes me wonder what the other members of this group do in their spare time. Javren might ride a Harley in his spare time.

I can't really picture him doing that. Then again, I never would've guessed Bob and Miriella get naked together, despite knowing they used to be a couple.

Miriella glides toward us. "We know why you have come here, but we cannot grant your request. You, Triskaideka, may not become mortal. But neither may Riley undergo the forging. Either outcome would prove disastrous for the Unseen and the mortal world."

"You're saying we can't be together. I love Riley, and I know we can find a way to—"

"Silence." Miriella raises a hand. "For once, listen before you comment."

One of the most powerful beings in the Unseen just told me to shut my trap—in a more courteous way. I stay quiet and just listen. But acid is rising into my throat, and I feel like I might throw up.

"If you wish to remain together," Miriella says, "without danger to either yourselves or the two worlds, only one path exists for you. Riley must become a copper fae."

Though I open my mouth to complain, I stop myself. She probably isn't done yet.

Miriella floats a little closer. "In all our existence, which stretches back further than the gods of the Unseen, we have recommended this method only twice before. But you and Riley are important to the future of both worlds. Therefore, we offer a radical solution. We have the power to transform Riley into a copper fae without undergoing the forging, but this act cannot be reversed. You must both be certain you wish to proceed."

I glance at Riley. "It's your decision."

"You must both agree," Miriella says. "Now, leave us. You need to consider this choice at length. Return to us only when you are certain beyond all doubts."

The Four Winds vanish.

Riley and I look at each other. Neither of us knows what to do or say right now. The Four Winds wouldn't command us to think about this option unless they believed it was a grave decision that requires a lot of consideration.

So I take us home—to my parents' house.

We materialize inside my bedroom, so I shout to make sure Ma and Pa know we've returned from our mission. "We're home! But we don't want to be disturbed right now."

"Don't you want a snack?" Ma asks.

"No. We need to talk. A lot."

"Of course, dear. You two *talk* all you want."

She assumes we plan to have sex. I wish that were the case, but we've got something way more important to think about right now. The fate of our relationship, and potentially two worlds, depends on our decision.

Yeah, we need a lot more time to think.

CHAPTER THIRTY-FOUR

Riley

TRIS AND I HAVE SPENT A MONTH MULLING OVER WHAT THE FOUR Winds have offered me. A chance to become an elemental, a copper fae just like Tris. But the decision has proved far from simple. There's my family and his family, but they all say they support whatever decision we make. Tris keeps telling me it's my decision, not ours. No matter how many times I insist we must decide together, he insists it's all up to me.

I love him more every day, but I need to know he'll be okay with whatever I decide. The only response I get when I bring up the topic is a reiteration of his claim that he has no place in the conversation. So, what, I'm supposed to hash out the pros and cons by talking to myself?

That's why I announced, two weeks after our visit with the Four Winds, that we need to take a break from the Big Decision and just have fun together. That worked for a while. But eventually, we need to bite that bullet. Today, we're relaxing in a hammock behind his parents' house in Coppertown when I broach the forbidden subject.

"We need to talk about what the Four Winds offered me," I say, while I have my body plastered to his and one arm draped over his chest. "I could become a copper fae like you. Why isn't that exciting news? You act like it's a death sentence."

"I don't feel that way about it. But I'm not sure you've really considered all the ramifications."

"Do you think I'm too dense to understand?"

"No. You're the smartest person of any species that I've ever met. But you're too excited about this."

I slide my body on top of his, which makes the hammock sway wildly for a moment. "I love you. I want to spend the rest of my life with you—or the rest of eternity. The Four Winds have given us that chance. Why are you still so worried?"

He grimaces. "It's dumb."

"Just say it. I won't get mad."

Tris lays an arm over his eyes. "I, uh, can't help thinking that once you're an elemental, you won't think I'm so great anymore. You might meet someone better, like an incubus, and dump my ass."

He seriously worries about that? Well, he did mention that he hasn't had many girlfriends. I can't figure out why other women, human or elemental, can't see how hot and amazing he is. But I understand why he worries.

I rest my chin on his chest. "I'm with you, Tris, forever. I've never felt this way about anyone else, and I know I never will. Don't you trust me?"

"Of course I do. But—"

"If you trust me, it has to be all the way. If I'm going to remake myself into a different species for you, I need to know you won't back out."

He gazes into my eyes for a long moment, his expression unreadable. His irises glow bright blue, and they swirl faintly. I've never seen anything more beautiful than the eyes of Triskaideka.

Finally, he smiles in the sweetest, softest way. "I love you, Riley, all the way and forever. And I trust you that much too."

"Good. Then it's settled."

He whisks us away without even telling his parents we're leaving, without even telling me that. We now stand on the jagged mountain that houses the Temple of the Four Winds at its summit. The swirling fog dissipates, allowing us to trudge up the steps to the portico. The doors are already open, so we walk inside hand in hand.

The Four Winds are hovering there, waiting for us.

"Welcome back," Miriella says. "You have reached a decision."

"Yes," I say. "I want to become a copper fae."

"Excellent. We knew you would make the right choice."

I bite my lip as I consider asking a question. Should I do that? What if they don't like what I ask?

"Go on," Miriella says. "We have anticipated your question, so do not fear the answer."

"Okay." I hesitate, but then I make myself just do it. "If you guys have done this only twice before, why did you choose me? There must be more impressive mortals who are more deserving of this gift."

"You are incorrect. No one is more impressive or more deserving." Miriella glides closer, lowering herself until her feet almost touch the floor. Her gaze meets mine. "We have watched you for a long time, Riley Jordan. And we knew before you were born that you would one day prove an invaluable resident of the Unseen. Your passion for studying and cataloging mysterious creatures led you to this world, where you met the only male in any realm who appreciates your gifts."

"I believe Tris and I were meant to meet and fall in love."

"And you are correct. But we do not offer you this opportunity because of that. Before we transform you, we must explain the caveat."

Why didn't they mention that before? I guess they needed to make sure I'm all in before they share the last requirement.

Miriella clasps my hand, her skin cool but somehow comforting. "We wish for you to continue your research here in the Unseen. Cataloging and studying the denizens of this world is a monumental but necessary task, and it could take an eternity. That is why we offer you the chance to become an elemental. Knowing what we desire from you, do you still want to do this?"

I glance at Tris.

He smiles and nods.

"Yes," I say. "I want to do this."

"The choice is irrevocable."

"I understand, and I consent to the transformation."

Miriella rises above the floor and floats backward to rejoin her fellow beings. They form a circle and bow their heads.

I sidle closer to Tris, and he slides an arm around me. Just feeling his body against mine gives me a sense of peace I've never experienced with anyone else. We belong together, and whatever happens from this day forward, we will deal with it together. Who knew my interest in cryptids would lead to this? I found my true love, vindicated my parents, and discovered strength I never knew I had inside me. I helped destroy a powerful dragon shifter, after all.

Maybe no one in the mortal world will ever know my parents were right. Who cares? We know, and that's more than enough.

"It is done," Miriella announces.

"But I don't feel any different," I say. "Are you sure it worked?"

Tris grasps my shoulders, turning me to face him. His eyes gradually widen, and a look of awe overtakes him. "Your eyes, Riley. They're glowing."

"Seriously?"

He nods. Then he grins and laughs. "You're a copper fae, baby. Try conjuring something."

I imagine a flower appearing in my hand—and it happens.

Tris laughs again.

And I leap up to fling my arms around his neck, shrieking and giggling like an idiot. I don't care if I'm behaving like a ditz. My dumb-blonde routine helped save the world. And now other elementals won't need to worry about me outing them with my research. My new mission is to classify and understand all the beings in the Unseen, however long that takes.

"You may leave us," Miriella says. "I imagine you have…things to do now. Do not let us delay you."

Did she just imply we should zip away to have sex? Well, yeah, we absolutely should. When I glance at Miriella, she's smiling. Really smiling. The expression dimples her cheeks.

I whisk us away, straight into Tris's bedroom in his parents' house. I've also made our clothes disappear, and we landed on the bed with me on top. "We need to find our own lair. Don't you think?"

"Yep." He grasps my ass. "After we celebrate."

Someone knocks on the door. "Tris, dear, did it happen? Is Riley a copper fae?"

"Yeah, Ma, she is. Now take Pa shopping or something. We're about to make a whole lotta noise."

"Frimis!" Nyara hollers. "We're going shopping."

"Right now?" Frimis says in a slightly grumpy tone. "I was watching that makeover show where they take an ugly house and—"

"Now, Frimis."

Silence follows.

I squint as I struggle to listen for any sounds in the rest of the house. My newly remodeled body comes with awesome hearing abilities. "I think they left."

He squints too for a few seconds, then he relaxes. "Yep, they're gone. Let's make noise."

"Lindsey told me she and Nevan once had sex on a cloud. Could we try it?"

He makes a derisive noise. "I can do better than that. Air fairies have no imagination."

"Show me what you can do, Triskaideka."

"I love it when you call me that." Tris teleports us to…a church. "What do you think?"

We're both wearing clothes now—a suit and tie for him, and a white, lacy dress for me.

"Am I wearing a wedding dress?" I ask. "And are we in the mortal world?"

"Yes and yes." He settles a hand on my back, guiding me into the adorable little chapel. "I wanted to surprise you, so you can't say no. When I told you that we need to celebrate, this is what I meant. And telling Ma we were about to make noise was our secret word. She knew that meant everyone should gather here immediately."

"Is this your weird way of proposing?"

"Kinda." He leads me into the main area of the chapel, where at least two dozen people sit in the pews. Travis and Nevan stand at the altar along with Lindsey and Ennea. "Hope you approve of your bridesmaids."

"Aren't you supposed to propose before the wedding?"

"We don't do anything the normal way, do we?" He drops to one knee in front of me and brings out a ring box, which he flips open. "Riley Jordan, will you marry me?"

This is totally insane, but I don't care. "Yes, I will."

He grins and slips the ring onto my finger. "Ready to get hitched right now?"

"Let's do it."

My dad walks up the aisle to us and offers me his arm. "May I escort my daughter to the altar?"

Tears sting in my eyes, but I blink them away. Then I hook my arm around Dad's.

My fiancé races up the aisle to take his place at the altar.

As my father guides me up the aisle, I notice who our officiant is. Bob the oracle stands there waiting for me to march up the aisle so he can solemnize our marriage. Maybe this is the weirdest marriage ever, but it suits us. We aren't a normal couple, and I love that. Of course we're getting hitched in a bizarre way. It makes complete sense in our world.

"Here's how this will work," Bob says. "I don't do all that nonsense mortals love. I'll keep it simple. Riley, do you want to marry this irritating fae?"

"Yes, I do."

Bob shifts his attention to my fiancé. "Triskaideka, do you want to marry this enchanting, newly created fae?"

"Absolutely, I do."

The oracle raises his hands, palms out. "I now pronounce you are wedded, bound to each other for eternity and beyond. May your love inspire the entire Unseen to discover the same joy you two share. You may now kiss the bride."

He winks, then vanishes.

And Tris pulls me into his arms to kiss me.

Our guests cheer and clap and whistle. We should probably hang around for a while since our friends and family have probably organized a reception somewhere. But we can't wait any longer to consummate our new marriage. Okay, we've had sex before. Often, actually. Once we destroyed Drakon, we had no reason to hold back. But today will be the first time we've made love as a married couple.

My husband spirits us away while still kissing me. And we materialize inside the bedroom of a house I don't recognize. We're lying on the bed, naked, with me on top. I'm straddling his hips. Wow, he really needs to teach me how to teleport into a specific position. And oh yes, his hard cock is already nestled deep inside me.

"Where are we?" I ask.

"Our new home. A lair wasn't good enough for you, so I bought us a house in Coppertown. It's two lots down from my Ma and Pa's place."

"Sounds perfect." I rock my hips just enough to make him gasp. "Are you finally going to show me how a copper fae can do better than an air fairy?"

"Oh, yeah, for sure." Tris conjures a glass bottle that seems to be empty. "Max gave me a little pre-wedding gift."

"A bottle with nothing in it? You got gypped."

"No, I didn't." He holds the little bottle between his thumb and forefinger. "This contains enough salamander pheromones to let me drive you wild for days. And now that you're an elemental, we can do that. No need to hold back anymore. I can fuck you so hard the earth will shake."

I snatch the bottle from him. "Let's do it."

"Take it easy with the pheromones, Riley. One whiff at a time. That's potent stuff."

"Okay, I'll be careful." I lick my lips while I admire his muscular body. "Will these pheromones affect you too?"

"Not sure. Max only told me it would make you insanely hot for me."

"I always feel that way." I start to unscrew the bottle's cap. "Let's both try it."

He grins and grasps my ass. "Do it, baby."

Now that I've unscrewed the cap, I crack it open just enough to release a tiny bit of pheromones, inhaling deeply as the erotic energy sizzles through me. "Oh, wow, this is incredible."

I offer the bottle to Tris.

He takes a sniff too. "Damn, that smells good. But not as good as you."

Sealing the bottle, I set it on the nightstand. "It's time. Come on, Triskaideka, make us both scream."

My husband's lips curve into a smile of carnal hunger that makes my clit throb. Then he proves he was right. A copper fae can do better than an air fairy—or a salamander. I don't need to sleep with a sylph or an incubus to know that. Nobody else in the multiverse could make me feel the way Tris does. He gave me more than his love and trust. He showed me I'm stronger than I ever realized, and I will always be grateful for that. Now it's time to express my gratitude in the one way I can.

And yes, we do make the earth shake.

Did you love

Visit
AnnaDurand.com

to subscribe to her newsletter
for updates on forthcoming books in this series
&
to receive exclusive content!

ANNA DURAND IS A BESTSELLING, MULTI-AWARD-WINNING AUTHOR OF contemporary and paranormal romance. Her books have earned bestseller status on every major retailer and wonderful reviews from readers around the world. But that's the boring spiel. Here are the really cool things you want to know about Anna!

Born on Lackland Air Force Base in Texas, Anna grew up moving here, there, and everywhere thanks to her dad's job as an instructor pilot. She's lived in Texas (twice), Mississippi, California (twice), Michigan (twice), and Alaska—and now Ohio.

As for her writing, Anna has always made up stories in her head, but she didn't write them down until her teen years. Those first awful books went into the trash can a few years later, though she learned a lot from those stories. Eventually, she would pen her first romance novel, the paranormal romance *Willpower*, and she's never looked back since.

Want even more details about Anna? Get access to her extended bio when you subscribe to her newsletter and download the free bonus ebook, *Hot Scots Confidential*. You'll also get hot deleted scenes, character interviews, fun facts, and more! Plus you'll receive the short story *Tempted by a Kiss* and mutliple bonus chapters in both ebook and audiobook formats.

VISIT ANNADURAND.COM TO SIGN UP.

www.ingramcontent.com/pod-product-compliance
Lightning Source LLC
Chambersburg PA
CBHW072129300726
48975CB00003B/985